The Old Ways

The Paladins, Book 3

DAVID DALGLISH

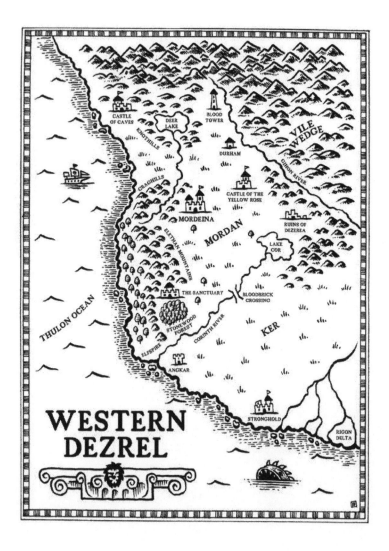

WESTERN DEZREL

BOOKS BY DAVID DALGLISH

THE HALF-ORC SERIES

The Weight of Blood
The Cost of Betrayal
The Death of Promises
The Shadows of Grace
A Sliver of Redemption

THE SHADOWDANCE TRILOGY

A Dance of Cloaks
A Dance of Blades
A Dance of Death

THE PALADINS

Night of Wolves
Clash of Faiths
The Old Ways

The Old Ways

1

Jerico reached for his shield as he heard the rider thunder into the dark village of Wilhelm.

"What's going on?" asked Darius, sitting up in his bedroll. "Is he one of Sebastian's?"

Jerico shook his head, peering through a crack in the door of the small shed that they slept in.

"No," he said. "I don't think so."

They'd been on the run since the battle between Arthur and Sebastian Hemman, the two paladins originally on opposite sides of the conflict. But Jerico had won his friend over, and together they'd defeated several faithful to Karak. Arthur's army had lost, however, forcing them to flee to safety. Sebastian's men had combed the surrounding forests, and it had taken a lot of running, and a bit of luck, for the two to reach Wilhelm without being seen. They'd rented the only room available in the farming village: the shed.

"I only use it when an animal gets sick, to keep it away from the others," the farmer had said. "Don't worry none. Been awhile since the last, and I changed the straw."

Jerico had been looking forward to his first peaceful night of sleep in what felt like days, but then the horsed rider had come, crying out something Jerico hadn't quite caught...

"He might be looking for Arthur's men," Darius said, rubbing his eyes.

"The village is loyal to Kaide," Jerico said, pressing open the door. The rider had stopped in the village square, and several older men and women were coming out to greet him in their bedclothes.

"You so certain?"

Jerico nodded. Kaide was a local hero in the North, a bandit who robbed Sebastian Hemman's caravans and gave away the wealth and supplies he didn't need. It was his private war against Sebastian that had started everything, with Arthur only recently taking up arms against his brother.

"We are safe, no matter the coin they offer."

"No matter the coin?" asked Darius.

Jerico shrugged.

"Well, within reason. Everyone has their price."

"That so? Then what is yours?"

"Eternity," said Jerico, stepping outside the shed. "I'd love to see Sebastian offer me that."

Given Jerico's prominent role in the battle, he knew he needed to be careful, in case the rider had been told his description. With his long hair, red beard, and blue-silver armor, he wasn't the most easily forgotten of men. Still, the night was dark, and his armor was in the shed. If he kept his distance, he should be able listen in without being noticed.

The rider was still gathering people, ensuring that there would be no need to repeat himself before riding off to his next destination. Jerico leaned against the side of a house, hidden in the shadows cast by the torchlight. The rider wore light armor, and he bore a crest Jerico recognized. Sir Robert Godley and his men had worn similar markings when they came to help fight off the wolf-men in Durham. It seemed like ages ago to Jerico, but he knew it'd been hardly three months. He felt his worry lessen. Robert was a friend, and had little to do with the brothers' conflict.

"People of Wilhelm, I seek a man responsible for a most terrible tragedy," the rider began. The speech was well-rehearsed, and though his words were fiery, he spoke them in a perfunctory manner. To Jerico, he sounded beyond exhausted. "Not long ago, a man helped burn down the village of Durham, and slaughtered many of its residents. This act was done without mercy and without reason. I've come offering a bounty of five hundred gold coins to whoever brings me, or any proper authority of the King, this man's head."

A gasp ran through the people. Five hundred gold was a fortune, a thousand times more than any farmers might see in their lifetime. Jerico felt something catch in his throat as he thought of Durham. He'd preached alongside Darius there, becoming friends with the people. He'd lost many fighting the wolf-men, succeeding only because of Robert's help. Now someone had attacked it again?

"Who?" asked one of the crowd, as if on cue. Who indeed, thought Jerico. He found himself wishing he held his mace in hand. Who would dare defile the sacrifices they'd made?

"His name is Darius," cried the rider. "A tall man with long blond hair. He hails from the Stronghold, and wears the cruel armor of their kind. He is extremely dangerous, and should be greatly feared. My master, Sir Robert Godley, offers this bounty so this vile criminal will be brought to justice for his terrible deeds."

Jerico felt like he'd been punched in the gut. His blood drained from his face, and as the people began to murmur, he remembered the words he'd spoken in jest not moments ago.

Everyone has their price.

Indeed. And the villagers' were just exceeded tenfold.

Jerico turned and ran for the shed, knowing time was not on their side. Darius waited for him, leaning beside the door with his arms crossed. Seeing Jerico's worry, he frowned.

"What's wrong?" he asked.

"Put your armor on," Jerico said, ignoring him. "Now."

The countless hours spent putting on and taking off the cumbersome plate and chainmail served him well as Jerico donned it in the darkness. Darius strapped on his greaves, then reached for his chestplate.

"What's going on?" he asked again.

Jerico knew he should ask about Durham, but wasn't sure he wanted to hear the answer. Still, he had to know.

"There's a bounty on your head," he said, not looking at his friend. "They say...they say you helped destroy Durham. Helped kill a lot of people."

He left his question unspoken as he pulled on his gauntlets. Torchlight flickered through cracks in the walls as outside the first of many arrived. They would not rush in until the whole town was gathered, Jerico was certain. Their little shed would be surrounded, with more coming every second, all to guarantee no escape. He grabbed his mace and his shield. Soft blue light shone across them. In the light, Darius met his gaze.

"I killed no one," Darius said. "But I was there, and I deserve their anger."

Jerico struck a board, felt the whole shed vibrate. Several people outside gasped.

"Come out, Darius," someone shouted. Jerico recognized him as the messenger from Robert. "There's no reason to spill any more blood."

Darius finished putting on the last of his armor, then reached for his weapon. It was an enormous two-handed sword, its edges serrated in sections. It shimmered with a faint light, far dimmer than Jerico's shield. The glow represented the strength of their faith, and Jerico felt worry squirm in his gut at how weak Darius's was. Whatever had happened at Durham, it still troubled him greatly.

"Darius!" cried the messenger amid an uneasy rumble of conversation.

"What do I do?" asked Darius. "They'll be knocking down the walls any second."

"We can't kill them," Jerico said. "They're just desperate."

"I'd say greedy. How much was the bounty?"

"Five hundred," Jerico muttered.

"Silver?"

"Gold."

Darius chuckled. "Damn."

"If you are guilty, they're just obeying the law. I won't shed innocent blood."

Darius shook his head.

"I won't give myself up for a hanging. You must trust me. I killed no one; even did my best to protect them. Don't you dare turn on me here."

The door rattled. Jerico kicked it open, and as the people scattered away, he stepped out amid the mob, his shield shining bright on his arm. There were over two hundred gathered, men and women of all ages. Those closest bore weapons, sickles, pitchforks, and staves designed for farming, not warfare. Only Robert's messenger wielded a blade, and he held it before him as if expecting Jerico to attack at any moment. Jerico looked into their eyes as they held their collective breaths. He saw fear, desperation, and a greedy hope for something far beyond their tired, meager lives. He could not blame them.

But that didn't mean he had to accept it.

"Go back to your homes," he told them. "We were offered safety, and a soft place to lay our heads. Will you betray that now, all for the promise of gold?"

"He's a criminal," said an older man. Jerico recognized him as the farmer who had lent them the shed. Several others murmured in agreement.

"As am I," Jerico said. "An outlaw, so says your Lord Sebastian. Will you turn me in next?"

Plenty looked unhappy at that. Support for Kaide ran deep, and Jerico had quickly become a hero for his pivotal role in the battle at Green Gulch. Only the messenger seemed not to care.

"That's different," muttered one of the farmers. "You ain't done what he's done. Send him out, and let it all be over quick."

Jerico felt torn, but knew he could show no weakness. He needed to hear it from Darius's lips, know for certain what had happened. Shed no innocent blood. If there was anything that had been hammered into his thick skull during his training at the Citadel, that had been it. But he was also trained to protect, and letting his friend be strung up by a mob felt a bit contradictory to that.

"The coin won't buy you happiness," Jerico said, his voice softer. "It will only tear apart the love you have for one another. It won't bring peace. It won't bring safety. Do not do this. You offered us shelter and safety. Don't stain your hands with treachery."

Before any could answer, Darius stepped out into the night. His armor, dark steel, shimmered in the torchlight. His hollow eyes looked to the crowd, which gave him a wide berth. Despite their numbers, attacking someone so well armored, strong, and skilled was something none of them were prepared to do alone.

"Enough," he said, his voice carrying authority. Jerico had always considered him the far better speaker, and a master at manipulating crowds. Many stepped back, as if expecting him to draw his blade, which so far remained on his back.

"Darius, you're under arrest," said the messenger. He was sweating, and his sword was unsteady in his hand.

Darius shook his head.

"I have too much to atone for. My life does not end here, not to a misled mob in the dead of night. I do not want to hurt any of you, and Jerico will insist the same. I have done many wrongs, but of this, I am accused unfairly. I took no lives. I spilled no blood. If you would hang me, or cut off my head, you end the life of the wrong man. The one who committed that deed is dead, slain by my hand. Move aside, and let us be. We still fight for you, for Kaide. But I will protect myself if I must."

He drew his sword and pointed ahead of him.

"Move aside."

At first Jerico thought they would. The speech was sincere, his certainty forceful. Jerico felt uncomfortable with the implied threat, but surely the people would understand. Surely they would realize the gold coin was not worth the bloodshed and betrayal of...

"Cowards," said the messenger, thrusting for a crease in Darius's armor. Before it hit, Darius stepped to one side and swung. The blade cut the messenger at the wrist. Blood arced across the grass as both weapon and hand twirled and fell. Jerico felt his heart stop, and his breath catch in his throat.

The mob saw blood, and it was like fire on dry leaves.

"Push through!" Jerico shouted, ducking his head and leading with his shield. His armor was thick, and his shield thicker. He felt blows strike him, mostly ineffective. A sickle scraped across his pauldron, and a pitchfork struck the shield before sliding to one side. Legs pumping, Jerico continued on, giving them no chance to resist, no chance to regroup. He burst through the other side of the crowd, feeling battered and bruised, but alive.

Spinning, he saw Darius trying to follow, but the crowd's attention had turned on him. Without a shield, he could only lead with his sword. He cut and parried, relying on his armor to protect him from fists and clubs, and his blade to protect him from all else. His armor had many sharp ridges and edges, and he slammed through people who tried to block his way. Blood coated the dark steel.

"Darius!" Jerico shouted as the way closed between them. He ran, using his shield to shove aside a group of three trying to stop Darius's exit. Two more blocked the way, both with heavy sickles. Darius smacked aside one, but the other slipped through his defenses. The curved end hooked over his chestplate, past his neck, and into the flesh of his collarbone. Darius screamed, and then whipped his sword around, cleaving the attacking farmer in half.

"No!" Jerico cried.

The way was clear, and Darius sprinted free. Jerico stood before the crowd, and he braced with his shield.

Forgive me if this is wrong, he prayed. Light swelled in the center of his shield, then burst outward with the strength of a lightning bolt. Blinded, the people staggered. Hooking his shield on his back, Jerico turned and ran, following Darius out of Wilhelm and into the wilderness beyond.

They ran for a long hour, both of them conditioned to such exertion as well as blessed with strength from their deity. Not a word was said between them. At last they reached the end of the farmland, and feeling confident they could lose themselves in the hills beyond, Jerico slowed. Bending over to catch his breath, he let his shield slip to the ground, glad to be free of its weight. Darius did the same, jamming his sword into the dirt and leaning on it, the handle pressed against his face.

"You're bleeding," Jerico said.

"Most of the blood isn't mine."

"No, your neck."

Darius pulled off his glove and then touched the wound at his collarbone. His fingers came back red.

"Not too deep," he said. "I'll live."

An awkward silence fell between them. Jerico felt he should be the teacher, Darius his student, even though Darius was actually older. He knew more of the world, understood better the politics of the North. But he'd erred, badly.

"Darius..." he started to say.

"Save it. I know. I made a mistake."

"A mistake? You cut a man in two."

Darius glared.

"I was hurt, and frightened. A second more, and they would have buried me. What would you have done then? Watched me die? Or risked dying yourself when you tried to save me? There was no reasoning with them, and you know it."

"They might have listened until you cut off a man's hand!" His voice was rising, and much as he knew he shouldn't, he continued anyway. "We're beacons, examples for others to follow. We're not executioners!"

"Bullshit!" Darius was in his face now, overcome with exhaustion and frustration. "I saw how many wolf-men you killed, far more than I ever did. I saw you slaughter Sebastian's men. You're just as good at killing as I am, if not better. I killed one man, *one man*, protecting my life. You think I'm happy about it? Think I enjoyed it? Gods damn it, if this world were just, they'd have killed me in my sleep without giving me the choice. You weren't there. You didn't see it."

He fell silent. Jerico took a deep breath and forced himself to calm down. He couldn't judge Darius harshly, not without knowing everything he'd gone through. This was a man turned from Karak to Ashhur. A dark paladin would have had no qualms about slaughtering an entire village to protect himself. That he felt guilt at all was a poignant sign.

"What happened in Durham?" Jerico asked softly. "I've not asked before, but now I think it best you tell me."

Darius looked back to the village, then sighed.

"A priest found me, wandering and lost," he said. "He offered me a chance to redeem myself in the eyes of Karak. He was a cold, cruel man, Jerico, if he was ever even a man. Very powerful, and worst of all, his words were like poison in my mind. I believed him. He was Karak's prophet, the voice of my god. And then he brought me to Durham, to make amends for my mistakes. I was to convert the faithful, make the entire village bend its knee."

Jerico thought of the many he knew there, and could guess their reaction.

"What happened then?" he asked.

Darius chuckled, and he wiped at his eyes.

"I couldn't do it. I tried, but they knew me better than I knew myself. Yet it didn't matter. The prophet...when he came back...damn it. Damn it all, I told them to run! I told them how dangerous he was. Some listened, but not enough. He came with fire and magic, and..."

He started laughing, despite his grief.

"You know what, Jerico? I'm glad there's a bounty on my head. It means a few made it out alive. It means at least I might have done something right."

Jerico looked back, and he saw a distant cluster of torches, about a mile away by his estimate.

"We need to continue," he said. "It looks like they're pursuing us farther than I thought."

"I don't blame them."

They gathered their things. They had terribly few supplies, and Jerico expected a very hungry day until they could reach another village, or trap a rabbit or squirrel.

"Darius," said Jerico. "Please, just promise me you won't kill anyone else coming after you because of that bounty. They're only obeying the law. I'll help protect you from the people, but don't make me protect the people from you."

Darius looked down at his armor, saw the blood on the sharp edges.

"I'll try," he said. "Forgive me. I've much to learn."

Jerico thought of his dilemma earlier and chuckled.

"I think we both have plenty to learn. Let's just keep the body count to a minimum while we do."

2

Sir Robert Godley was at the top of the Blood Tower when Karak's army arrived.

"Robert?" asked Daniel Coldmine, Robert's most trusted companion. The lieutenant stood at the half-open door, his fingers still wrapped about the handle.

"I know," Robert said, staring out the window at the reinforced doors of the walls surrounding the tower. Beyond were tents, caravans, and many, many armed men. His heavy hands lay flat across his desk. Between them were a bottle and an empty glass. "Send whoever is in charge up to me."

Daniel hesitated.

"Sir, we still have the option to turn them away. The worst they can do is voice their complaint back at Mordeina. They can't be mad enough to attack servants of the King and expect no retribution."

"I said bring their leader to me," Robert said, still refusing to turn around. "I will show no fear, not to the likes of them. Now go."

Daniel bowed.

"I'll return shortly."

"Take as much time as you need," Robert said to no one. He reached for the bottle, then pushed it away. He wasn't drunk, but he was getting damn close. It was shameful enough using the liquor to bolster his courage. Confronting the priests shit-faced was an embarrassment he'd never let himself live down. He was better than that, and more importantly, he owed his men better than that.

It hadn't taken long. Within two weeks of his bounty on the paladin Darius, he'd received message that an envoy from Mordeina would soon arrive to represent the Stronghold. Robert had put a death sentence on the head of one of their own. At the time, Daniel had warned him such an action would not go unnoticed, and he'd been right. As to how Karak's children would respond, he could only guess, but seeing over five hundred private soldiers bearing the mark of the Lion surrounding his tower, Robert's imagination didn't need to work too hard.

A knock at the door sent him slowly to his feet.

"Enter," he said.

The door opened, and Daniel escorted two men inside. One was older, with thin gray hair that hung down to his bony shoulders. He stood straight, though, and walked without a limp. He offered a wrinkled hand, and when Robert shook it, he squeezed with impressive strength.

"Greetings, knight," said the priest. His voice was deep, well-aged. "My name is Luther, priest of our glorious god, Karak. With me is my pupil, Cyric."

The other man stepped forward. Unlike Luther, he looked young, barely into his twenties. He bowed low, in a manner more respectful than Luther had shown. His hair was a deep brown and cut short, so that his forehead seemed much larger than it was. Combined with his blue eyes and slender nose, it gave him an awkward, youthful look. When he spoke, though, his voice echoed with an authority and a certainty that immediately revealed why he'd been chosen as Luther's pupil.

"I am honored to meet the man who devised the banishment of the heathen elves from our lands," said Cyric. "You did Mordan a great service."

"You'd have been at your mother's breast when that happened, if not still in her belly," Robert said. "How could you know much of that?"

"He's a voracious reader," said Luther. "I doubt there is a book in our library he has not read. But come, we have not traveled all this way to discuss forgotten battles. Word of your bounty on one of the Stronghold's paladins reached us quickly, Sir Godley."

Robert exchanged a look with Daniel, who shifted his stance so his hand rested on the hilt of his sword.

"I'm not a fool," said Robert. "I knew you'd come, but if there were ever a guilty man in the North, it would be Darius. I have over a hundred people who'll swear that he..."

"We have not come to question his guilt," Luther interrupted. "Darius is a fallen servant, and has rejected Karak's teachings. We have reason to believe he killed several of our paladins, good men sent to find and ascertain his faithfulness to our ways."

Robert's eyes narrowed. They weren't here to argue, or to protect Darius? It sounded too good to be true, which made him all the more suspicious.

"Then why have you come, Luther? I can see your armed men from my window. The North is dangerous, but not so much to require that large an escort for only two priests."

"Indeed," said Luther, smiling. "I pray we have not frightened you, but yes, we have come with a request. You handed Darius a sentence of death, but we ask that you deliver him unto us instead."

"You want to spare his life?" asked Daniel, and Robert could see his anger ready to burst forth.

"Spare it?" asked the young Cyric, laughing. "Our tomes detail quite clearly the fate blasphemers and traitors must suffer. Whatever death you think Darius deserves, I assure you, ours will be worse."

Luther shot his pupil a look, and Robert recognized it well. It was a warning against speaking out of turn. Robert had just sent Daniel that same look for his own outburst.

"This is about more than punishment," Luther said, clearing his throat. "Darius is a dangerous man, and your bounty invites much unnecessary death. If he can kill our skilled paladins, then poor farmers and soldiers desperate for a bit of coin stand little chance. I ask that you retract the bounty, and instead make it for information only. Let the Stronghold deal with Darius. He will not remain hidden for long, not from me."

Robert crossed his arms and tried to think. The offer was tempting, but something about it bothered him. The two priests were acting too kind, too understanding. No doubt they were trying to save face for their order by having Darius executed in private. Hardly the example Robert wanted to set.

"His crimes are against the King's citizens," Robert said, trying to stall.

"Whose protection has been left to Lord Sebastian," said Luther. "But has he done anything? Of course not. He's too busy squabbling with his brother for land, leaving this matter to you. Speaking of which..."

The old man walked over to the map on the far side of Robert's wall, and he rubbed his chin as he stared at it with bloodshot eyes.

"How goes the North?" he asked. "We hear only rumors in Mordeina, and struggle to know what is true and what is not."

"Lord Arthur met Lord Sebastian in fair battle, and lost," Robert said. "He retreated to his castle, which Lord Sebastian has put under siege. That is the last I have heard, but I expect it to take months before the Castle of Caves falls."

"Sebastian is a good friend of Karak," Cyric said, more to Luther than Robert. "We must ensure his victory over his brother."

"I thought the priests and paladins of Karak remained neutral in political matters," Daniel interrupted again. Robert knew well his distaste for the priests, and if he couldn't hold his tongue...

"Go prepare lodging for Luther's men," he ordered. Daniel looked displeased, but he bowed low and left to carry out his orders.

"A rebellious man," Luther said, softly chuckling.

"He only asks what I myself am thinking," Robert said.

"And you are right, in a way. We are neutral in most politics, but when it comes to Karak and his children, we are ever vigilant. Sebastian is a faithful servant, whereas Arthur is under the delusion we are a ... detriment to the North. Besides, is Sebastian not the lawful ruler of these lands? We only uphold the law, Robert."

"As do I," said Robert. "And Darius has broken it. Forgive me, but my bounty stays. If he is no longer a paladin of the Stronghold, then he should be of no concern to you."

"We do not operate under your laws," Cyric said. "We live under the law of Karak, which is wise as it is..."

Cyric looked furious, but Luther remained calm, not even turning from the map.

"Enough, Cyric," said Luther. He gestured to the door. "Leave us. I will speak with our host in private."

Cyric's look was bitter, but he bowed low and obeyed. As the door closed, Luther sighed.

"May I sit?" he asked.

"By all means."

Luther walked over to a chair pressed against the wall that was usually reserved for Daniel. His joints creaked as he sat. His eyes bored into Robert, who sat at his desk. Something about that look shriveled his testicles and made him wish he could call Daniel back in.

"You must forgive my pupil," Luther said. "He is still young, and has difficulty understanding that the way of the world is rarely as easy as his books would imply."

Robert grunted.

"Very little of the world is easy, especially here in the North."

"Indeed. I do not think he would understand what I have to say to you, for I know what he expects me to say. The will of Karak is lord of all things, and for you to resist speaks blasphemy against that which is holy."

Robert decided to the Abyss with it, and poured himself another glass.

"And what would you say?" he asked before taking a drink.

"That such a claim would be an insult to your honor. You have the safety of many people in your hands, and the lawful authority to do what you have done. You also fear our power, for you know how strong our influence is in Mordeina. You also fear Karak. I can see it in your eyes. Yes, what you did is within your power, but not all we do is wise. You may have the authority to lay judgment on a priest or paladin of Karak, but it is not your *place* to do so. I need to be convinced you are aware of that."

"You just said Darius was no longer a paladin of the Stronghold."

"Something you were unaware of when you offered that bounty."

Robert tried to summon fury at having his station challenged, his authority mocked. Instead he could only stare into Luther's eyes and feel the power of the entire priesthood prepared to move against him.

"I fail to see how you are any different from your pupil," he said, putting aside his glass.

"Cyric would view your resistance as blasphemy, worthy of punishment and purging with cleansing fire. He would threaten you with the Abyss, and escalate this into a conflict of wills and pride. I only hope that we might see eye to eye. You do not have to agree with me, Robert, only acknowledge who wields the greater power, and act as the pragmatic man I know you are."

Robert swallowed. There was no doubt about who wielded the greater power. It took months of begging just to get King Baedan to send a fraction of their needed resupplies, yet meanwhile, the priests of Karak whispered into his ear day and night.

"You want the bounty changed to capture only, correct?" he asked.

"I do," Luther said. He smiled, as if sensing Robert's breaking resolve.

"I want you to make me a promise," Robert said, "and swear to it in writing on the same parchment upon which I alter the bounty."

"And what do I promise?"

"That your order will execute Darius for his crimes. I don't care how, and don't care when. I just need to know he will suffer for what he did to Durham."

"He has turned his back on our god," Luther said, rising to his feet. "The stars may fall from the heavens, and our sun dwindle and die, yet his suffering will continue amid darkness and fire. Never ending. Never relenting. If you wish, you may write so on your parchment, and I will sign it with my blood. Will that suffice?"

"It will suffice," Robert said, but he felt no comfort. Cyric may have been a fanatic, but this man...he truly believed what he said, that he would capture Darius and force him to endure such tortures. But even amid the fanatic belief, he could still see through Robert's eyes, understand his motives, and react accordingly. Luther had left him with no argument against accepting his request other than basic pride. Should he resist anyway, it would only take the time for a letter to reach King Baedan and back before he was reprimanded and overruled.

"Excellent," Luther said, clapping his hands. "My men will stay here while we await word of Darius's location, as well as plan our conflict with this rebellious Lord Arthur. Oh, and before I forget..."

He pulled out a scroll from one of his lengthy robe pockets.

"I know your provisions are low, so as a measure of gratitude, we have brought gifts from Mordeina."

Robert accepted the scroll, unfurled it, and began to read. His jaw dropped. Bread, butter, caskets of ale, jars of honey, clothes, coats, furs, blankets...He could reinforce nearly every tower along the Gihon for the winter, just with what their wagons had brought.

"Thank you," he said, stunned.

"No, thank you," said Luther, "for your cooperation."

Robert heard his meaning loud and clear.

"My men thank you as well."

Luther smiled.

"I am glad. Do not worry about finding my men a place to sleep. They will bunk in our wagons and tents, to lessen our burden upon you. I must insist upon a room for Cyric and myself, though. Now, if you do not object, I must oversee my companions."

He left, and Robert leaned back in his chair. His eyes flicked over the list, still stunned by the donated wealth. A rock built in his stomach as he thought of how refusing the priests would have kept him from receiving a single crumb of bread. His men would have found out, too. His blood chilled. They'd hear of the warm coats, the abundant food, and then hear how they'd lost it all because of a single criminal. As dissension spread, Luther would have remained outside his tower, surrounding it with his wagons...

"Damn it," he said, tossing the scroll to his desk. It had never been an option. The result had never been in doubt. In time, Luther would have had his way.

Once more he felt the power of the priesthood arrayed against him, and knew how helpless he was before it. His only consolation was knowing that that same power had turned its focus to Darius. Deep down, he believed Luther would find him, and bring him back to the Stronghold in chains. It would only be a matter of time.

⊲⊳⊲⊳

Valessa stood naked before the door of the farmhouse. She wanted to barge in, but knew she had to find out for certain. She had to know how much was left of her humanity. Her knuckles rapped against the wood, its solidity against her touch reassuring. At least there was that. As the door opened, she tried her best to act the poor, wounded girl. She held her daggers behind her back.

"Bandits," she stammered to the heavyset farmer and his wife.

Her body shivered like she was cold, yet her red hair was singed in places as if by fire. The husband set aside the dagger he'd been holding while the wife reached for her, sympathy in her eyes.

"You poor dear," said the woman. "Come in, please. Cale, go see what you can find for her to wear."

The ceiling was low, but the house was large enough for several rooms. The walls were old wood, but clean, as the floor was meticulously swept. A fire burned in the hearth, and she fought an urge to sit beside it. As Valessa stepped inside, the woman reached for her. Both flinched at the contact, the woman's fingers touching her shoulders only briefly.

"Oh my," she said, pulling back and rubbing her hands together. Her face looked a mixture of sadness and fear. "By gods, you're cold."

Cale returned holding a blanket, and he made a point to stare at her eyes instead of elsewhere.

"Here you go, miss," he said, wrapping it about her shoulders. As the blanket settled over her, she forced herself to concentrate, to remain calm. Part of her expected it to fall right through her, as if she were a ghost, but it did not. There was no warmth to it, no comfort, but at least she wasn't standing there naked.

"Care to sit with me by the fire?" asked the woman. She gestured to two chairs carved of wood, each on opposite sides of the fireplace.

"I...yes," said Valessa. She shuffled as if she had been wounded. In a way, she had been, though of her own volition. Every time she closed her eyes to rest, she relived the memory of impaling herself on Darius's blade. Darius, the betrayer...

"My name's Dora, and this is my husband, Cale," said the woman, settling down in her chair. "Might I have your name?"

"Valessa," she said, wrapping the blanket tighter about her. It wasn't her nakedness she was trying to hide. It was how with every movement she made, her skin thinned, its color draining away as it became liquid shadow. She was darkness given form, and a soul. That she could hold the blanket gave her hope. Perhaps there was still a chance she might have some decency and normality, even in the form her god had cursed her with.

"Forgive me," she muttered. *Blessed,* not cursed. She'd been given a chance to hunt down the traitor, to make amends for her failure. Never should she spit in the face of her god and his gifts.

"Oh, it's no bother," said Dora, misunderstanding her. "Truth be told, neither of us were sleeping. The older we get, the more the night seems to like us better than the day."

Valessa settled in the chair, focusing on every inch that touched her body. There could be no give, no shift. There was still plenty she had to experiment with, but if she were to be the assassin she needed to be, simple acts like sitting in a chair needed to be mastered. So far, so good. Feeling confident, she set her daggers beside her, still hidden by the blanket.

Cale returned, a meager assortment of clothes in his calloused hands.

"It's not much," he said, holding them out for her to take. "But it'll do until we can get you back to your family."

Valessa tried to smile. As a gray sister, she'd been trained in a hundred different personas, from obedient servants to wealthy noblewomen. She tried to be the wounded victim, to keep her motions quick and startled, her eyes wide, her speech rare. Concentrating amid the pain, though...

"Thank you," she said, reaching a hand out from underneath her blanket. Her reaction was too fast, despite it being appropriate to the persona she channeled. A wisp of smoke trailed over her skin. Cale didn't seem to notice, and she thanked Karak for that. Grabbing the clothes, she felt the rough fabric, its touch almost painful. She set them on her lap, and assumed correctly the couple would understand if she remained there, still warming.

"I'm hungry," she said.

Dora stood, and she motioned for Cale to take her seat.

"I think we still have a bit of soup from earlier," she said, nodding to a pot set near the fireplace. Retrieving a wooden bowl and spoon from a cupboard, she knelt and scraped up a meager portion of soup. It was a dark brown broth, with hints of meat and vegetables floating inside. It looked appetizing enough. Valessa had yet to eat or drink a thing since her...what should she call it? Resurrection? Recreation? Salvation? It didn't matter. That was over a week ago. She should have been dead, but she was not. Or perhaps she was.

She took the bowl, slowly. This was it, she knew. She dipped the spoon into the bowl, then brought it to her lips. Her hand shook, and its color faded. Opening her mouth, she slipped the spoon inside. She imagined the taste, heavy and meaty, but it was not there. No sensation, just the texture, and an awareness of its lukewarm temperature. The only thing she felt was pain. Every second, day and night, she felt a throbbing ache everywhere she once had muscle and flesh. The taste of food was just another sensation, without pleasure or satisfaction. She wanted to cry, but tears would not come. Her new form refused such a weakness.

Valessa swallowed. Instead of traveling down her throat, the liquid passed through the bottom of her chin and neck, dripping across her blanket.

"Careful dear," Dora said when she saw the mess. Cale had not seen at all, too busy staring into the fire with a half-asleep expression on his face. Fighting down her fury, Valessa offered the bowl back to Dora with one hand. Too fast, her hand became shadow and smoke. The bowl fell right through her, hitting the floor with a dull thud. This time Dora saw, and her mouth dropped open.

Valessa moved before she could scream. She grabbed her daggers and shot from her chair. She didn't cast aside the blanket, for she passed right through it. In a single smooth motion, she slashed open the woman's throat, then turned to Cale. The man was still trying to get up from his chair when she jammed a dagger into his chest and twisted. He coughed once, his knuckles white as he clutched the arms of his chair, and then he died. Blood poured across the handle of her dagger, but when it reached her quivering flesh, it slid past and down to the floor.

She dropped the dagger, and naked on her knees, she howled out in mindless fury. Softness, pleasure, comfort, a loving embrace...all denied to her. And why? Because she had failed her duty, failed to kill that bastard, Darius. Hatred seethed in her heart at the mere thought of his name. He'd suffer, oh, how she'd make him suffer. Her new form might be a penance imposed by Karak, but there would be no penance for Darius, only torment. When finished, she'd use her daggers to send him to Karak, and let her deity deliver for an eternity all the suffering Darius deserved.

Stop it, she told herself even as she continued to shriek. Karak was not a god of love. He was a god of order. Darius had broken that order, as had Valessa in failing to kill him. She couldn't be angry. Not at Karak. No, that wasn't fair. It took all her willpower to choke down her fury at her beloved deity. Now was not the time for weakness. It was time for revenge.

She looked down at her naked form. Valessa was not ashamed of exposing her body in any way (and in truth, had seduced many in the name of her god, all to execute the unfaithful), but trying to go about unnoticed would be impossible. She needed clothes. Returning to her chair, she grabbed a shirt and slid it over her head. It was too big, and left much of her breasts exposed, but it was better than nothing. Pausing for a moment to focus her thoughts, she took a single step. Every inch of fabric brushing against her shadowed flesh itched in her mind, but she remained solid. Another step, still good. But she could not waddle everywhere like a lame animal. The real test came as she lifted her arms above her head and twirled in a half-remembered dance that had been common in court.

The shirt fell through her to the floor, her body a whirling creature of shadow and smoke.

"Why?" she shrieked. Her fists pounded against the floor until her hands began to pass through, striking nothing. It made no sense! How could she perform her god's will when saddled with such difficulty? How could he expect her to stroll naked through open streets in a hunt for his fallen paladin?

"Please," she prayed. Her body might not create tears, but she was sobbing anyway, her grief overwhelming her. "Please, help me, Karak. Show me the way."

She heard no answer, which perhaps she deserved. Trying to overcome her grief, she looked at her naked body and began to think. Her body was not real, only an illusion. She could make parts of it solid, particularly through concentration. Was her skin not also an illusion? As she stared at herself, she tried to see what she truly was, not what she remembered. Before her eyes, she became darkness. The sight terrified her, but in it, she found hope. Perhaps there was more to it than that. Closing her eyes again, she imagined her old leather armor, covered with dull plain clothes, and a long gray cloak wrapped about her shoulders. She'd worn such an outfit so often it was natural to her. She could still imagine the way it felt, and how her cloak would billow in the wind.

When she opened her eyes, she was no longer naked.

"Thank you," she whispered. She moved her arms, watched the sleeves fade along with her skin. Her body was just an illusion, a projection of how she imagined herself. Which meant...

She closed her eyes again. Thinking of her former partner, Claire, she tried to imagine Claire's blonde hair falling down to her shoulders over her more slender form. And then she opened her eyes, saw the hair, saw the subtle shift of her hands. The true power of Karak's gift came to her then, and she might have wept for joy. Yes, she would have to endure pain, but all gifts came with a price. She could be anyone, limited only by her imagination.

Valessa retrieved her daggers. Only they would remain in her grasp when she moved at full speed, somehow blessed by Karak during the process of her...revival. One last thought came to her, one she had to finally test. Turning to a wall, and without any time to think, and therefore frighten herself off her course of action, she ran straight at it. No slowing. At the last moment, she closed her eyes.

When she opened them, she was outside, daggers still in hand.

She laughed.

"Where is he?" she asked, looking to the stars. "Where is the traitor?"

When she lay down to sleep, she relived her moment of death, thrusting her neck upon his blade. But when she focused on his name, his face, she could always look to the sky, day or night, and see a red star burning, showing her the way. Sure enough, she saw it, and forgetting her hunger, her pain, her sorrow, she left the corpses inside the farmhouse and headed southwest.

Toward Darius.

3

As the two paladins walked into Stonahm, Jerico did not wonder about linking back up with Kaide, or worry that the villagers might hand Darius over for coin. All he cared about was finally getting himself a decent meal.

"You sure they won't try for the bounty?" Darius asked as they passed the nearby homes. "I'm not too eager to repeat what happened at Wilhelm."

"Neither am I," said Jerico as he glanced about. "But this is Kaide's home, his family." The last time Jerico had been in Stonahm was not long after Sebastian's army had come and pillaged it. Much of the damage had been repaired over the past two weeks, and as faces peered at them from windows and doorways, he saw no anger, only fear. "I've helped them, fought for them. To go against me, and turn over an enemy of Sebastian, wouldn't even cross their minds."

He stopped in the center of the village, with not so much as a word spoken to them in greeting. Everyone seemed eager to either avoid them or pretend they were not there.

"I think," Jerico muttered as a group of men came around a corner and approached. He recognized their leader, the elderly Kalgan, the closest person the village had to a healer.

"I see you survived," Kalgan said, hardly sounding pleased by that fact. Jerico tried not to feel angry with him. Jerico's protection of a woman from one of Sebastian's knights had caused the lord to send his army down to punish them in the first place. As much as he tried to convince himself he was in the right, it did little to sway his guilt, and he well understood Kalgan's ire.

"We've come for shelter," Jerico said. "We've traveled far, and are hungry."

Kalgan eyed him and Darius, and the other men with him shuffled nervously.

"Follow me," he said. "We need to get you out of sight."

Jerico glanced at Darius, who only shrugged. They followed the elderly man back to his empty hut. Opening the door, he gestured for them to enter. Once inside, Kalgan waved away the others, then joined them, shutting the door after them.

"You have a lot of nerve to return here," Kalgan said, his voice more tired than angry.

Jerico sat on the bed, glad to be off his feet, while Darius remained standing in the corner, clearly on edge.

"I never fled the battle, if that is what you're thinking," Jerico said. "I was there to the end, but Sebastian had too many. It was Kaide who called for the retreat, not me."

"It's not that. I've heard what you did. You are a two-faced blessing, Jerico, sometimes bringing joy, sometimes sorrow. Sebastian has sent knights to all corners of the North looking for, as they put it, 'the man with the god shield'. His reward is substantial, though I wouldn't worry about any of the villagers here turning you over. Should you travel beyond Kaide's influence, however..."

The old man looked to Darius, and his frown deepened.

"And you. You look like the man Sir Robert is searching for, the one who supposedly burned Durham to the ground. Are you Darius of the Stronghold?"

When Darius nodded, Kalgan rubbed his eyes and swore.

"Two wanted men appearing in our town. Ashhur help us. Sebastian already fears us rebelling. To have both of you out in the open...damn it, do neither of you have any sense?"

"I thought you said no one here would turn us in," Darius said.

"I meant Jerico, not you," Kalgan said. "And it doesn't matter. One errant word, one man with more greed than sense, and Sebastian's knights will ride in again, and this time they may not stop at just rape and fire. You two must leave now, before you cause any more trouble."

Jerico leaned against the wall and sighed. So much for a night of relaxing and enjoying a bit of corn meal, warm soup, and maybe a roll of bread...

"Where is Kaide?" he asked. "That is why we're here. We separated after the battle, with Sebastian's army between us."

"He's back in the forest," Kalgan said. "Not sure how long he'll be there. He's trying to recruit more men. The gods help him, he thinks he can break Sebastian's siege of Arthur's castle."

Jerico frowned, though he wasn't surprised by the news. With Arthur's defeat, he'd have little choice but to flee. A lengthy siege would be expensive and draining for Sebastian's men, but he had the patience and manpower to do it. Victory would only be a matter of time.

"We'll leave for his camp, then," Jerico said, slowly rising to a standing position. It felt like every muscle in his body ached from the constant walking, and his stomach growled, as if realizing its good meal had been delayed. Kalgan opened the door, glanced about to make sure no one waited for them, and then gestured for them to leave.

"A fine welcome for one who fought and bled for you," Darius said as he brushed past the old man.

"There have been enough of both in this village," Kalgan said, unimpressed. "Forgive me for hoping we might have peace for a change."

As they headed for Stonahm's limits, someone cried out Jerico's name. He turned, then smiled, as Beth came running up to him. Without slowing, she hugged both her intact arm and her stump about him. That she was not self-conscious about the injury brightened his mood considerably.

"You're back," she said, all smiles.

"I promised, didn't I?"

"Beth, don't you have work to do?" Kalgan said. Beth took a step back and nodded curtly to him.

"I do, but Katie said she saw Jerico, and I wanted..."

"Enough. Go on."

She nodded again, then turned back to Jerico.

"My father will be so happy you returned," she said. "Tell him I miss him."

"I will."

He kissed her forehead, then continued on toward the forest.

"A fan?" Darius asked, eliciting a chuckle from Jerico.

"A spider bite nearly killed her. I saved her life, but still had to take her arm. She's Kaide's daughter."

"That makes a bit more sense. I'd be interested to meet this Kaide. How does he compare to his rumors?"

"He doesn't care for honor, has no qualms about killing, and is driven by revenge. But he's not a cannibal, if that's what you're wondering."

Darius smirked.

"Well...I guess there's that. How far a walk is it?"

"Better part of a day."

The other paladin sighed.

"We should have asked for food before we left."

Despite Kalgan's obvious impatience, Jerico rubbed his eyes and sighed as well.

"Yeah..."

They slept at the forest's edge, eating a few berries they found as well as some roots that Darius was certain were the most bitter thing he'd ever tasted. They built a large fire, Jerico hoping the smoke might alert one of Kaide's gang of their approach, but come morning, there was no one. Jerico tried assuring Darius it would be no problem, and with their things packed, they trudged into the forest. There appeared to be no path, though a couple of strangely cut branches might have been a marking.

"You do know where you're going, right?" he asked Jerico.

"More or less."

Hardly the confidence Darius was hoping for.

"'More or less'?" he asked as they pressed through the rough thicket. "Jerico, what does 'more or less' mean?"

"I've been this way a couple of times. I'm fairly certain I can find it."

Darius winced.

"And if you can't?"

"Kaide's men will find us," Jerico said, grinning at him.

"Find our starved corpses, you mean," Darius muttered.

They walked for an hour, at a fairly slow pace, as Jerico kept checking the surroundings. What his friend was looking for, he didn't have a clue. At last they stumbled upon a stream, which Jerico insisted was a great sign. They stopped to rest. Darius yanked off his armor and dipped his head into the wonderfully cold water.

"What I'd give for a mule or something to carry my armor instead," he said.

David Dalglish

"Not much of a luxury either of us can afford. I'd sleep in it if it were at all comfortable."

Darius grinned at him as water dripped down his face and hair.

"That worried about daggers in the night? If you're asleep, wearing armor matters little when the assassin stabs you through the eye."

Jerico chuckled, then turned his attention to Darius's armor. He nodded toward the chestplate.

"You should do something about that," he said.

Darius followed his gaze and saw the lion painted across the chest.

"Would you have me paint a golden mountain there instead?" he asked.

"Honestly? Yes."

Darius shifted uncomfortably, and he ducked his head back into the river to stall. As the cold seeped into his pores, he tried to think. In Jerico, he'd seen something he knew he wanted, a hope for a dark world far more sacred and meaningful than the fire and order Karak promised. But he still felt uncomfortable calling himself a servant of Ashhur. Ever since his childhood he'd been a warrior for Karak. It was hard not to consider himself a traitor, no matter how terrible some of Karak's servants had been, or what Karak had shown in blessing him for the killing of innocents because they worshipped Ashhur, the enemy. And now he was sworn to that enemy. According to his teachings in the Stronghold, he was doomed to an eternity of torment. Was that still true? Or would he escape to the Golden Eternity?

Pulling his head free from the cold water, he gasped in air. While wiping at his eyes, he inspecting his armor. Jerico had a point. He looked so much darker, so much more dangerous than Jerico when they stood side by side. There was little he could do about the color, which was stained into the armor during its crafting. The symbol of the lion, though, he could remove with enough diligence and the scraping of a knife. No matter how hesitant he might be to publicly announce his worship of Ashhur, he was certain he wanted to claim no allegiance to Karak.

"Give me time, and I'll get it off," he told Jerico. "Might make it a bit easier to go unnoticed without it, too. Robert's looking for Darius of the Stronghold, not the Citadel."

At the mention of the Citadel, Jerico's mood darkened.

"Forgive me," Darius said. "I'm sure such a loss will take a long time to heal."

Jerico nodded, then reached for his shield, flinging it across his back.

"I must go back there sometime," he said. "I must see for myself its ruin. But Arthur needs my help more urgently than I need some shallow confirmation. Are you ready to go? If we follow the stream, I believe I can find their camp."

"Just let me get dressed. Daggers in the night and all."

Darius put back on his armor, and for the first time felt uncomfortable with the lion on his chest. To be sure, he touched his greatsword, and saw the faintest of blue light shimmer across its edges. He still believed, at least some small part of him did. He held on to that, and followed Jerico.

Another hour later, Darius felt the hairs on his neck stand on end. Long used to trusting his combat instincts, he looked about, then spotted a man in a distant tree. In his hands the man held a bow, the arrow already nocked and ready to fly.

"Jerico," he started to say.

"I see him," Jerico said. "Let's pray he's a friend. Hail!"

He waved, while subtly letting his shield shift to his other arm, in case he needed its protection. The man tensed for a moment, then relaxed as he caught sight of the blue glow.

"Jerico!" cried the distant man, shimmying down the tree. He was a far bigger man than Darius expected, and his was face covered with scars.

"How have the past few weeks treated you, Adam?" Jerico asked, clasping the man's wrist and pumping it up and down.

"Like shit," Adam said. "Was hoping to be stomping Sebastian's ass all the way from here to Mordeina. Instead we're stuck waiting."

Jerico nodded to the weapon slung across his shoulder. "I didn't know you could use a bow."

"Gotta hunt to eat, don't you?"

Darius thought of their meager meals the past few days.

"Not necessarily," he said. This brought the big man's attention over to him.

"Who the fuck are you?" he asked.

"Darius," he said, offering a mock bow. "Consider me flattered to finally meet one of Kaide's most infamous knights."

Adam paused a moment, as if still thinking over the words, then his face spread into a giant grin.

"Funny man," he said, punching Darius in the shoulder, despite his armor. "But if you're half as good as Jerico, and willing to fight, we'll treat you fine as any prince."

Darius raised an eyebrow at Jerico, who only shrugged.

"Better than being chased out by people eager for a bounty, right?"

"If you say so."

"Come on," said Adam. "Follow me. Kaide'll want to know you made it out of the Green Gulch alive and breathing."

The paladins let him lead the way away from the stream and into Kaide's camp. Darius was surprised by the amount of buildings, all built of wood and straw. He'd expected a few tents, maybe a single home, but not this. More surprising was how many wandered about, working at various tasks. Nearly everyone stopped what they were doing as Adam led the newcomers to the camp's center. Darius could hardly believe the hero's welcome they received. Even Durham had not been so thankful after they'd protected them from the wolf-men's attack.

"Where's Kaide?" Adam roared as the people began to crowd them.

"Out back, training," said one of the men.

Darius could only guess where 'out back' meant, but Adam seemed to know. They followed, curling around one of the buildings to a large open stretch between the trees. Twenty or so men stood in a line, old metal swords in their hands. A man walked before them, barking out orders while making slow motions in the air with his dirk. He was lithe, well fit, with his prematurely gray hair bound into a ponytail. He moved with such authority, Darius knew immediately that he had to be Kaide. His eyes carried such an intensity, it left him with little wonder how the man had managed to raise an army against Lord Sebastian, however ill-equipped and meager it was.

"Jerico," he said, sheathing his dirk. He wiped his hands on his tunic, and, unlike the others, he seemed only mildly surprised that the paladin had returned. "So you survived after all."

"There any doubt?" Jerico asked, and he smiled as the two embraced. "It'll take far more than a couple thousand soldiers to bring me down."

A half-hearted cheer came from the men training. Kaide turned on them, whatever joy had been present in his composure immediately gone.

"Back to training, all of you," he said. "Pat, you lead until I get back."

Kaide thanked Adam for escorting them to the camp, then sent him back to his hunt.

"Takes a lot of food to feed so many," Kaide said as he headed to his quarters with the two of them in tow. "Thankfully the deer here are plentiful, and even in winter we can usually capture a few squirrels."

"Venison sounds wonderful," Jerico said as they stepped inside the small log cabin, and Darius heartily agreed. Once the door shut behind them, Kaide turned and swung. His fist crunched into Jerico's jaw, the blow knocking him a step backward so that he thudded against the door. Instead of retaliating, Jerico stood there, mouth agape, and rubbed his face.

"When you tell me to flee, you don't stand there and keep on fighting yourself," Kaide said, jamming a finger in Jerico's face. "We fight together, you and I. If you're going to hold a line until death, then I stay at your side, and if I retreat, then your ass follows. Whatever miracle allowed you to survive, I don't want to have to rely on it again. You're the heart of this band now, the one thing that gives them hope, and your stand at the Green Gulch only solidified that. Do we understand each other?"

"You going to hit me again if I say no?"

The tension continued for a few more seconds, and then Kaide broke out into a laugh.

"No, but Sandra might. She missed you. We all have." He turned his attention to Darius. "I see you brought a friend."

"My name is Darius," he said, bowing. "Jerico saved my life, and I seek to return the favor."

At hearing the name, Kaide froze, and his eyes seemed to sparkle.

"Darius," he said. "As in Darius of the Stronghold, from Durham?"

Darius swallowed, and he tried not to show any emotion.

"Yes. Will that be a problem?"

"A problem? Depends. Who'd you piss off to get that bounty on your head?"

Darius thought it might be prudent to lie, but he immediately felt ashamed for even entertaining the notion.

"I was once of the Stronghold, but no longer," he said, standing up straighter so his full height towered over Kaide. "Karak's followers have never taken kindly to one who leaves the fold."

"That's strange," Kaide said, rubbing his chin. "Report I heard said the bounty came from Sir Robert at the towers."

"I was there when one of Karak's greatest priests burned it to the ground. I'm sure the blame has been cast upon me."

"Enough," Jerico said, standing between them. "We've come back to help, in whatever way we can."

Kaide shifted his attention to his friend, but Darius felt no comfort. It lingered in the air, that unspoken challenge, the question of his guilt, his role in Durham. No doubt Jerico saw the strong leader that Kaide was, but Darius also saw in him a greed and a hunger that set his nerves on edge. He saw a man with a cause, yet no ideals. The whole world might burn while Kaide waged his war on Lord Sebastian, and it wouldn't matter, so long as in the end he found victory.

"We don't have enough men, not yet," said Kaide. "But soon, we'll move out. We'll starve Sebastian's army of supplies, hit their caravans, set fires when they sleep. Anything to make their lives miserable. With each passing day, my men scour the North, telling tales of Sebastian's depravity. We'll build another rebellion, one that won't be stamped out after a single battle. But we can talk about those details later, once Bellok comes back with more supplies. For now, let's get you something to eat, and find you a room."

He opened the door, then glanced back at Jerico, whose face was starting to swell on one side.

"You tripped crossing the stream on the way here," he said, then exited.

"Aren't you the clumsy one," Darius said, following Jerico out, but there was no humor in his voice, only unease, as the rest of the camp cheered once more for their arrival.

4

With how many Kaide had gathered, there was no more room left in the few cabins. So they were given heavy blankets and bedrolls, which Jerico accepted gladly.

"We've both had plenty of experience sleeping on the ground," he said.

"Still prefer a bed, though," Darius said. Jerico chuckled, smacked him on the shoulder, and found a spot to make his own. It was at the outset of the camp, and he wasn't surprised when Darius didn't follow him. The man had been sullen since Wilhelm, and they'd been traveling together since the battle in the Green Gulch. No doubt Darius wanted to have some solitude for once, and, to be honest, Jerico felt the same. The near-worship Kaide's followers gave him didn't help much. By the way they acted, it was as if they thought Jerico could singlehandedly win them the war.

Which he couldn't. He'd try, of course, but even he had his limits, and he felt safe in assuming that taking on an army by himself was one of them.

As he was smoothing out the grass and weeding out any rocks or sticks that might make sleep difficult, he heard a woman call his name. He turned to see Kaide's sister, Sandra, weaving through the trees toward him. He raised his hand in greeting, but she ignored it, instead wrapping her arms about him. Her smile was the finest thing he'd seen in weeks.

"They told me you stayed behind when everyone else fled," she said, slipping out of his arms.

"I did. I tend to do stupid things like that."

"I should slap you for worrying me so."

He turned his head so she could see the light bruise on his cheek.

"Your brother beat you to it."

She laughed, and they embraced once more.

"I'd say he is only under stress, and worried about you, but I think I spend too much time apologizing for my brother's behavior as it is."

Jerico found himself increasingly aware of the feel of her in his arms, the way her silver hair curled about her face before falling past her shoulders, and the scent of flowers crushed into a perfume that wafted up from her neck. It made him feel awkward, and his mind failed to think of conversation.

"It's been rough since the battle," Sandra said. If she noticed his sudden awkwardness, she gave no acknowledgment of it. She sat down in the space Jerico had cleared and leaned back against the nearby tree he had planned to use to prop up his pillow. He took a seat next to her, thinking of the aftermath he'd seen: Arthur's men in flight as Sebastian's cheered in victory.

"I can't imagine," he said. "Did Kaide's men escape the fight cleanly?"

Sandra shook her head.

"Sir Gregane gave chase, and while my brother led them on a wild hunt, the rest started filtering back here." She shuddered. "So many were wounded, and there was no one else. I kept hoping you'd return, be there with those healing hands of yours. That light...but you never came. Just me. That was all. I sewed and stitched everything I could, but we didn't have enough herbs for the pain, not for any of them..."

She looked at him, and her eyes had tears.

"Tell me of other things, of a world so much better than this one. I want to think of anything else but the bloodshed and heartache of the North."

Jerico took her hand in his, and she did not protest, only squeeze hard against his fingers.

"I've not traveled much," he said, forcing a smile to his lips. "But I did visit Ker before heading north, and traveled to Angkar's harbor..."

He told of men and women he'd met, a few strange creatures kept in cages as pets, of Ashhur, and even how he'd defeated a gang of thieves with nothing but a wooden spoon. They talked, and the sun swung low across the sky.

Darius chose a place to sleep on the far outskirts of the camp. It felt as if eyes lingered too long on him, and conversations turned to whispers just by his passing. He ate around the main bonfire when they served supper, hoping that he might acclimate Kaide's men to his presence. He expected Jerico to help, but the other paladin was nowhere to be seen.

"Thanks, Jerico," Kaide muttered as he prepared his bedroll and blankets. "Just leave me out to dry."

The sun was just setting, but he was tired from the travel, and the many people had worn him thin. He sat down, removed his armor, and then held his chestplate in his lap. He stared at the sigil of the Lion, and wondered what it meant to him anymore. Was it just a dead reminder of what he had been? Did it represent the enemy? Or was it nothing but paint, a useless symbol given far too much importance?

It didn't matter. He wanted it gone. Slowly, carefully, he scraped away with the thick edge of his greatsword near the hilt. Chip by chip, the paint vanished, and the stars came out above the forest canopy. He thought Jerico might swing by at some point, but he did not. Darius knew he shouldn't be upset, but was anyway. Yes, he'd come to help, but he didn't know these people, and they certainly didn't know him. Well, other than that tiny fact of a bounty. The gold glinted in their eyes when they glanced his way.

He lay down, and thought to pray to Ashhur. But what was he to pray for? Every night, it seemed he begged for forgiveness. Every night, he reopened old wounds and felt his soul bleed. The scars Velixar had inflicted ran deep. Even in his dreams, he remembered the fire and bloodshed at Durham. In his mind's eye, he saw the innocent family praying to Ashhur, Velixar peering through a dirty window like a hunting animal, a locust, an evil beast come to consume everything pure and good. And now he was there, on his bedroll, in a dark forest, trying to pray just the same. Darius would have rather been the child, to have known nothing, for how did he go to Ashhur as anything other than a miserable wretch?

"I'm sorry," Darius whispered to Ashhur. "Jerico insists I feel no guilt, that I am redeemed. But he wasn't there, and sometimes I wonder if you were either..."

Enough, he thought. He laid his sword above his head, the handle in easy reach, and closed his eyes. It took plenty of shifting and turning, but at last sleep came to him.

It didn't last long.

His eyes opened, and his instincts fired off commands he did not understand. His hands flung above him, and only then did he realize a club swung for his face. It hit his arms hard enough to make his bones ache. His legs kicked out, but someone was on top of him. He felt rope and fists, and his eyes hurt in the light of torches. His groggy mind yearned for his armor, and reaching for his sword did nothing but expose his face to another blow of the club.

Blood splashed across his lips as it connected with his nose. He gagged, and then the rope was about his neck.

"Quiet now," one of the men said as he felt himself pulled to his feet. "Don't want him hearing."

Him? Him who?

He opened his mouth to ask, but one of the men shoved a thick wad of cloth between his teeth. He spat it out, but they struck his cheek with a club, then shoved it in again. Slender rope looped about his face, holding the cloth in place. Tears ran down, but he finally could see. A group of ten men surrounded him, with two of them holding his arms at either side. A heavy rope wound around his knees, waist, and arms. Several held torches, and others held clubs. Many bore splashes of his blood.

Who? he thought again. Kaide? Or did they mean Jerico? Who was it that had sold him out? He looked to the men, and he felt anger stirring in his heart. These fools, these men he'd come to help, now sought to sell him for coin? So much for the incredible loyalty Kaide supposedly instilled. So much for a noble war against Lord Sebastian.

"Hurry," said the same man, apparently the leader of the group. Squinting, Darius realized it was the one who had found him, the enormous, ugly man with the scars. Adam. That was his name.

And then someone who looked just like Adam grabbed the front of his shirt. At first he thought he saw double, but no, there were two, both alike but for their scars. He remembered the twins, having seen them briefly when eating around the campfire.

"Bring the horses over, Griff," Adam said, and the other nodded.

"Don't let him make a sound," Griff said.

"I'm not a damn fool, now go."

Two men restrained his arms, plus the huge Adam held him by the shirt. It didn't matter. Darius felt his anger growing. He struggled. The knots weren't the tightest, and they'd been hastily tied. Adam struck him across the mouth, and Darius's chest heaved as he gagged on the cloth. But his legs were gaining strength, and he flung himself to one side, knocking the two men off balance. They fell, Adam cursing as his fingers caught in the rope. That curse turned to a cry of pain as one of the fingers dislocated.

Darius rolled as the rest of the men swung their clubs, as if to beat him into submission. When he hit a man's legs, he curled onto his knees, then kicked. The top of his skull rammed into the man's groin, dropping him like a log. The knot at his heels loosened even more, and he freed his right leg. His arms were still bound, and he could only breathe through his nostrils, but at least he could run.

Not that he had anywhere to go. The men still surrounded him, and more worrying, Adam had regained his composure and grabbed a club from one of the others.

"Don't be a fool, Darius," Adam said. "We're hoping your bounty's worth more with you alive than dead, but we still get paid even if we drag your corpse to Robert. Drop to your knees, before I crack your fucking skull like a walnut."

If Darius had his armor and sword, he'd have laughed, and dared the man to try. Instead, he tensed with all his strength. With Karak, he could have called upon his deity for power, and filled his hands with fire to burn away the cords. But what did Ashhur offer? He didn't know, but it was time to find out. His neck muscles tensed, the rope dug deep into his wrists, and he snarled into his gag like an animal. Adam shook his head, as if disappointed, but his grin was ear to ear as he stepped forward to swing.

The rope snapped, the club hit his left forearm, and even though he felt bones snap, Darius struck Adam with his right fist, throwing all his weight into the blow. The roundhouse sent the big man staggering, and blood splattered across the dark earth as several teeth flew. The sound of the punch seemed to freeze the others, as if they could hardly believe what they'd seen.

"Goddamn," Adam sputtered, his hand against his mouth. Blood dripped through his fingers. "You hit like Jerico."

And then he swung his club. Darius ducked underneath, falling back into a retreat. The rest moved to join, his advantage of surprise finally lost. He shifted and parried blows with his right arm, keeping his left tucked against him and using it to absorb hits only when he had to. He head-butted one man, spun, and then rammed his elbow into the neck of another. Two bandits with torches tried to burn him, but the torches made poor weapons, and Darius pushed them aside. A club struck his back, but it hit thick muscle, not even knocking the air from his lungs. Spinning, he kicked the man in the knee, hard enough that he could hear the joint crack.

Adam closed the distance, but Darius caught him with a knee to the groin, and as he bent over, Darius uppercut him in the throat. Adam's mouth opened and closed, trying for air, but he remained eerily silent. The rest backed away, and Darius felt his rage overwhelming him. Don't kill, Jerico had said. Protect the innocent. But what of these bandits, these pathetic cowards who would steal him away in the night? Did they deserve his protection?

When he saw that none were moving against him, he reached up and yanked the rope from his head, then spat out his gag.

"Is this the best you can do?" he asked, gasping in air. The pain in his left arm was growing, and he felt his fingers shaking. "No wonder Sebastian doesn't give two shits about your army."

"It ain't that," said Griff, returning with a horse he led by a rope. In his other hand he held a long blade, and he pointed it at Darius. "We wanted to do this with you alive, outta respect for Jerico. But looks like you ain't giving us much choice."

"Seems so."

Griff suddenly crumpled to his knees as the sound of metal rang out through the forest. Behind him stood Jerico, his shield in hand. He looked about as mad as Darius felt. He lacked any armor, but his mace was clipped to his belt. So far he hadn't drawn it. So far.

"All of you should be ashamed," Jerico said, the light of his shield washing over them. He joined Darius's side, and he winced at the sight of all the blood. "How could you turn on one of your own?"

"He ain't one of us," said Adam, sounding funny with the missing teeth and his swelling lips.

"We're just following orders," said another.

"Orders?" Jerico looked about, and somehow, his anger grew. "Whose orders?"

"Mine," Kaide said, stepping through the ring of men. His hand was on the hilt of his dirk.

"I'm not going in as your little prize," Darius told him, grinning despite the pain. "I hope that won't be a *problem*."

"I don't understand," Jerico said, approaching Kaide. The rest of the men tensed. "How could you do this?"

"How could I not?" said Kaide, drawing his dirk and pointing it toward Darius. "Do you know what he is? He's months of food. He's an arsenal of weapons. He's a mercenary band that could break the siege at the Castle of Caves. Everything I need, right here, just by slitting his throat."

"Do it, and I'll kill you," Jerico said. He looked about the gathered group, and Darius found himself stunned by the sheer fury in his eyes. It felt as if the air about them thickened, and no fool, Darius moved to his bedroll and lifted his greatsword into one hand. He might have trouble swinging it, but it'd be better than fighting unarmed. Jerico freed his mace.

"Don't make this worse, Jerico." Kaide took a step back, among his men. "I tried to take him alive, for your sake. We still need you, but we owe this stranger nothing. He helped burn Durham to the ground, and if he is innocent, then let him plead his case to Robert, not me. I'll take the gold. It doesn't mean a damn thing to me if I have to buy my revenge with blood money."

"Move aside, Jerico," said Adam.

"Yeah, get on out," added Griff.

The two paladins shifted so they stood back to back. Jerico tilted his head, and spoke to Darius.

"I'm sorry. I thought them my friends."

"So am I allowed to kill them?"

Jerico shook his head.

"I'd still prefer not."

"I think it's up to them."

Darius pointed his greatsword at Kaide.

"Move aside," he said. "I'm leaving, tonight, and you will not stop me."

"Kaide," Jerico said, and he met the brigand leader's gaze. "Don't do this. Don't make me do this, not after all we've suffered through. You're better than this. You know I will defend him. I don't need my armor to bring you all down, not when I have my shield."

Kaide jammed his dirk back into its sheath and shook his head.

"I told you, Jerico," he said. "There's no honor in our war, only justice. But for your sake...so be it." He turned to Darius. "Leave here, tonight, as you said. I will send no man after you, so long as Jerico stays with me."

"You're too kind," Darius said.

Kaide left, and at his absence, the rest of the men dispersed, leaving the two paladins alone at the dark edge of the camp. Darius kicked, scattering his armor, then collapsed to his knees. Jerico knelt beside him, setting aside his shield to examine Darius's many wounds.

"Some friends," he said as Jerico's hands began to glow with blue-white light.

"Quiet."

Darius relaxed as the healing light shone across his arms, then plunged into his muscle. He felt a sharp snap of pain in his bones, and then it faded. He stretched the arm, the limb tight and sore, but otherwise healthy. He wished the same could be done for his mood.

"We can't go on like this," Darius said.

"Of course. We'll both go, and find..."

"No." Darius shook his head. "That's not what I mean. This bounty is absurd. No matter where we go, I'll stick out like a sore thumb."

"We can repaint your armor, maybe stash it on a horse or donkey."

"And accomplish what? What can we do when I must hide, and fear the very mention of my name? No, I'll fix this, one way or another."

"How?"

Darius leaned his sword against a tree, then began gathering his things.

"I'm going to the Blood Tower," he said.

"What?"

"I'll speak to Sir Robert face to face. Whatever crime he believes I've committed, I'll hear it with my own ears. I'll tell him of the horrors done by Karak's prophet in return. Either he rescinds the bounty, or I'll…"

"Or you'll what?" asked Jerico.

Darius struck the tree with his fist. The bark tore into his hand, and he clenched his teeth against the pain.

"I don't know how you do this," he said, his voice lowering. "How do you expect me to leave them alone, to forgive these unjust accusers, thieves and murderers?"

"What did you once tell me?" Jerico asked, taking Darius's sword and offering him the hilt. "Our path is a hard one. Nothing's changed, not with that. Mercy over vengeance. Grace over condemnation."

Darius drew his sword and held it before his eyes.

"A light in the darkness," he whispered, seeing its glow.

He sheathed it once more, then held the rest of his things.

"Farewell, Jerico," he said.

"What? I'm coming with you."

"I won't argue this. Sebastian is dangerous to the North, and his allegiance to Karak is only the beginning. You must stop him any way you can."

"Even if it means helping the men who just tried to kill you?"

Darius chuckled, and he clapped Jerico across the shoulder.

"Never said it'd be easy."

He turned to leave.

"How will we find each other again?" Jerico asked as Darius ducked his head and marched into the forest.

"I'll listen for the stories," Darius called back.

5

Hunger had grown a constant to her, a sensation now as meaningless as the feel of wind across her skin, or the pain that flared from every inch of her body. Valessa used it to propel her onward. She longed for the comfort of sleep, for a respite from the pain and guilt. But it would not come, so onward she followed the red star. It led her through plains, farmlands, and at last to a forest whose name she did not know. The sun and moon rose and fell, their light and darkness just as meaningless to her as bread or water.

The thick branches and leaves proved problematic at first, for they blocked the light of the star. But she found that when she stopped to focus, to demand its crimson light, it could pierce even the forest canopy.

"Praise be, Karak," she whispered. "Praise be."

She ran, at first weaving through the trees on nothing more than instinct. When she realized how pointless that was, she might have laughed, but even laughter caught in her throat. Her body was meant for slaughter and pain, not humor. Not pleasure. Penance.

Her path lost its weave, and she plunged through the trees, feeling the trunks and low branches pass through her. She was smoke, shadow, an incorporeal being. Her speed increased, distant wolves howled, and the red star shone on. Its light was so bright, she knew Darius had to be close. His presence burned in her mind like a beacon. Her hands clutched her daggers, and with near ecstasy, she imagined plunging them into his throat. The sensation of pleasure overwhelmed her. She hadn't realized something like that had been left to her, but it seemed she was wrong. She could still feel joy. She could still know Karak's love. All by repenting for her error. All by slaughtering Darius the traitor.

In the distance, she saw a camp, and she slowed her run. It had to be Kaide's, she realized. Who else would have a miniature village lost in the woods? It certainly explained Sebastian's difficulty in finding him. Had Darius taken shelter with them?

Up ahead, she saw two figures, a man and a woman. Valessa slowed even more, and she let her presence fade away. Gone were her clothes, her pale flesh, replaced only with darkness. Unseen, she crept up on the couple. The way the red star flared, she'd hoped it was Darius, but it was not. Her disappointment did not last long. She recognized that red hair, that enormous shield strapped to the man's back.

"Jerico," she whispered, the word curling off her tongue like a purr. The paladin of Ashhur was equally as responsible for her failure as Darius, all because of his meddling, and that damn shield of his. He spoke with a silver-haired woman, who looked upset but was hiding it well. Valessa glanced to the sky, saw that the red star beckoned further, but she could not deny herself such an opportunity. How might Karak bless her for defeating such a terrible foe? How much joy would soar through her shadowy soul when her daggers tore the life from his veins?

She looked to the nearby camp, then smiled, a plan already forming...

Jerico watched until Darius was gone, and then shook his head. Darius was right; Sebastian was trouble. But Darius was young in faith, and it'd been mere weeks since he'd been in the prophet's thrall. To separate now felt risky, but in the end, he had to hold faith in Ashhur. It was the right thing to do, letting him go. So was this.

He gathered his things, pulled his shield across his back, and waved goodbye to the camp.

Kaide had threatened to send men after Darius if Jerico did not stay. *Good luck,* he thought. Any fool that went after Darius now deserved the beating they received. But he could not stay. They'd betrayed his trust, and no matter how important Kaide claimed he was, that importance was not enough for them to take Darius under their protection.

Barely beyond the light of the camp's torches, Jerico heard Sandra call his name. He turned, steeling himself against any guilt.

"Jerico, wait," she said, hurrying after.

"What is it?" he asked. "Are you here to apologize for your brother again?"

Sandra shook her head, and he realized she carried a small bundle against her stomach.

"You didn't know, did you?" he asked.

"I'd have stopped him if I did," she said. She looked back to the camp, and he could see the sadness in her eyes, and the way her lips quivered. "I've been at his side for years now. Always the older brother, the one who would save our family. But I don't know who that man is, not anymore. I once told you I thought he knew nothing but revenge. Tonight proved that."

Jerico stopped, and he put his hands on her shoulders.

"Are you sure?" he asked. "He's your family, and they're your friends. I understand their desperation, as much as I might loathe their actions. Don't risk whatever happiness you know just for my sake."

She shook her head.

"Our town is gone. My parents are dead. Whatever happiness I knew, it died that winter. Kaide's just kept that pain fresh. We gave him his battle, and I saw the dead and the dying. It did nothing, only fed the beast that's taken over my brother."

She brushed her hair away from her face and behind her left ear.

"Let me come with you," she said. "I don't care where. Just let me follow you until I can find a new home, free of all these memories."

She stepped closer, and Jerico felt his throat tighten.

"Shouldn't you say goodbye?" he asked her.

"He'd never take it well."

Jerico sighed. He knew his path was dangerous, and he had no intention of giving up the fight against Lord Sebastian.

"All right," he said. "But we need to hurry, and put as much ground between us and here by morning. Because you're right...there's not a chance Kaide understands."

She smiled, and he accepted her embrace. As his arms wrapped about her, he saw a figure walking toward them from the camp. He tensed. Sandra sensed it and turned. The figure grew closer.

"Shit," said Sandra. "It's my brother."

"So much for a romantic flight through the dark forest."

She punched his chestplate, then pulled free of his arms.

"Let me talk to him," she said, approaching Kaide. The moonlight fell across his features, and seeing them, he clearly did not look happy.

"What are you doing?" he asked.

"Don't be upset," Sandra said, crossing her arms over her chest. "I'm allowed to make my own choices. You're not our father."

He never slowed. Never stopped. His hand dipped to his belt, then thrust. Jerico felt his heart shatter. Sandra gasped as the dagger pierced her belly. Jerico was too shocked to scream. Time crawled still, and she fell to the ground, blood pouring. Kaide looked at him, and he smiled, but suddenly he was no longer Kaide. He was a creature of shadow, his clothes melding and changing into the face of a woman he thought had long since departed for the Abyss.

"Valessa," he said. The woman Darius had killed. The word stuck in his throat. His arms felt like they were made of stone. Valessa's now feminine body shimmered, and fading in and out of dark smoke he saw her gray clothes and leather armor. Her daggers shimmered with crimson power in her hands.

"You killed Claire," she said, yet it was still Kaide's voice that spoke. "You killed me. I've come to return the favor."

"What are you?" he asked. It was the only thought that he could manage. Behind her, Sandra wept in pain, her life bleeding out her stomach. *Still alive,* thought Jerico. Praise Ashhur, she was still alive. His hand shifted for the complicated straps of his shield.

"I'm Karak's judgment," she said, now in her own voice. The daggers twirled in fingers that lost all color and texture. "His executioner. His beloved."

She lunged, and he yanked free his shield. The light flared amid the darkness, and Valessa let out a shriek. Her dagger struck the center and slid to the side. Jerico grabbed his mace and swung twice. The first missed, Valessa ducking beneath with a bend of her back that looked beyond humanly possible, but the return swing clipped the side of her face. Instead of shattering her jawbone, it passed right on through. Her face reformed, and it grinned at him despite the obvious pain the light of his shield caused her.

"Not good," Jerico muttered, flinging himself backward. His shield blocked the next flurry of blows, but one twisted about, and Jerico had no choice but to try a parry with his mace. It connected with the dagger and batted it aside. His relief was palpable. Her flesh might defy reason, but at least her weapons still made sense. Confidence growing, he took the offensive. He swung his mace in arcs, using it not as a threat but a means to keep her daggers engaged, for as he anticipated, she fought with the finely honed instincts she'd had when still alive. Still human. He couldn't tell what she was now, other than that her whole being was composed of Karak's raw power and fury. The light of his shield, that was his weapon, and he wielded it accordingly. Anytime she pressed close, he saw the pain on her face, saw the way she twisted and turned to add distance and keep herself from staring into its center.

"You'll die," she cried as her daggers struck his shield amid a shower of sparks. "You, your whore, the bastard Darius...all of you will die, sacrificed in Karak's name!"

Her movements grew faster, a twirling monster of smoke. But time was running out, and Jerico no longer had the patience.

"No," he said, lifting his shield high, then slamming it to the ground. "We won't."

He cried out the name of his god. The light on his shield flared, brighter and brighter, until the clearing shone as if a blue sun had risen in the sky. Valessa let out a cry akin to a cat in pain. Her flesh peeled, and her daggers lost their glow. Jerico swung, his mace passing through her chest. Valessa stumbled, and it seemed to take longer for her shadowy body to put itself back together. Her legs wobbled, and Jerico flung his shield toward her as the light dimmed. She shrieked again, then was gone.

Jerico gasped in air, his shoulders heaving, as he looked about the clearing. In his mind, he felt no danger, heard no warning from Ashhur. He forgot all about the gray sister, for he heard Sandra weeping. He clipped his mace to his belt, flung his shield onto his back, and then rushed to her side. A lump in his throat, he knelt and took her hands in his. They were soaked with blood.

"Don't," she said.

"I must."

He pulled her hands apart to look. The stab wound was wide, circular. Valessa had twisted the blade on the way out, he realized. He clutched Sandra's hands tighter, and did his best to keep down his hatred. No matter what, it wasn't right.

"I can save you," he whispered, making sure none of his doubt crept into his voice. "Trust me, Sandra. You won't die here. I've got you."

He pressed his hands into the wound, the blood, and the exposed intestines. His fingers shook, and he clenched his teeth and closed his eyes to keep them still. Fear and doubt would ruin his ability to be a conduit of healing power.

"Please Ashhur," he whispered. "Please, this is all I know to do."

Light shone, and his tears fell upon her chest. When he opened his eyes, he saw blood, and a vicious scar, but the bleeding had stopped. She'd still be weak, and he knew it would take several days before she recovered from the loss of blood. But her pulse was strong, and when he touched her face, she smiled at him.

"Do strange men and women attack you often?" she asked, her voice hoarse.

"More than I'd prefer. Can you stand?"

Sandra nodded. He stood, gently took her into his arms, and lifted. Her feet were unsteady beneath her, but he kept her still. She looked like she might vomit for a moment, but it passed. Her whole body trembled as if she were cold.

"Who was that?" Sandra asked, glancing about the forest.

"Someone with a grudge."

"Is she dead?"

He shook his head.

"I don't know."

She tried to step away, but it was too much. He caught her, and looked back to Kaide's camp, torn. Could he really take her with him, wounded as she was? A day or two of bed rest was what she needed, not rough travel.

"Sandra," he started to say, but she cut him off.

"I'm going," she said. Her fingers clutched his arm in a vise-like gripe, and her other hand pressed against her stomach. "If not now, I never will."

Jerico couldn't believe her strength. If that was what she wanted, what she was capable of, then who was he to deny her?

"So be it, but we rest whenever you cannot go on. If your brother gives chase, he will catch us, no matter how much we hurry. Are you prepared for the consequences?"

She smiled a delirious smile and pulled her hand away from the hole in her dress.

"How could he do any worse to me than what he already has done?"

Jerico chuckled, then patted his shield.

"We'll just have to be careful. Take my hand."

With the rest of her things tucked away on his back, she accepted his aid, leaned much of her weight against him, and followed him out of the forest.

Kaide stood before the dwindling campfire, hands clasped behind his back. The stars were out, but they'd soon vanish, the morning sun only an hour or two away. He should have been asleep, but one of his scouts had woken him, fearful to say what he'd discovered. Kaide had had to badger it out of him.

"It's Jerico," said the scout.

Now Kaide waited as several men searched the surrounding area. He'd known Darius was leaving, but he thought Jerico would stay to ensure his friend's safety. It seemed that was not the case. Was it a bluff, a reproof? Or perhaps Jerico's pride was injured? It didn't seem to matter. After twenty minutes of searching, he knew for certain Jerico was not just sleeping in the distance. He'd left for good.

"Damn you, Jerico," he said, sadly shaking his head. The paladin had meant so much to him, but that was his fault for putting his faith in a man who valued gods above all else. Ashhur couldn't care less for his plight, couldn't care less for his quest of revenge. Where had the god been when the deep snows piled up around Ashvale after Sebastian's knights had ransacked every bit of their food and livestock? Where had Ashhur been when they threw the first of the dead upon the fire? When the smoke wafted up, and their stomachs growled, and their children cried in hunger?

Adam approached, looking tired and angry for the disruption of sleep. His lips were still swollen, and he had done a poor job cleaning off the blood from his chin.

"You're not gonna like hearing this," Adam said.

"Out with it."

"It's your sister."

He started to ask what about her, but Adam's look was enough. A stone shifted in Kaide's stomach, and he looked to the dying fire.

"Do we go after them?" Adam asked. "You did say..."

"I know what I said."

Adam shifted, his arms crossed.

"Then what do we do?"

Kaide drew his dirk, and he twirled it before his eyes, staring into the multitude of reflections cast by the light of the dying embers before him.

"Let them go," he said, jamming it back into its sheath. "Call off the search. Bellok should be back soon, and we'll need to be rested. We've wasted enough time. Tomorrow we march, and we'll bring the Abyss to Sebastian and his men."

"You're the boss."

Adam left, and once more alone, Kaide cursed the paladin's name.

"Take good care of her," he whispered, looking up to the night sky. "Otherwise I'll kill you myself."

He returned to his cabin, hoping for a few more hours of sleep. After tossing and turning for an eternity, he gave up hope, and only stared at the ceiling until at last daylight streamed in through a window.

6

Daniel put on the last of his armor, then left his room. The morning was young, and he had men to train. His mood was foul, but not because of the training. He'd had a horrible time avoiding the two priests and their men. It seemed every hour they came to Robert with new demands or expectations, and it seemed every time Robert conceded. The idea of pandering to Karak's fanatics burned his gut. He'd warned Robert of the Stronghold's strength, yet he'd gone ahead with the bounty on Darius's head. Now look what it'd gotten them.

He turned a corner, approaching the bottom door to the Blood Tower, when he encountered one of the priests. It was the young one, Cyric. The way he leaned against the door with his arms behind his back made it seem like he'd been waiting for him.

"Morning," Daniel said, hoping to barge right past without conversation.

"Morning," Cyric said, stepping in the way. "A word, if you please?"

Daniel's jaw tightened, but he nodded.

"Of course. What do you need?"

Cyric rubbed his knuckles against his robe and then looked at them, as if oblivious to Daniel's impatience.

"Something has been bothering me. Luther insists I not worry, but perhaps you might indulge me anyway. I would like to speak with the witnesses of the attack on Durham."

The young man looked up and smiled. Daniel felt his blood chill. It was a serpent's smile, a killer's grin.

"For what reason?" he asked. "Sir Robert has already judged they speak truthfully."

"I do not mean to doubt Robert's decision," Cyric said. "Only to hear with my own ears what happened. I find it hard to believe that just one man caused such destruction. Don't you?"

Daniel swallowed. The townsfolk had spoken of another man that came after Darius's warning. Fire had leapt from his hands and demonic words from his tongue. They'd given no name, and among them all, couldn't even agree on a description, other than the color of his eyes: a deep red that shone as if the fires of the Abyss burned behind them. With so little to go on, Robert had restricted the bounty to the one person whose blame no one could deny: Darius.

"A paladin of Karak can be a very powerful foe," Daniel said.

"Indeed," Cyric said, his smile growing. "I am not ignorant of their power. Five traveled with Luther and me from Mordeina, after all."

Daniel sensed the implied threat and did his best to pretend he hadn't.

"That's fine, but I don't think it appropriate you speak to the townsfolk. They have suffered enough without you bringing up bad memories."

"I am afraid I must insist, Daniel."

"Then insist to Robert. You have my answer."

He grabbed the handle to the door. Cyric remained leaning against it, as if daring Daniel to pull it open.

"We'll be holding a service tomorrow," said the fledgling priest. "You should attend."

"The Abyss will freeze over before I do."

"Careful," said Cyric, stepping out of the away. "The time of judgment approaches on the backs of lions. I would hate to be caught unaware."

Daniel stormed outside, glad to be away. He'd hoped to take his frustration out on his men in a grueling training session, but it seemed one of the gods was conspiring against him, and it took little wit to guess which one. Normally they held practice in a wide area of trampled dirt, within the small courtyard that stretched between the tower and the outer walls. That morning, Luther stood in its center, a book in hand. A tenth of the Blood Tower's fighting men stood about, listening as Luther preached in a firm, steady voice. The mere sight sent Daniel's blood boiling.

"What is going on here?" he asked, pulling one of his men aside.

"Just listening," said the man, though he looked away, as if guilty of something. Daniel bit his tongue as he realized Luther was in mid-prayer. He felt awkward interrupting it, especially when he realized several others were praying along. Karak or Ashhur, Sir Robert had never cared, so long as it didn't interfere with his soldiers' duties. Despite his anger, Daniel tried to honor that, and let the priest finish.

"...and may we always abide by the strength and wisdom of the Lion," said Luther. "And all those with wisdom say amen."

Five or six echoed the word 'amen', and for whatever reason, it set the hair on the back of Daniel's neck to standing. The prayer over, the men scattered, all shooting glances toward Daniel, who approached Luther.

"A word," he said, grabbing Luther's robe by the shoulder.

"Of course," Luther said, nothing but calm. "Though remember whose robe you grab, and perhaps show wisdom the next time you would act in anger."

Daniel accepted the rebuke, and forced his temper in check. Their situation was no less precarious now than it had been at the priests' first arrival.

"My apologies," Daniel said dryly. "But this place is for my men to train every morning, and I cannot have you occupying them with speeches and sermons."

"Does the soul not need training as well?" Luther asked as he led him toward the gate to the outside. "What good does it to teach men how to kill if they know not when or why to use those abilities?"

"That's why we have a chain of command, why we teach them to follow orders."

"Exactly," Luther said, sounding pleased. It made Daniel feel like he was just another of the old priest's students, and he didn't like it. "Chain of command. Such a good term to describe what we do. Imagine the Blood Tower represents our world. You are to your men as I am to my flock, a teacher. Above you is Sir Robert, just as above me are the old masters in Mordeina and the Stronghold. And as the King is above Sir Robert, so is Karak above us all. We are in the same field of work, Daniel, and I would hope you appreciate my difficulties."

"I'm training men to defend all the West from the bloodthirsty creatures in the Vile Wedge."

"And I'm training men to defend their souls from the evils of the world. I dare say that my task is more important, wouldn't you?"

They stepped out the gate. Across the lush field fed by the Gihon was Karak's encampment, formed of several dozen tents. Over five hundred men were there, well armed and armored. Their very look made him uneasy. They were like private mercenaries, only worse. The Stronghold might pay them with gold or jewels, but they viewed their service as a religious duty. They served no king, only Karak. The very notion made Daniel nervous. Once a man invested his loyalty in something other than his own king, it made him unpredictable and dangerous.

"What is it you're here for?" Daniel asked as Luther stopped to view his camp. He kept his voice low, as if they were discussing secrets. "You have what you wanted. We'll take Darius alive, and deliver him to you. Why do you stay?"

"There is the matter of the two Hemman brothers."

"Lord Arthur is trapped in his castle, and will starve in the next few months. You have nothing to fear there."

"Do we not?" Luther turned to face him, and with those eyes staring into him, Daniel felt naked. He tried not to meet his gaze, but was powerless against it. "This is more than a mere squabble between brothers, more than a war between fellow lords. I have long heard of the North's faith to Karak. We believed it, for the tithes were great, and Lord Sebastian was ever eager to please. But now that I walk these lands, I find myself doubting. So few of your soldiers practice *any* religion, let alone the truth of Karak. In the villages we stayed in during our journey here, many harbored hidden sympathy for Ashhur. When most spoke of Karak, I heard no love, no loyalty. A sickness grows in our most faithful of territories, and I must find out why."

"Fascinating, but why should we give a damn?"

Luther smiled.

"You're much like Sir Robert, and if you would trust me, we might get along well. You are a practical man, as am I. Perhaps I deal with spiritual matters, but I understand we will never achieve perfection, and there will always be men like you who, as you might say, don't give a damn."

Luther gestured to the three hundred. Daniel watched them closely, and realized they were preparing their things to move out.

"Where will you be heading?" he asked. "To the Castle of Caves?"

"You are correct," Luther said. "Most of them will leave tomorrow. They'll go to ensure victory for the lord that is most obedient to Karak, at least on the surface. I now wonder how faithful Sebastian is, but even if he is false, his actions and tithes are real enough. My student will stay here, for there is still much work to be done."

Daniel didn't like the sound of that, but he feared to say so. If the three hundred men were leaving, then at least he might walk about Robert's tower without fear of an impending coup. But what work remained? Would he proselytize the rest of his soldiers? Or would they strike out for the nearby villagers in an attempt to root out the reason for the 'sickness', as Luther put it?

"For all your gracious gifts, we will try our best to accommodate your student," he said, bowing slightly. "For now, I must go train my men."

"Of course."

Daniel started to hurry back, but Luther spoke his last parting words of wisdom.

"You are a good man, Daniel, but you must soon bring your mind to the things beyond this world. The hour comes when a war will bathe Dezrel with blood, fire, and death. I would hate to see you caught on the wrong side."

Daniel couldn't help himself.

"And what side would that be?" he asked, glancing back.

"There is safety in Karak's arms," said Luther, his smile kind but his eyes glinting with danger. "Good day, lieutenant."

Daniel snorted and pulled at the collar of his shirt as he returned to the Blood Tower.

"Safety," he muttered, thinking of those cold eyes. "Bullshit."

❖

Valessa had thought she knew pain. She thought she understood torment. But she'd never known this. In the light of the moon, she knelt on her hands and knees and prayed for death. It didn't matter if it was a blasphemy. It didn't matter if she cursed the gift her god had bestowed upon her. She wanted the agony to stop. That was all that mattered. To make it stop.

Her form shifted and twisted, and she felt every interminable inch. It throbbed, unending, with pain and failure. She felt knives twisting inside her, felt fire burning outside her, felt hatred within her non-existent veins. The light of Jerico's shield had left her weak, and nearly broken whatever essence kept her together. It had taken all her focus to flee, and in the shadows of the forest she waited for her strength to return.

"Damn you," she whispered. She felt her lungs solidify by her thoughts so that air might press through, felt her tongue gain form so that it might speak the curse. Each moment was torture. But she said it anyway. "Damn you, Jerico, damn you to the Abyss a thousand times."

This was her failure, of course. She'd been given a second chance at taking down Darius, not Jerico, but she had ignored the wishes of her god. She'd thought to impress him, as if that were possible, using a life and form granted by *his* hands. She was nothing without her deity, and despite the hatred and agony, her confrontation with Jerico had helped her remember that. She tried to be thankful. It was better than crying out her fury against Karak. She worshipped him, loved him, accepted his

73

authority over her, but never before had she hated him so. Not like this.

It was no longer a matter of pride, revenge, or faith. She needed to kill Darius for her freedom. The fires of the Abyss surely would not burn her so. She was a child of Karak.

Valessa focused her prayers, begging for forgiveness, begging for his touch. Day and night swirled over her, but she was aware of it only distantly. She did not sleep. She did not eat. She did not *live*. With each minute, each prayer, she felt herself growing whole. Her skin regained its color, and her naked form assumed the clothes she once wore. Her daggers, having never left her hands, started to glow once more. The pain in the center of her being faded, becoming only the constant ache she had learned to accept. Looking to the sky, she hoped Karak had not yet abandoned her, had forgiven her for her weaknesses.

Seeing the red star, she smiled. An even greater surprise, she felt liquid running down the sides of her face. Valessa touched her cheek, and when she pulled her fingers away, she saw them stained red. Tears of blood. Perhaps grief was not yet lost to her.

"Thank you," she whispered to the night. "I will make you proud."

It had been several days, though how many she did not know. But darkness was about her, the red star above her, and with a single-minded purpose she ran.

7

The days had not gotten any easier, despite Sandra's hope otherwise. The flesh around the wound in her stomach had tightened and scarred. After mere minutes of walking it would start to ache. Teeth grinding together, she'd fought on, and it wasn't until the second day that Jerico noticed how badly it hurt her.

"You should have told me," he berated her as she lay down on a soft patch of grass. His hands pressed against her waist, and she shivered.

"I didn't want to worry you."

"Worry?" said Jerico as his hands began to shine white. "I could have helped you, Sandra. Besides, worry's what I do."

His healing prayers subdued the pain, but when he finished, she saw the look on his face, the trepidation. Something was wrong, but he wasn't telling her what. Night after night he had to pray over her so she could sleep without sobbing from the pain. The scar continually flared red, as if trying to reopen. She'd seen Jerico close the most brutal of wounds. This shouldn't have been beyond him, yet, somehow, she sensed it was.

She tried to not let him see her fingers brush the scar from time to time, each touch always more painful than the last.

"Enough," she told him as the sun dipped beneath the horizon on the third day after leaving her brother's hideout. "I can't...my legs can't take any more."

Jerico nodded, and as she sat, he began preparing a fire. She rubbed her calves and watched him. It hadn't been a lie. The constant walking was murder on her body, something she was far from accustomed to. Again, she'd hoped it'd improve with time, but that didn't seem to be the case. Jerico looked spry as ever as he gathered kindling for a fire, and that was with him wearing armor and carrying their supplies on his back. Whatever the paladin was, Sandra was starting to believe he wasn't human. He unwrapped a small strip of dried, heavily salted meat he'd bought from a town they'd passed through. Stabbing it with a stick, he held it over the fire, and its smell awakened Sandra's hunger.

"Kaide must not be tracking us if he hasn't found us by now," she said, staring into the fire. "We don't need to use such haste, nor avoid every village we encounter."

"The northern folk are loyal to your brother," Jerico said, turning the meat. "I'd rather he not know our every move."

She pulled her knees to her chest and curled her arms around them.

"You speak as if he were an enemy."

"I pray he isn't."

She ate her portion of the meal, surprised as always by how hungry she felt come nightfall. Jerico finished before her and began removing his armor piece by piece.

"Why do you always wear it?" she asked him.

"Easier than carrying it. Besides, ever since the Citadel fell I never know when the next fight will be. I'd sleep in it, if it were at all comfortable."

"And use your mace for a pillow?"

He chuckled.

"Help me with these straps, will you?"

With the rest of his armor piled to the side, she made a show of waving her hand before her nose. In truth, the smell of leather and sweat didn't bother her much, but the gesture always earned a smile from Jerico. She removed her own worn shoes, stretched out before the fire, and closed her eyes. It felt so good to be still, and if not for the pain in her stomach, she might have drifted to sleep. Instead, her mind wandered. She thought of the Irons twins; her niece, Beth; and most of all, her brother. With each day of travel, the Castle of Caves neared, and her friends grew that much farther away.

Jerico sat beside her, and she shifted so she might rest against him. She felt his hand stroke her hair once, gently. His fingers were rough, calloused from his gauntlets and the constant training.

"Do you wish you had stayed?" he asked her softly.

A tear ran down her face, and she nodded.

"It doesn't matter," she said. "I knew I would regret it when I left. Maybe when Kaide has finally won, and this whole damn fight is over...I just want my brother back, Jerico. I hope my leaving hurts him. I hope it eats at him, makes him realize just how much he's lost because of it. Is it wrong for me to pray for his misery?"

"I think your heart's in the right place," he said. "Though I'd prefer you pray for his vengeance to leave him, instead of misery taking its place."

"I just want to slap some sense into him," she said, and she laughed to force away the rest of her tears. "Truth be told, this is the first time I've been on my own in years. We've always been so close..."

"Sandra," Jerico said, his voice still soft, but now with a barely contained urgency. "Sit up, right now. Don't ask why."

He was looking beyond her, into the distance. His left arm was slowly reaching for his shield beside him. Suddenly afraid, she sat up, wincing at the pain in her stomach.

"Who is out there?" she asked, ignoring his instructions otherwise.

Before he could answer, Jerico shoved her hard with his right hand. His left clutched the handles of his shield and pulled it before him. As Sandra landed on her back, she let out a cry, and she heaved from the pain splitting across her stomach. Light flooded their campsite and illuminated the surrounding grasslands. An arrow pierced that light, struck the center of Jerico's shield, and then ricocheted harmlessly into the dirt.

"Stay down," Jerico told her as another arrow sailed in, this one missing the mark. He moved toward the fire, where his mace lay beside their rucksack of things, but a third arrow flew in, and its aim was far better than the last. Jerico dropped to one knee, the bottom of his shield clipping the arrow just in time. Without his armor, he had only his shield to protect him, and their conversation earlier didn't seem quite so entertaining now.

"Where is he?" Sandra called out, still lying low. The grass was tall, but there weren't any trees or large rocks for someone to hide behind. He had to be crouched down, standing only to fire.

"Right here, girl," a voice said, mere feet behind her. Sandra's blood ran cold. She whirled, already kicking. A large man towered over her, his face unshaven and his left eye scarred over. He held a short sword in his left hand, raised to swing. Her kick caught him in the thigh, doing little. Down came the swing, but then Jerico was there, slamming in with his shield. The swing halted in midair. The man let out a cry, and then both continued out of the campsite and into the tall grass.

Sandra rolled to her knees and watched as Jerico crouched, his shield constantly shifting. He kept the thug with the sword occupied, but she realized others were out there, at least the one with the bow. She looked, saw a shorter man standing in the grass thirty yards out, barely visible in the flickers of their firelight.

"Jerico!" she cried as he nocked another arrow.

Jerico shoved away another thrust, then spun, his shield intercepting the arrow just in time. The other thug's sword slashed in, and it cut across Jerico's arm before he could turn. Furious, he struck the man's jaw with his fist, then pressed in, punching and slamming with his shield. He was trying to take out the one opponent so he could deal with the archer, but the man with the sword knew they had numbers and remained on the defensive, always retreating.

"Shit," muttered Sandra. She wouldn't sit by and watch him die, nor let him protect her on his own. Kaide had raised her better than that. Near the fire was Jerico's mace, and she ran for it. Another arrow flew, but it was for Jerico, not her. She heard a cry of pain and prayed it wasn't the paladin. Clutching the mace, she lifted it, surprised by how light it felt. Holding the handle with both hands, she looked for the archer.

This time he had noticed her movement, and the bow swiveled toward her. She dropped to her knees, the sound of her heartbeat pounding in her ears. The arrow flew past her head, the wind of it tugging against her hair. And then she was up, sprinting as fast as her aching feet could manage. Gasping for air, she crossed the distance, feeling interminably slow despite all her efforts. The archer readied another arrow, and he pulled the string tight as she closed in for a swing. She saw his size, his long hair, and the slenderness of his body.

Not a man, Sandra realized. A woman.

The mace pushed the bow aside, the arrow releasing just above her left shoulder. Then the flanged edges struck the flesh of the archer's face, tearing holes. The weight of its center hit bone, and the woman's jaw cracked. Sandra saw this in the span of a single breath, such a quick moment, but the sight burned into her, a memory that hung before her eyes like a brutal painting. The body collapsed and lay still. A smell hit her. The dead archer had shit herself.

Footsteps behind her. She swung again, but a strong hand caught the hilt. She pressed harder, then saw it was Jerico, his shield slung across his back. Blood covered the front of his clothes, but it wasn't his blood. She released the handle, glad to be rid of the weapon. Her arms shook as she stood there, feeling dazed and confused.

"It's all right," he said, clipping his mace to his belt and then holding her against him. This smeared the blood from his shirt against her arms, and she pushed him away. "The shakes will go away in time," he told her. He looked down at the body and shook his head. "Are they with Kaide?"

Sandra glanced at the woman, then shook her head.

"No. I don't recognize her, nor the man."

Jerico sighed, and he sounded relieved.

"Good."

He knelt down and pulled the corpse into his arms.

"What are you doing?" she asked.

He didn't answer, and instead walked back to their campfire. She followed, still trembling. It was as if her pulse refused to slow despite the battle ending. Back at the fire was the body of the man who had attacked her. She saw no outer wounds, but the way his throat was bruised and misshapen told her enough of how Jerico had killed him.

"I had to," Jerico said, putting the woman's body down next to the man's. "I feared you might not reach the archer in time, might be...I had no time to be careful."

"You won't receive any judgment from me," she told him.

"It's not you who I fear judgment from." He pointed to a distant cluster of trees several hundred yards out. "Grab a branch, biggest you can find."

She did not ask, only obeyed. The walk there helped calm her down, and the last of her shakes faded. As they did, though, she felt the pain in her stomach flare. Reaching the trees, she stopped to press her hand against her abdomen. She felt blood. Was it from Jerico's embrace, or herself? She didn't know. Didn't want to know. Finding a half-broken branch, she tore it free and carried it back. Jerico took it, lit it in their fire, and handed it back.

"Go start another campfire," he said.

"Why?"

"Because it will take all night and day to dig a grave for them, time we don't have. I won't leave them here for the carrion."

She thought of the look the man had given her before he'd tried to take her life with his sword.

"They don't deserve it," she said, crossing her arms, feeling very cold.

"They were bandits, probably husband and wife. I don't know what family they have, what life they've led. Children may starve now because we killed them. If only they'd asked, I would have given them what little coin I had. If only they'd asked..."

Jerico sighed.

"I hate this world sometimes. Now go on, before that branch burns too low and hurts your hand."

Sandra nodded, but couldn't go just yet.

"You really hate this world?" she asked him.

Jerico grinned despite his apparent exhaustion.

"Yeah," he said. "I do. But I love the people in it. Now go."

She set up camp farther away, near the cluster of trees, so she might have ready kindling. When finished, she looked back, saw Jerico tending the pyre. Her stomach heaved, and she turned to vomit. In the light of the fire, she saw it was a deep red. Blood. She felt like crying. Instead she lay down, closed her eyes, and waited for Jerico. The paladin returned long after, though she could not say just how much time had passed.

"Sandra?" she heard him ask. His shield thudded into the ground beside her, and then his palm was against her forehead. "Sandra, you're burning up. Why didn't you tell me?"

"Didn't know," she murmured. She felt very tired. Jerico carefully lifted her shirt so he might examine the wound on her stomach.

"Oh god," he whispered.

She was scared to look, to see what frightened him so. All she knew was that it hurt like a blade driven deep in her belly. Eyes closed, she thought of the bandit woman as her mace struck her face.

"I've never killed anybody before," Sandra said, feeling as if she'd drunk too much of Griff's personal stash of hard liquor. "I've seen people die; saw plenty after the Green Gulch...but never killed before."

"Don't dwell on it," Jerico said as he pressed his palms against her abdomen. She screamed, but wasn't sure why. All she felt was a sharp pressure.

"Can't...help it," she said. White light shone, and she relaxed. The healing magic would flow into her, banish the pain like it had the past several nights. She was safe with Jerico. Safe...

"Sandra," he said after several minutes. Sweat lined his forehead, and he wiped it away with his wrist. "I don't know what's wrong. I'm not sure I can heal this."

She swallowed, tried to remain calm. Panic swelled in her breast, coupled with anger.

"You've healed worse," she said. "I've seen it. I've seen it! Why me? Why this?"

Jerico grabbed her hand and clutched it with both of his.

"Forgive me," he said. "I can do this, but I need you to stay with me. Can you do that, Sandra? Talk to me, Sandra. Sandra!"

A river ran through her mind, softly swaying side to side, and in it she was free of the pain, the fear, and the anger. She closed her eyes and let it carry her away.

Sandra!

Sandra...

She opened her eyes, that river suddenly gone. She knew time had passed, dimly aware of it in some instinctual way. Jerico knelt over her, and she saw his hands pressed against her stomach. His head was bowed, his eyes closed. Guilt washed over her, for she realized he was praying, and it felt wrong to be present in a moment so private. But his words struck her, and she realized he was crying as he spoke.

"Don't let me fail her," Jerico said, his jaw trembling. It seemed like every part of him was fighting against losing control. "Don't do this to me. I don't know what I've done, where I erred, but don't let her suffer for it. I can be stronger. I can do better. Please, your strength, not mine. Your strength, not mine..."

She reached out and touched his face. He stiffened, then looked to her, eyes red. He smiled.

"Sandra," he said, and it seemed as if her very name swept away his sorrow.

She kissed his lips, then held him tight against her as the pain in her stomach slowly returned, and she was once more aware of the chill of the night, the soft cries of the crickets, and the way his strong arms kept her close.

"What happened?" she whispered.

"I don't know. I think you were stabbed with a cursed dagger. I've done what I can. Everything else is in Ashhur's hands."

"Am I cured?"

"I don't know. I'd need to examine the wound to be certain."

She kissed him again.

"Not now," she said. "Let me sleep without knowing."

He gently lowered her back to the grass, then lay beside her, his arms carefully wrapped about her chest, his face pressed against her neck. The heat of the fire washed over her face.

"Thank you," she said.

He gave no answer, only kissed the back of her neck. She fell asleep not long after, the rhythmic warmth of his breath against her ear.

8

Cyric helped his master and teacher prepare for departure, and did his best to hide his excitement. It wasn't that he bore any ill will toward Luther—far from it. But this meant a chance to finally be on his own, to have a measure of trust placed upon him. With it came expectations, but he felt confident he could handle whatever the world threw at him. His faith in Karak was strong, after all.

"Remember to keep your patience when speaking to Daniel and Sir Robert," Luther said as he folded together similar colored robes, then cinched the container tight. "They will never be faithful to Karak, but they can still be of use in our crusade against chaos."

"They should be replaced if they will not bow to the true god," Cyric said, hoisting a trunk of Luther's things onto his shoulder.

"In time, my student. In time, all the world will bow. But it does not yet, and expecting perfection from this chaotic world will only lead to disappointment."

Cyric led the way down the stairs to the outer wall, where the wagons waited.

"What you say sounds like defeat," he said. He didn't like arguing with Luther, but today he felt confident, proud. Luther was to leave fifty men in his care. He had every intention of using that gift to its utmost potential.

"Defeat and acceptance are not the same thing," Luther said. Cyric could not see him, but he heard the impatience creeping into his voice. "You'll understand one day, when you have walked across Dezrel as much as I."

Cyric put the chest into the wagon and shoved it into place, then took Luther's bag and gently tossed it in as well. That was the last of it, and all around them the armed men of Karak prepared to leave. Luther crossed his arms and looked Cyric over. The younger man held down a shiver. He hated when his master analyzed him so.

"What will you do?" Luther asked. Cyric stood up straight, and did not hide the pride in his voice.

"Continue to spread the faith. Weaken Sir Robert's control over the Blood Tower until he acknowledges our right to rule over him. With that done, I will find the remnants of Durham. They will learn the folly of accusing a paladin of Karak of causing chaos and destruction."

"And how will you do that?"

Luther's voice had grown quieter, more guarded. Cyric knew he was treading on dangerous ground, but didn't care. He'd put much thought into this, and it was time to reveal the truths he'd uncovered.

"I've read the older tomes," said Cyric. "There are spells in them, rituals of such power and strength it overwhelms the mind. That strength will be mine. With it, I will renew the faithful, and crush those that worship the false god, or deny Karak's power. It is time to bring the old ways back to the North."

"I told you to avoid those tomes," Luther said. "Our council has deemed them too dangerous to the cause of Karak."

"But why? With them, I can force the will of Karak upon all chaotic life!"

"You would *enslave* them, Cyric! Don't you understand? We must use a firm hand when reshaping this world, but we must also ensure that there is still a choice, no matter how illusionary it may be. Man will struggle against foreign chains about his neck, but if he binds himself willingly, humbly, he will remain free of chaos forever. That is why you must not use the old ways."

Cyric felt his temper rise at such a rebuke, and his pride stung deeply.

"Not all the priesthood feel as you do," he said, trying to stand tall before his imposing master. "Hayden often laments the loss of the old ways, and I've read Pelorak's teachings from..."

"Enough," Luther said, striking the wagon. Dark magic flared across his fist, and the wood splintered from the blow. "You are *my* disciple, not theirs. How can I pass on my wisdom to you if you would ignore me, and go only by the books you read and the dreams that fill your head? If you resurrect the old ways, you will bring about terrible ruin, to yourself, and to the North."

He stepped into the wagon and called out for the rider to begin.

"You may not approve," Cyric said, walking behind it as it started to move. "But I am yet to hear you forbid me from doing so."

Luther leaned back, his arms crossed.

"It is still your choice," he said. "I will not deny you that. Be mindful of your prayers, and listen for the whispers of Karak. I trust he will dissuade you from this naïve hope. If you find yourself lost, trust in Salaul's advice."

Cyric bowed respectfully, but the moment Luther was gone, he shoved his teacher from his thoughts. He would not listen to a man so closed-minded against the wisdom of the great fathers of their faith. Hurrying through the now largely abandoned campsite, Cyric searched out the man left by Luther to aid him in spiritual matters, the dark paladin Salaul. He found him reorganizing the layout of the camp because of their far fewer numbers, relocating them into the inner walls of the Blood Tower.

"My friend," Cyric said, bowing to the paladin. Salaul leaned back and crossed his arms. He was an older man with graying hair, now living a life of training and teaching instead of actual combat. But he was a paladin of Karak, and his strength was still greater than that of most mortals. A greataxe hung on his back from several leather straps. Cyric could only begin to guess how many lives it had claimed.

"Young priest," Salaul said, his voice incredibly deep. "Luther told me you would be assuming control of the situation here at the Blood Tower. I offer you my wisdom, for I have seen much in this world, for good and ill."

"Your wisdom will aid me greatly," Cyric said, trying to sound even half as authoritative as Salaul. "But for now, I have a task for you, one that must be done away from prying eyes."

Salaul narrowed his gaze.

"I will do nothing that might dishonor my god," he said. "What is it you would ask of me?"

It was a gamble, Cyric knew. He'd learned everything he could of Salaul, of his many battles against bandits, his periodic trips to Mordeina to preach on the streets, and most of all, of his total lack of hesitation in using that greataxe of his to enforce the will of Karak.

"Tonight, I will cross the Gihon and into the Wedge," Cyric said, nodding toward the river. "I wish to communicate with our god. All I require is one man or woman to accompany me, someone loyal to Karak above all else."

"Any of our men would gladly volunteer," Salaul said, gesturing about the camp.

"Then find me the most faithful, and have them meet me at the river come nightfall. Understood?"

Salaul tugged at his armor, adjusting the padding underneath.

"They will want to know what it is they volunteer for," he said.

Cyric sensed the real question beneath it, the paladin's desire to know the truth. He had to be careful here, but his gut told him Salaul would be open to the old ways, more so than many.

"I will not say, but you may accompany me, Salaul. Karak surely will hear my prayer if you are there to lend it strength."

"Perhaps."

Salaul bowed, and Cyric returned to his room in the Blood Tower. His heart raced. It was time. All his patience would now be rewarded. In his room, he retrieved a book from his satchel. He'd read many things in the Stronghold's library, as well as the priests' library in Mordeina. In the dark corners, he'd found tomes untouched for over a hundred years. At the Stronghold, he'd discovered one in particular that had sent his fingers tingling just by touching its leather-bound frame, and set his heart racing by reading the faded cover.

The Collected Words of the Prophet.

It had no drawings, no gold lettering, nothing that might indicate the immense knowledge within. He still remembered the first sentence, the moment that had put his entire life into order, and given him a purpose for his discipleship. He opened it now, fingers lovingly touching the paper, and then read aloud.

"To the best of my abilities, here within I recount the wisdom granted to me by the man with a thousand faces, Karak's most holy servant..."

He flipped through, stopping at a section he'd marked with a thin, dried leaf.

Tonight, he thought. *Tonight!*

The hours crawled as in seclusion he read over passages he'd studied a hundred times. There could be no error, no slip of the tongue. This was the first of the rituals, his childlike step into the old ways. Should he be successful, all of Dezrel would soon know his name. Within the temple, he'd be revered for his accomplishments.

At last the sun began to set. He closed the book and tucked it under his arm. Before going, he reached into his trunk and pulled out a bundle of cloth tied shut with string. Hiding it within his robes, he left the Blood Tower. Waiting for him at the river was Salaul and another man who Cyric did not recognize.

"We are here," Salaul said at his arrival. "Cyric, this is Pat Arenson."

"Karak saved me from my sinful life of murder and rape," said Pat. He was a shorter man, with black hair that curled about his neck and ears. "I owe everything to you priests. Whatever you need from me, I'll do it with a song on my lips."

Cyric smiled.

"Excellent. I can sense your faith, Pat. Stand tall, and be proud. I have selected you for a great honor, unbestowed for far too many years."

"Very good," Salaul said, hardly sounding impressed. He gestured to the river. "Do you have a way for us to cross? Otherwise, I procured us a boat."

"A boat will suffice."

The three men rode to the opposite side, Cyric standing in the center while the other two rowed. He felt the cold night air blowing through his hair, and it did nothing to diminish his smile. Instead, it made him feel more alive, closer to the stars and, therefore, closer to his god. When they hit the shore, Salaul hammered down a stake in the dark earth and tied the boat to it. Meanwhile, Cyric hurried across the grass, searching for a flat section. It was all flat, so he chose a spot at random upon which to begin.

"Be with me, Karak," he said, closing his eyes in prayer.

Priests of Karak could wield great power, but so far Cyric had been given little chance to demand it. It was not something that could be practiced, for Karak frowned on pointless use of his power. But now—now was the time. Fire burned across his hands, and he felt pride at its strength. The grass caught, and he controlled it like he might his own limb, guiding it in a circle. The heat grew, the fire roared, and then the interior of the circle was also consumed. With a clap of his hands, it died, leaving him a space to perform his ritual.

"Clear out the ash," he told Pat.

The man knelt and scooped away with his hands without complaint. Meanwhile, Cyric flipped to the marked section and fought down a last moment of nerves. This was it. He would show no fear, no hesitation. The words of the prophet soothed him. When Pat finished, Cyric glanced at Salaul, who was watching with his arms crossed. Was that mistrust in his eyes, or merely boredom? The paladin might not be impressed yet, but he would be soon. Cyric read aloud a passage, feeling the power of Karak flowing through him. The burned ground flashed red for the briefest moment, then faded.

Falling to his knees, Cyric slowly dipped a finger in the dirt and scratched a symbol. It was as if he were opening a wound into the world, revealing an angry red glow burning across melted rock. Cyric hurried about the circle's perimeter, drawing rune after rune. His confidence grew as each one flared with power. There was no boredom in

Salaul's eyes when he finished, only a growing awareness of the momentous event.

"You dabble in ancient powers," he said.

"I awaken what was forgotten," Cyric said. "I practice what our god once preached. Will you stop me?"

The paladin shook his head.

"I still remember a time when the Stronghold held to the old ways. I was only a child, but I remember their faith."

"What would you have me do?" asked Pat.

"Step into the center," Cyric said, pointing. "Close your eyes, lift your arms up and your head to the stars. Pray to Karak with all your strength. Beg for his mercy, his wisdom. Let it flow upon us all."

"As you wish."

Pat hesitated only a moment, impressing Cyric with his determination. The runes shone about him, bathing him in crimson light. Pat lifted his head, closed his eyes, and began to pray. It was a constant drone, but it was sincere. Heart pounding in his chest, Cyric pulled out the cloth package and broke the string with his fingers. He let the wrappings fall, and he held the dagger hidden within.

There was a time when Karak himself walked the world, and he gave his wisdom to his priests and followers. There were a few who recorded those words, and the rituals demanded therein. Time had diminished their power, and council after council had challenged their use. They were rules for a more barbaric time, they claimed. Primitive practices, filled with superstition, exaggerations, and uncivilized ways. The priesthood had moved on. It had evolved. But Cyric knew the truth.

The world had not changed. People had not changed. Only their faith, their determination, had changed, and it was not for the better.

"Place your blessing upon me," Cyric said, lifting his dagger to the heavens. "Let it flow upon us, opening our eyes, our hearts, and our minds."

This was it, the only time Salaul could stop him. But he did not.

Cyric stepped forward, into the circle, where Pat continued to pray.

"Praise be," whispered Cyric, and he felt a chill run up his spine at the words.

He slashed open Pat's throat, then grabbed his jaw and held him still. Pat's eyes opened wide, and his arms convulsed, but he was helpless before the power that flooded into the runes. Blood poured down Cyric's arm, and it splashed across the circle. The runes burst with fire that stretched ever higher, but the heat did not burn—at least, not him. Pat's body flickered orange and red. The skin blackened. In Cyric's hand, the sacrifice was consumed.

The Lion roared.

Cyric felt a force fling him to his knees. The stars were gone, replaced by a solid black sky that rumbled angrily. Red lightning crackled, though there were no clouds. The ground shook, and he realized it was from the approach of a great stampede in the distance. He saw their eyes, their molten skin. Lions, thousands of them, racing toward him. As one they roared, and it seemed all of Dezrel quaked with their fury. The pack grew closer, swirling about him like a river. He did not see Salaul, and in truth, hardly even remembered he had been there.

What is it you seek?

The voice came from everywhere, as if spoken by the sky, the earth, the lions, and his own mind. It overwhelmed him to tears. He struck the ground with his fists, crying out for strength. The voice was so deep, so cold, but he would not be afraid. He would not cower.

"I am a servant," he shouted, but his voice was lost in a sudden wind. It blew in from the west, and in its fury came fire, consuming the very air. Cyric closed his eyes as he felt his hair burn away, and his flesh peel.

Whom do you serve?

"You!" he cried. "I serve Karak!"

The fire poured down his throat, igniting his insides. His tongue dried to dust. The ground beneath him turned molten, and he sank within. His legs were gone, his arms...

What do you desire?

He opened his mouth to scream, but he had no tongue, no voice. It didn't matter. He cried it out with his heart, with the last vestiges of his strength. It was the truth, for he could not lie, not in that storm. Not with the fires of the Abyss consuming the chaos of his very soul.

"To bring order to all I touch!"

The wind blew again, and it left a shocking cold. He saw nothing, heard only the growls of the legion of lions. Their tongues licked at his flesh. Their teeth bit into his bones. Again he shrieked his cry for order. He would banish the chaos by blade and fire. He would take life away from the unfaithful, deny them the gifts their wretched, ungrateful souls did not deserve. All of it, he screamed, he would do all of it in Karak's name.

And then, in a sudden silence, he was given his wish.

Then stand.

The vision left him. The pain was gone. Cyric looked about, feeling tears running down his face. It was still night. The circle at his feet was gone, the runes smeared with dirt. They no longer shone with power. Before him knelt Salaul, his greataxe laid flat across his knee. Nothing remained of Pat, not even dust.

"Blessed be," said Salaul, looking up to him with nothing but admiration. "I am honored to serve."

Cyric lifted his hands, and as he looked at them, he felt the immense power dwelling within. Karak's strength flowed through him, giving him a confidence he could hardly comprehend. Whatever he wished, he could make it so. He knew this, somehow. Overcome with a desire to test it, he told the paladin to stand.

"How long was I...gone?" he asked him.

"I do not know, milord," said Salaul.

"Lord? Why do you call me lord?"

Salaul swallowed. Something had clearly shaken him, but what?

"You disappeared among the fire," he said. "But Karak spoke to me, and told me to remain. I did, for many long hours. I heard lions roaring, and then you were here, within the blink of an eye. I heard Karak speak one last time...I heard him call you beloved."

Salaul knelt once more.

"You have been to the fires of the Abyss, and then returned. I cannot imagine being worthy of such a gift, but you are. You are worthy in Karak's eyes. Speak the word, and I will obey."

Cyric looked back to where the Blood Tower rose high above the river, its lanterns shining bright amid the night.

"Let us earn their faith," he said, thinking of Sir Robert's soldiers. "Let us show them miracles, show them power."

"As you wish, milord."

"Lord...yes. There is no other lord but Karak, but you are right to call me that. He is here, isn't he?"

"Cyric...your eyes!"

Cyric did not know what he saw, but he assumed it was another sign. Returning to the river, he saw their boat, then chuckled.

"Take my hand, Salaul."

The paladin did so, and together they walked across the river to the other side, where the faithless waited to be converted.

9

Despite what he'd told Jerico, Darius was in no hurry to reach Sir Robert at the Blood Tower. He traveled east, through the forest, but spent plenty of time setting up traps and catching rabbits and squirrels for his meals. He even found a bush of crimsonberries, and stuffed himself to the edge of vomiting. He kept several pocketfuls more, and crushed them across the rabbit he cooked on the third night after leaving Kaide's village. The stars were twinkling into existence, and he watched them through the branches as he ate.

"Think I can just stay here awhile, Ashhur?" he asked, then chuckled. As nice as it might be, he'd grow bored with the solitude and lack of conflict. He was a man of action, always had been, always would be. Hopefully his actions might lead to a bit more substance than they had before.

He closed his eyes to pray, and immediately opened them. An impulse echoed in his head, new to him, but he knew what it was. Ashhur crying out a warning. Darius stood and pulled his sword off his back. The soft light shone across his meager campsite. The stars were bright, and in the distance, he saw the approach of a man robed in black. He felt his throat tighten, and he prayed it be anyone other than him. But the man looked at him from across the distance, and his eyes shone like fire.

"No," Darius whispered. "It can't be. I killed you."

Karak's most fanatical servant...how was he alive? He'd cut his head off, watched his body burn. No one was immortal. It couldn't be him. But who else was it? The man in black drew nearer, and with each step, Darius felt

Ashhur screaming warning. It had to be him. His face shifted, each feature changing in the tiniest of ways. His hood dipped low, and then he smiled.

"You failed me, Darius," said Velixar, Karak's prophet.

"You're dead," said Darius.

"You failed me, and you failed your god."

Darius shook his head.

"Karak is my god no longer."

Velixar continued his approach. He stood at the edge of the campfire, the light shining over the black robes and pale white flesh.

"That isn't true," Velixar insisted. Another step closer. "You can still turn back to him. You can still accept my embrace, and return to the one true faith."

"No closer," Darius said, pointing his sword toward the prophet's throat.

"You do not need to remain a failure. You do not need to wallow in guilt. Lower your weapon, and listen to my words. I never lied to you. I would never lie..."

Darius prayed for strength, for courage. His time in Durham flashed back to him, and he thought of the innocent family he'd butchered in Karak's name. He used that anger, that shame, to keep his sword raised. Still, Velixar was there, smiling, stepping closer. Always there to discuss, to speak his truth. Darius would not listen. He would not!

"Do not be afraid," Velixar said. His throat was mere inches from the tip of Darius's sword. "You have nothing to be afraid of...traitor!"

Velixar lunged, his face locked in a horrific scowl. Darius started to thrust, but saw that the prophet wielded daggers. He almost didn't block, for it made no sense. His instincts ruled in the end, and he pulled back, his sword whirling. He blocked the thrusts, parried another, and then retreated closer to the fire. Velixar remained back, but he was no longer Velixar, and no longer smiling.

"You could never just die, could you?" asked Valessa.

"I could say the same for you," Darius said, trying to remain confident. The black robes were gone, as was the ever-changing face. She wore her gray cloak and plain leather armor. Two wicked daggers twirled in her hands. Darius felt like he was trapped in a nightmare. This hardly made any more sense than Velixar returning to walk the lands.

"You flung yourself against my blade," he said. "You killed yourself rather than accept defeat. What magic lets you live again?"

"Magic?" she said. "This is no magic. No blessing. No curse. This is vengeance."

When she moved, it was as if she became a shadow, her armor fading, her flesh a blur of darkness. Her daggers shone red, and he focused on them, nothing else. His greatsword had benefits of reach, but it lacked in speed. Protecting himself from her barrage involved a constant retreat, a step back for her every step forward. She twisted and struck with inhuman speed. Could he hurt her, he wondered?

At last he saw an opening. His counter-riposte slashed across her arm. The blade passed right through her, as if she were only smoke. At first the lack of blood and flesh disheartened him, but then he heard her scream. She pulled back, clutching at the wound, which was a deep gray scar compared to the rest of her body. He gave her no reprieve, thrusting for her chest. He thought her helpless, for she'd pressed against a large tree to avoid the thrust. He swung wide, a chop that would remove her head from her neck...he hoped.

But instead it thunked into wood. Before his very eyes, she'd sunk into the tree, as if it had been nothing but a mirage. He freed his sword just in time, for Valessa burst forth from the trunk, daggers leading. Darius blocked both, and he pressed against her crossed blades, strength against strength.

"What are you?" he asked through gritted teeth.

"Your better," she said.

"Not a chance."

The light of his sword shone against her in such close contact. The flesh of her face peeled away, revealing the darkness beneath. She let out a cry, then retreated beyond the edge of the firelight. Darius did not chase; he was too busy catching his breath.

"I do not sleep," she told him, pacing along the camp's edge. "I do not eat. I do not tire. Walls mean nothing to me, Darius. Nothing. What hope do you have? Your death is only a matter of time. I will send you to Karak's Abyss, and enjoy watching you burn."

"You're wrong, Valessa," Darius said, watching her, his sword still held tight. "You won't kill me, and even if you do, Karak won't have me."

"You will go to the Abyss if I have to drag you there myself!"

She attacked, her daggers arcing for gaps in his armor. Darius twisted so one scraped harmlessly against the platemail, then smacked aside the other so he could counter. His sword cut across her breast, white light shining. Again she shrieked, and fled out of his reach.

"What was it you'd do to me?" he asked her, laughing despite his tired limbs. At first Valessa looked ready for another assault, but she pulled back further, shaking her head.

"I endured death so I might kill you, Darius. I can wait a few more hours. You must sleep, and when you do, I will be watching. I will always be watching."

Valessa faded away into the darkness, her voice lingering in the night. Darius lowered his sword and took a breath.

"Damn."

He thought to put his back to a tree, then realized how foolish an idea that was, given that he faced an opponent who moved through trees as if they were not there. He stood in the open beside his fire and scanned his surroundings. He didn't see her, but that meant nothing. His instincts told him to flee, but where? If he pressed hard, he might reach the edge of the forest, but what did that gain him? Where might he sleep in safety, assuming she did not ambush him while he stumbled along? Not even castle walls could protect him. No amount of guards might keep her away.

And she was right. No matter how strong he was, he had to sleep eventually.

"Could really use you here, Jerico," Darius said, settling down beside the fire on his knees. Ashhur would warn him of any danger, he knew, but would it be enough if he were asleep? If only Jerico were there. They could spend the night in shifts, one awake, one asleep. But he was alone, and days away from civilization.

"This isn't how it should end," he whispered. It didn't seem fair. Didn't seem just. He had but one idea left, and that was to bait Valessa into combat. If he could kill her, assuming she could be killed, then that removed the threat of her ambush. He stood again, lifting his sword above his head.

"Is that it?" he cried to the darkness. "You're going to run? You're going to play the coward? What does that prove? You were weaker than me in life, and even with Karak's strength, you're weaker now. With every moment you hide, you accept Ashhur's greatness!"

Darius tensed, expecting her to launch at him with those blasted daggers. But instead, he heard her laughter from amid the trees.

"Do you think I am a fool to be baited?" she asked, momentarily appearing at his right before vanishing. "A child to be made reckless? You bear the gifts of Ashhur, and I of Karak. Your training may be better, your armor superior...but we still bear our gifts. And mine will send you to your grave. Lie down, Darius. Let Ashhur protect you. You're his beloved, aren't you? We'll see how much he cherishes his children...and make no mistake, Darius, you are the last of his children, you and Jerico. For such a victory, I can wait. And wait. Can you?"

Darius swallowed.

"Damn."

He stabbed his sword into the earth, grabbed its hilt, and knelt before it. He was already tired from the several days' journey, and the fight with Valessa had only worn him out further. His eyelids felt heavy, worse with each moment now that the excitement of battle was fading. No solutions came to mind, no matter how much he tried to think. Despair threatened him, but he refused it. This was the life he had chosen. When Jerico had offered his hand, and a hope for something better, he'd taken it, and he would not question the decision now.

"You won't win," Darius said, closing his eyes and trusting Ashhur to warn him if she were to attack again. "Even if you kill me, you won't win."

The night droned on, silent but for the crickets and the rustle of nocturnal birds. He clutched his sword, gripping the hilt hard enough to hurt his hands. He couldn't sleep. If he made it to daylight, perhaps he would think of something. Retreat back to Kaide? No, they'd only kill him as well. His mind couldn't focus. Everything about him was too calm, too quiet. Valessa no longer made her presence known, did not speak to him. Part of him wanted to believe she was nothing but an illusion, a terrible dream he'd slipped into as he lay beside the fire.

Maybe it wouldn't be so bad, he thought. Maybe dying wouldn't hurt at all.

He slapped himself to push the thoughts away. Another hour passed, dreadful in its tedium. His nerves could no longer take the wait, the constant anticipation of an attack from the shadows. He had no ideas, no solutions. The metal was cool against his skin as he pressed his forehead against the hilt of his sword.

"I have nothing left," he prayed. "No way to go. What do I do, Ashhur? Tell me, and I'll do it. Don't let me die here, not like this. Surely I have something more, something better to achieve. Tell me what to do. Just tell me."

Expecting nothing, he shuddered when he heard Ashhur's voice.

Sleep, it said. And he did.

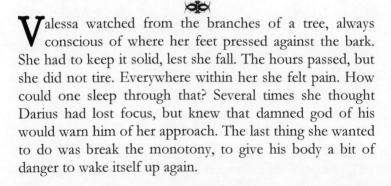

Valessa watched from the branches of a tree, always conscious of where her feet pressed against the bark. She had to keep it solid, lest she fall. The hours passed, but she did not tire. Everywhere within her she felt pain. How could one sleep through that? Several times she thought Darius had lost focus, but knew that damned god of his would warn him of her approach. The last thing she wanted to do was break the monotony, to give his body a bit of danger to wake itself up again.

"It doesn't matter the wait," she whispered, watching the way his eyes remained shut for longer with each closing, and how his head drooped ever further. She knew men could stay awake for lengthy periods of time, but it usually involved actual combat, arduous travel, or constant danger. She'd give him nothing. Already she felt foolish for not waiting for him to be asleep before she attacked in the first place, but her pride burned inside her belly. She wanted to prove to Karak she was the superior, and Darius's challenge had stirred shame and fury. Still, what would it matter if she beat him in combat, or forced a dagger through his eye while he slept? He was a traitor, a coward, and deserved an eternity of torment for his betrayal. What did honor or fairness matter compared to that?

And then his eyes remained closed for too long. Her body tensed, and she clutched the branch with a shadowy hand. Already? He'd fallen asleep already? She'd expected him to last the night, and perhaps much of the following day. How could someone so weak have defeated her?

"Accept this blessing, my glorious Karak," she whispered, slinking to the ground. She passed over leaves without making a sound. Her daggers shook in her hands, not from fear but from excitement. This was it. A single thrust, and she'd be free of her torment, of a form that knew only cold and agony. Darius's head dipped lower, his hands still clutching the hilt. His breathing was deep, rhythmic. Forcing herself to be calm, she waited, watched. She would not be tricked, not so close to victory.

But another ten minutes passed, and he did not stir. Lifting her daggers, she stepped into the dim light of his fire. The kill was hers.

And then the sword flared.

The pain overwhelmed her beyond words. She could not even scream. The blue-white light around his blade

shone brighter than any torch, any sun, any star. It flooded
the forest, washing over it in waves. Valessa tried to flee,
but it held her prisoner. The illusion of herself burned
away, until she was only darkness, only pain. Her thoughts
scrambled as her form weakened with every passing
moment. The Abyss awaited her, she knew, and she would
go there a failure. Her punishment would be beyond
reckoning. That terror gave her strength, and she stepped
away, dimly aware of her frantic, jerky movements.

And then the light diminished, became once more the
faint glow that barely lit up Darius's armor. She fell to her
hands and knees. It was hard to describe, but her body felt
loose, barely hanging together by threads of shadow. Every
shift, every twitch, elicited pain far beyond the constant
ache she had grown accustomed to. She'd felt the glare of
Jerico's shield as it pressed against her, but this was nothing
compared to that. Whatever she'd witnessed, it wasn't the
same. She didn't want to imagine the torment if she'd been
beside the blade when the light erupted.

"Damn you, Darius," she said, struggling to stand.
"You'll bleed by my hands. Ashhur won't protect you
forever."

Deep down, she could feel Karak's anger growing.
Thrice a failure...how long until he revoked his gift from
her completely? She didn't want to know—to ever know—
but glaring at the dimly glowing blade, she feared for the
first time that she might actually fail. Looking to the sky,
she hoped for comfort in the shining red star. It was there,
but another star was beside it, one she had never seen
before. The sight of it filled her with fear, and she swore
not to look on it again, nor think on what it might mean.

10

Jerico woke before Sandra did, both of them covered with a fine, cold layer of dew. He shivered, then carefully pulled his arms free of her. She stirred, repositioned her head atop her hands, and continued to sleep. Jerico rubbed his eyes, glancing once at the rising sun. The clouds were thick, yet the sun burned a deep red. A bad omen, Jerico knew. Had another of his brethren died in the night? Or perhaps Karak moved again, further sealing his victory.

In the end, it didn't matter. Jerico's task was to worry about himself, and those with him. Glancing at Sandra, he felt hesitation building in his chest. Better to pray first, he thought, or prepare breakfast. He knew that would be stalling, though, and let out a sigh. He was hardly perfect, and the last thing he wanted was to see what he feared most: an angry red scar, the skin about it darkening purple. He'd cured disease, venom, and wounds of battle...but could he defeat Karak's own curse?

"Just normal skin," he prayed while she still slept. "Normal skin. Not too much to ask, right?"

Knowing time was short, and Sandra would wake soon, he carefully knelt beside her and grabbed the bottom of her shirt between his fingers. He didn't want her to see his reaction if it was bad. He needed to be strong. At least, that's what he thought she needed.

Realizing he was stalling again, he swallowed, then slowly revealed the skin of her stomach.

The sight hit his gut like a club. It was worse than he'd expected. The wound wasn't even scarred. It looked like it was still trying to heal, swollen flesh leaking pus. The skin around it was a dark purple, with red veins snaking through the bruises.

"No," he whispered.

"Jerico?"

Sandra was awake, and lying very still. Her jaw trembled, but there were no tears in her eyes.

"It's bad, isn't it?" she asked.

Jerico licked his lips, and begged for strength.

"Yes," he said. "It is."

She laid her head back on the grass and closed her eyes. Her hand clutched his, and it held him tight.

"I thought so," she said softly. "It hurts so much, Jerico. So much."

"Lie still," he told her. "Let me do what I can."

He prayed over the wound, and watched the healing light about his hands plunge into the skin. He did this again and again, refusing to let anything of Karak's defeat him. Not now, not when a life was at stake. The purple faded, and the wound closed back to an angry scar. Each time drained him, laid an extra layer of exhaustion across his mind. He'd endured worse, especially after the wolf-men attacked Durham, but he knew there was little more he could do for her. Standing, he let her examine the wound.

"The pain's mostly gone," she said.

"Mostly? It should be gone completely. Dark magic must have been in that dagger, Sandra. It is the only way to explain why I can't heal it."

"You're keeping it under control though, right? Maybe it just needs time..."

Jerico bit his tongue and nodded. It was getting harder every day to heal it, but he didn't want to tell her that. He could see the way she looked at him. She was grasping at hope, and if there was anything Jerico was supposed to represent, that was it. Arguing with her about it seemed beyond childish.

"Come on," he said, offering his hand. "Let's get you something to eat."

After they'd eaten and prepared for travel, Jerico pondered their destination. He'd originally meant to go after Lord Arthur, and do what he could to break the siege. But now?

"We need to find a stronger healer," Jerico said as he scattered their fire with his foot. "A priest, maybe even a wizard. Whatever has infected that wound, be it a curse or spell, might be familiar to someone with a better background in the arcane."

Sandra put her hands on her stomach and nodded. He'd wrapped it tight with clean bandages, but it still looked like it bothered her. He felt so helpless. How was it he could heal broken bones, but a single stab wound defeated him so?

"I thought you were heading toward the Castle of Caves," she said.

"That was before."

"I told you, I'll be fine. I just need some time. I promised to be no burden, and I won't have you changing your plans now."

Jerico shook his head.

"I won't..."

"Won't what?" she asked, stepping face to face with him. "Watch me die? Is that what you think will happen?"

He looked away, and that was answer enough.

"We could go back the way we came," he offered. "Bellok might know a way..."

She was crying, but she let none of it affect her voice as she shook her head.

"I'd be dead already if not for you," she said. "I'm not going back. You may doubt, but I trust you. I've seen what you can do. Whatever this is, you're stronger. We're going on, to where you're needed most. All right?"

"Yes milady."

She smiled, stood on her toes so she could kiss his lips. Jerico smiled back, but there was little joy in it. He'd seen the grimace that flashed across her face when she stepped away. He saw how blood was already starting to seep through the bandages around her waist.

"Let her live," Jerico whispered as she led the way west. "Otherwise you're going to have one pissed off paladin to deal with when I walk through your gates."

Jerico followed Sandra, wondering what his teachers at the Citadel would have said upon hearing him issuing threats to his own deity. He had a feeling they would have been amused.

They walked for several hours, often stopping to rest. When they ate at midday, Sandra only nibbled on the hard bread. The lack of appetite worried Jerico, but he said nothing. They continued on, their pace growing slower with each mile. Jerico prayed over Sandra's wound, and when it showed only marginal improvement, he said nothing, only accepted her thanks with a smile.

The day wore on, and they passed field after field. When they saw a distant farmstead, Jerico led them there. He saw many children working the fields, and the first to see him bowed low, his eyes nearly bugging out of his head.

"Are you a paladin?" the boy asked. He looked like he was nine at most.

"I am," he said, smiling. "Is your pa about?"

The boy nodded.

"I'll get him."

He ran off. Jerico took Sandra by the hand and led her toward the farmhouse.

"We're fine on food," she said, but she sounded distant.

"That's not why we're here."

They reached the home, but stopped when they heard a man call a greeting from the fields. Jerico turned, then bowed low to a man who looked to be on the verge of his fiftieth birthday. His skin was tanned from many hours spent in the sun, and his back was stuck in a stoop, but he moved easily enough, and when he shook Jerico's hand, his grip was strong.

"Welcome," said the man. His demeanor was friendly, but Jerico sensed the apprehension hidden behind it. After all, here he was, a simple farmer greeting an armed stranger wearing platemail.

"Forgive us for intruding," Jerico said. He kept his tone warm and hoped the farmer would realize he meant no harm.

"No intrusion," said the farmer. "My name's Cobb Williams. What can I do for you? If it is food you want, I have a bit to sell, though I'm not in the way of much else."

"This is Sandra, and my name is Jerico." He debated a moment, then added, "Of the Citadel."

Cobb's eyes widened a moment, and then he grinned.

"Gods be good, you telling the truth? My oldest joined up with that bandit, Kaide, and came limping back from the Green Gulch with fewer fingers and a lot more sense. Mind if I see that shield of yours? He's always talking about it."

Jerico obliged, pulling his shield from his back and holding it before him. Light shone across its surface. Cobb reached out to touch it.

"It safe?" he asked, just before making contact.

"Depends how dark your heart is."

Cobb laughed.

"Perhaps I better not," he said, pulling back his hand. "I'm a simple man working the fields, but I know when not to press my luck. Please, come inside. I can get my wife to make you all a fine meal, and perhaps you can tell me how the battle at the Gulch really went. Never know if my son's speaking truth or telling tales, if you get my meaning."

Jerico glanced at Sandra. He'd planned to buy a horse, even a donkey, so long as Sandra would have something to ride. No matter how much she might deny it, he knew the lengthy walks were aggravating her wound. Yet her skin had grown pale, and he doubted they could go much further that day. Perhaps eating some fresh food and sleeping in a comfortable bed would do her good.

"Our food has been poor, and rationed," Jerico said, returning his shield to its spot on his back. "I hope you understand what you're offering."

Cobb grinned.

"Mister, you won't eat more than what my Debra can cook. When you feed as many mouths as we do, two more don't matter much."

They entered into a large family room, which looked to take up more than half the house. Cobb left them there to talk with Debra. Their furnishings were meager, but Sandra sat on a cushioned chair, closed her eyes, and slowly rocked.

"Are you all right?" Jerico asked her.

"That's a stupid question, even for you."

She smiled, and even with her eyes closed, she looked so beautiful. Jerico's hatred grew in his heart at what Valessa had done. He knew his hatred was wrong, that it went against all he believed...but damn it, sometimes it seemed so appropriate.

Debra came to greet them, wiping her hands on her apron. She was as worn and tanned as her husband, though she looked to be a good ten years younger. Jerico took her hand, bowed on one knee, and kissed her knuckles. Debra giggled as if she were but a young girl yet to leave her father's home.

"You're just like Jeb described," she said. "Be honored if you stayed at least a night. We don't hear much beyond our neighbors, and they'd rather talk about the harvest than what the Hemman brothers are up to."

She turned her attention to Sandra, and her giddiness vanished, replaced with a distinctly motherly attitude.

"Are you feeling fine, dear?"

"Just a little ill, that is all," Sandra said. "Honest."

"This is Sandra Goldflint," Jerico said. "Kaide Goldflint's sister."

That raised some eyebrows, but the couple held their questions as to why she was there, traveling with Jerico instead of her brother. Sandra kept silent, and soon she slept.

"It has been a long trek," Jerico said.

"The road is hard on everyone," Cobb agreed, and let the matter drop.

Come dinner, the whole family gathered. The room was cramped, but none were willing to eat outside or in a different room, not with Jerico there to entertain. Jerico counted four sons and one daughter. The oldest looked to be in his late teens, and was already married. They also lived there on the farmland, though Cobb insisted the boy would soon have land and a house of his own. Hardly a year separated him from the second oldest brother, Jeb, the one who had joined Kaide's army when the bandit leader had gone recruiting on his way to join Arthur Hemman's army.

Truth be told, Jerico didn't recognize him at all. He'd been just one of many amid the battle.

"I didn't get a chance to fight much," Jeb explained. "Stayed near the back, but I did help hold the line when you said. You shoulda seen yourself, that shield glowing as we fought. Even when I took a hit to my hand and lost half my damn fingers, I'd still have gone on fighting. We all thought you died when you stayed back after calling for a retreat."

"I'm too stubborn for that," Jerico said, earning a laugh from around the table.

When Jerico brought up purchasing a mount, Cobb would hear none of it.

"Far as I'm concerned, you're why my boy's still alive," he said. "I got an old ass that doesn't care too much for plowing anymore. He'll still let you ride him, long as the burden isn't too much. I don't think Sandra will upset him none."

The food was delicious as promised, particularly the bread. Jerico devoured slices until it was gone, though the same could not be said for Sandra. She ate little, nibbling at her food before pushing it away. Her skin had grown even more pale, and he caught her staring at the table as if amid intense concentration.

"Sandra?" Jerico asked, hoping not to alarm his hosts. She looked up at him with a blank expression, then shook her head.

"I'm sorry," she said, standing from the table. "I need some air is all. Just need..."

She fell to one knee, remaining upright only because one of Cobb's sons grabbed her arm and held her. Jerico shot from his chair and hurried to her side.

"What's the matter?" Debra asked. "Can we help?"

"It's nothing," Sandra said, weakly pushing Jerico away. "I'm fine."

Her forehead was slick with sweat when he touched her, and it burned his hand like fire.

"Fever," he told the couple. "I hate to ask, but..."

"But nothing," Cobb said. "Put her in our bed. Barely sleep as it is, and the floor suits me just fine."

Jerico scooped Sandra into his arms and stood. Debra scattered the rest of the children as Cobb led him into the small bedroom to the side. Laying her atop the blankets, Jerico brushed his hand against her forehead and tried to focus his thoughts for another lengthy bout of prayer.

Cobb crossed his arms and nodded toward Sandra.

"Sir, I don't mean to pry, but I know you're not telling me everything. She's got more than a fever. My old eyes can still see those bandages."

"She was stabbed," Jerico said, lifting Sandra's shirt. "Normally I could handle it, but something's wrong. It's fighting me somehow."

"Those bandages need to be cleaned," Cobb said, leaning closer to inspect them. "I'll grab a knife, and then we'll take a look."

He stepped out, only for Debra to replace him at Sandra's side. She laid a cool cloth over Sandra's forehead, then told her to hush when she protested.

"I've got Jeb heating some water over the fire," she told Jerico. "When it gets to boiling, I have a few herbs that should help bring down her fever."

"Thank you."

Cobb returned, knife in hand. Debra scooted over to allow her husband access to the bed. With slow, deliberate movements he sliced off the bandages. They smelled sickly sweet, and were soaked with blood and pus. Jerico winced when he saw the first patch of flesh beneath. More and more bandages fell to the floor. Cobb leaned in, examining every inch, close enough for his nose to nearly touch her skin. When done, he looked at Jerico.

"The wound's gone bad," he said. "I'm not sure how she's even alive."

Jerico nodded, for he'd thought the same thing. Her entire stomach was purple, and in its center, like a cat's eye, was a weeping cut. Its edges were yellow, and the veins about it a violent red. Jerico couldn't begin to imagine the pain it caused her.

"Jeb said you can heal people," Debra said, guarded optimism in her voice. "Surely she's not too far gone for you?"

"No," Jerico said, taking a deep breath. "But each day she gets worse, and my prayers lessen in their effect. Something's inside her, fighting against every bit of healing."

"Maybe so," Cobb said. "But I've seen something like this before. Not so terrible, of course. We need to open her up, or she'll be dead soon."

The farmer leaned down so he could whisper to Sandra.

"I need you to lie still," he said. "I'll have Jerico hold you down if I have to. If you don't trust yourself, just say so, and we can go ahead and have him do it now."

Her breathing had grown shallow, and when she spoke, it was too soft for Jerico to hear. Cobb heard, though, and closed his eyes and sighed.

"Hold her down," he said.

Jerico took Sandra's hands, lifted them over her head to the pillow, and leaned his weight on her forearms. Debra left, then came back with her oldest, ordering him to help her hold down Sandra's legs.

"I'm sorry I have nothing for the pain," Cobb told her.

"Wait," said Jerico. He released Sandra's arms and placed his palm against her forehead. He closed his eyes and tried not to tremble. Never the best when it came to the non-physical aspects of being a paladin, he still knew many useful prayers. Normally he focused on healing, but for now...

Numb the pain, he prayed to Ashhur. *Numb the hurt. Give her strength.*

A dim light shone across her eyes, and then Jerico nodded.

"Go ahead."

He held her wrists and watched as Cobb's knife pressed against Sandra's skin. It pierced, drawing blood. Sandra tensed, and let out a whimper, but did not struggle much. Debra left her son to hold her legs, and instead took out a second cloth and used it to mop away the blood and pus. With grim determination, Cobb reopened the wound in a single smooth cut. Jerico watched, wondering what the famer hoped to accomplish. The foul smell in the room worsened, as if by cutting into Sandra they'd opened a rotten fruit.

Cobb stepped back and let his wife wipe away at the blood so he could see. He stared, and stared, and then grunted.

"There you are, you son of a bitch."

He reached his fingers into the wound. Sandra let out a cry. Jerico stroked her face, and pressed his cheek against her burning forehead.

"Be strong," he said, closing his eyes. "You're strong. You're stronger than this. You're Kaide's sister, and he only wishes he was as strong as you. It's almost over, I promise. Hold on, Sandra. Hold on."

He heard a sound, like metal scraping against bone. When he looked up, Cobb held something aloft with his blood soaked hand. It was smaller than a pebble, metallic, and shone a soft red that immediately made Jerico feel ill in his stomach. Cobb looked around, then wrapped it with a bloodied cloth.

"Can you handle the rest?" he asked. "Otherwise, Debra has a way with stitches."

"She needs more than stitches," Jerico said, shaking his head. "Leave me be. Ashhur will make her well."

The three left. Alone with her, Jerico knelt by the bed, put his hands across her stomach, and prayed. Healing light poured into her, and strength out of him. The minutes passed, but he paid no heed. His hands shook, and they were stained with blood, but he ignored that as well. For over an hour he stood vigil, watching as the vicious wound closed, and the purple flesh and red veins faded away. Her fever lessened. Her eyes closed, and sleep came to her.

At last Jerico knew he could not continue. His mind felt raw, his throat dry. He tried to stand and stumbled. Gripping the bed, he rose slower, took a deep breath, and then left the room. Darkness had fallen, and the family gathered in their thick blankets across the main room. Debra leaned back in the chair, softly rocking. Cobb stood by the door, and when he saw Jerico exit, he beckoned him over.

"Outside," he said.

The cool night air felt good against Jerico's sweat-soaked skin. He stretched his back, then leaned against the side of the home. Standing was a chore, but it felt good to no longer be on his knees. Cobb chewed on something tough and watched the stars. After turning to spit, he held out a small cloth bundle.

"Take it," he said. "I don't feel right having it around."

Jerico accepted the cloth, then unwrapped it. Inside was the metal piece that had remained inside Sandra, poisoning her from within. Its red glow had dimmed, as if it were losing power.

"I believe it's the tip of a dagger," Cobb said, not looking at it. "But that's thick metal. Don't see how cutting through something soft as a woman's belly would have broken it."

"It was no ordinary dagger," Jerico said, thinking of the strange magic that had possessed Valessa. Hearing this, Cobb chuckled.

"You're telling me things I already know. There's something foul about it. Stuck in her, it must have been killing her every moment."

"It's no wonder I couldn't heal her," Jerico said, staring at the metal as if it were a sentient evil. "I feel so foolish for not thinking to check her as you did."

"Doubt you've ever needed to. Your abilities are amazing, Jerico. You probably could have stuck my son's fingers right back on his hand if you'd been there, and had the time. But sometimes a good knife and a pair of eyes have their uses, too."

Jerico put the metal piece into his palm and clenched his fist. Holy light shone through his fingers, and he directed every bit of his anger toward the metal. When he reopened his fist, nothing but dust remained. He lifted his hand and blew it on the wind, let it carry far beyond the farm. Cobb nodded in approval. Silence stretched between them, until Cobb turned, spat, and began again.

"Forgive me if I'm prying," he said. "But what is Sandra doing with you, and not her brother? Last we heard, he's still fighting Lord Sebastian. He set her out on a task? Are you some sort of bodyguard?"

"Why she is with me is her own affair. But I'm on no task from Kaide."

"Then where are you headed?"

"To the Castle of Caves, to help Arthur."

Cobb sighed.

"Not surprised, though I was hoping a good man like you had seen the senselessness of it all. All lords are the same. I told Jeb that when he rode off to fight, kill, and die like a bloody fool. They all want their taxes, all demand our worship, and all see us as nothing but cattle. The sooner this ends, the sooner the North returns to peace."

"I've spoken with Arthur. He's a good man, a better man."

"Those not in power always seem so," Cobb said. "Funny how all that fairness and honor vanishes once they're the one sitting on a throne."

Cobb turned and spat out whatever he'd been chewing on, then wiped his lips on his sleeve.

"Forgive me," he said. "You're a good man yourself, and I'm sure you're doing what you think is right. I've got a few more years on you though, and I think they've hardened me like leather over a fire. Seeing Jeb get caught up in it didn't help none, either. Reason why I ask...I doubt Sandra's going to be ready to travel anytime soon. If whatever you're doing is dangerous—and it sounds like it is—she can stay here. We could always use another if they're willing to work hard, and she's a pretty lady to boot. If she wants a normal life, I'm sure I could find a dozen men eager for her hand."

"I'm not sure that's what she wants."

"Then what does she want?"

Jerico chuckled.

"I'm not sure I know that, either."

Cobb shrugged.

"Just giving you the option. It looks like she's already been hurt once traveling with you. I'd hate for it to happen again. Promise me you'll think on it."

"I will."

Cobb stretched, and his back popped several times.

"I should join my family."

"I'll sleep on the floor in Sandra's room, if that's all right with you."

"I thought you might," Cobb said, and he smiled. "And Jerico...if it's *you* she's wanting, you might consider just how important taking down Lord Sebastian really is."

He went inside. Finally alone, Jerico looked to the stars. He wanted to pray for guidance, but he was too damn tired.

"Tomorrow," he promised the stars. "And thank you."

Jerico returned to Sandra's room. He put his hand against the side of her face, checking there was no fever. She slept deeply, with no appearance of pain. For that, he was thankful. Cobb's words came to him, but he pushed them away. He had no energy for that. Beside her bed he found a blanket laid out for him, when and by whom, he could only guess. Wrapping himself in it, he closed his eyes and fell asleep within moments.

11

Darius was stunned to be awake. His back hurt like the Abyss, his left arm was asleep, and the red mark on his forehead would probably never vanish...but somehow, he was alive.

"Huh," he muttered. "I'll be damned."

Well, maybe not quite, he thought with a chuckle. That was, after all, the entire point of what he was fighting against.

He ate his meager breakfast, always with an eye out for Valessa. It made no sense, really, why she hadn't killed him in his sleep. How she'd mocked him, taunted him with that fate. She could wait, she'd said, yet Ashhur had commanded him to sleep, and no dagger had found his throat. It was a miracle, one he felt woefully unworthy of. Not that he'd complain. It was still vastly better than the alternative.

Darius caught sight of her only once as he gathered his things, watching from behind a distant tree. She looked like herself, plain-garbed and furious. When she realized she'd been spotted, she vanished. Darius saluted her direction, then continued east, toward the Gihon River. Once he reached it, he could follow it north to the Blood Tower. Sir Robert Godley, issuer of the bounty on his head, would be there. As he'd told Jerico, he'd explain everything and demand that the bounty be removed before anyone got hurt.

And if Robert refused...

Darius tried to not think about that.

Valessa bothered him little as the next days passed. Several times Darius felt a tingle in the back of his mind, and he'd turn, readying his sword. If she'd been planning to attack, she backed down at his reaction. At no point did he feel safe, nor relinquish his weapon. Even when he took a piss, he held the hilt in one hand, his dick in the other. Valessa might not think it honorable killing a man while he relieved himself, but he'd seen the madness in her eyes. As long as he died, he felt pretty sure she'd be content.

Every night he knelt in an open space or field, for he'd left the forest long behind him. He stabbed his sword into the dirt before him, closed his eyes, and slept. Every night, he expected death, and prayed Ashhur would take him. Every morning, he awoke shaking his head and chuckling.

It wasn't until the fourth day that Darius encountered another human being. He walked a dirt path between great fields stretching north to south on either side. Gold wheat blew in the wind, and he ran his hands across their stalks. Half a mile beyond the Stronghold there had been a field, and a long time ago Darius used to play in it, weaving hidden from the world through the wheat when he was supposed to be performing his daily prayers. He'd been caught once, and that once was enough to ensure he never did it again.

His hand dropped to his side. Karak had stolen away his childhood. Surely that alone proved the destructiveness of the Stronghold. Lost in memories of rigid canings, forced prayers, and constant reaffirming of the chaos in his heart, he barely noticed the approaching wagon until it was right on top of him.

"Hold!" Darius called out, waving his arms at the approaching driver. A wagon meant supplies, and food, both of which he was running low on. What little coin he had should get him to the Gihon, and from there it was just a matter of time until he spotted one of their patrols along the river.

Two men sat at the front of the covered wagon, which was pulled by a pair of heavily panting oxen. Their clothes were the color of dirt and toil, their faces unshaven. They said something to one another, then issued a command with the reins. Darius knew nothing of how to drive a wagon, but he could tell when one wasn't slowing. Frowning, he waved his arms again, making sure to keep his sword sheathed.

"Hold, I wish to trade," he shouted. "I am a paladin, and mean you no harm!"

The men appeared unwilling to run over a champion of the gods, and finally slowed, close enough for Darius to reach out and touch the noses of the oxen.

"Could you move?" the driver asked Darius.

"Certainly," Darius said. "Though I'd prefer we talk first. I've run low on supplies, and wonder if you have any to spare?"

The men exchanged a look.

"I can pay," he insisted.

"Not got much to trade," said the larger man beside the driver. "I suggest you move on. Town's not far back behind us. Buy your fill there."

Darius tried to show no insult for their inhospitable nature. While at times he'd received preferential treatment for his allegiance to Karak, he also knew there were plenty who wished nothing to do with the gods' champions, or any matter of faith. With dark paladins hunting those of Ashhur all across Dezrel, they also might not wish to traffic with either side, lest they be caught in the middle.

"Just a scrap of food," Darius said, doing his best to show he posed no danger. "I will pay fair prices, and be grateful for your kindness."

Still they looked at one another, neither saying a thing.

"It's that, or you run me over," Darius said, his patience wearing thin. "I'm not moving."

"Fine," said the driver. "Grick will see what we can spare, if you'll curl around to the back."

"Much appreciated," Darius said, bowing. He walked past the wagon, smacking one of the oxen across its muscular side. Grick vanished into the covering. For a brief moment Darius thought the driver might resume now the road was clear, but he did not. At the rear of the wagon, Darius peered inside. Various bags and crates were stacked to either side. Many of them were already open. Grick wandered around them, as if unsure of what he was looking for.

"On the way to market?" Darius asked.

"Huh?" Grick looked over at him, then shrugged. "Yeah, right. Been lean, so me and Gacy thought to take some things to sell down at Murkland. Now where..."

Darius watched him search as a cold feeling settled in his stomach. When Grick turned aside, Darius stepped closer, and peered at the visible boards of the wagon.

Dried blood.

"So are you and Gacy brothers?" he asked, swallowing hard.

"Brothers?" Grick chuckled. "Yeah, we're brothers. Ain't we brothers, Gacy?"

"Just shut up and sell him what he wants," Gacy shouted from the front.

A strange sensation hit Darius, though it was less of a sensation and more of a certainty. He knew, without a shred of doubt, Grick had just spoken a lie.

"Poor wagon looks like it's been through plenty of hard winters," Darius said, making casual conversation. "Had it long?"

"Yeah," Grick said, pulling out two loaves of bread from a sack. "Had it forever, it seems."

Another lie. Darius knew that Jerico had always possessed the ability to detect truth, and now it seemed Ashhur had granted him the same gift. Darius slowly pulled his sword off his back and rested it across his shoulder.

"Where'd you get it?" he asked.

Grick was about to offer the bread, but paused. Something in Darius's voice must have set him off, for he pulled back.

"Asking a lot of questions, mister," Grick said. "Why you care about my wagon?"

"I don't. I care about what you and Gacy did to the original owners."

"Go!" Grick shouted, ducking further into the covering. Darius climbed after him. On his knees amid stolen goods and atop wood stained red with blood, he felt his anger rise. Before he could take to his feet, Grick was back, knife in hand. He lunged, the small blade aimed for Darius's throat. It was a meager weapon, suitable for robbing peasants, not combat with an armed professional. Darius smacked it aside with his gauntleted hand, then kicked himself forward. The headbutt knocked Grick to his rear. The ensuing kick sent the knife flying.

The wagon shuddered as it started to move, and then Gacy was there, climbing over the divider between the front seat and the rest of the wagon. He wielded a heavy club, and swung it overhead with all his strength. Darius blocked it with his sword, kicked Grick again when he tried to get up, and then swung. His sword slashed across Gacy's arm, severing tendons. Howling in pain, Gacy leapt at Darius, his hands reaching to strangle him.

Darius reacted as he'd been trained to a thousand times. Stepping back, he put the tip of his sword between them and let the man impale himself on the blade. Gritting his teeth, he kicked the man away and pulled his sword free. The body collapsed on the floor beside Grick, arms and legs sprawled atop various crates. Grick's lower lip quivered, and he pushed at the corpse.

"Don't kill me," he pleaded. "Take it. Take the wagon; it's yours, all of it, yours. Just don't kill me!"

Darius pressed the tip of his blade against Grick's throat. Blood trickled down the sword, obscuring the blue glow beneath. His pulse pounding in his ears, Darius tried to think, tried to decide what Jerico would do.

"You're thieves, aren't you?" he asked.

"Yes," said Grick.

"You stole this wagon, didn't you?"

"Yes. I...I didn't want to, it was Gacy's idea, I swear."

"Shut up!"

Darius felt his jaw begin to tremble, so he clenched it tighter. He ground his teeth as he fought for calm.

"What did you do to them?" he asked. "What did you do to some poor farmers on their way to market? Tell me, Grick."

"We just roughed 'em up," Grick said. "I swear, roughed them up, but they're alive. We left them alive."

Again came that certainty. The man spoke a lie.

"They're dead," Darius whispered. The tip of his sword pressed harder against Grick's neck. "That makes you a thief and a murderer."

"Please, no," the man said, barely understandable between his sobs. He was a wretched man, poor, uneducated, without a shred of courage. His skin barely clung to his bones. Yet he had taken a life. Many lives, most likely. Gacy was already dead, and Darius could only imagine Jerico's unhappiness at that. But what was he to do? Turn them over to the law, and risk capture himself?

Let them go free, with an easily broken promise to do no wrong?

Mercy over vengeance, Jerico had said. Grace over condemnation. But what of justice? Grick continued to sob, and in Darius's mind, he became the wounded stranger that Karak's prophet Velixar had brought him to on a dark night. Velixar's lesson was that killing could be done for good, that the ending of a life was a mercy. How could Darius reject Karak's teachings, yet desire nothing more than to shove his sword right through Grick's throat? He would not be a hypocrite. Darius would rather be a failure—or a weakling—than a hypocrite.

"Get up," he said. He saw a coil of rope in the corner and gestured to it. "Grab it, and step out of the wagon. Slowly. If you run, I will chase you down and make sure you get every scrap of pain you deserve. Have I made myself clear?"

Grick nodded.

"Good. Now do it."

The man slowly stepped out from the wagon, wincing every time the tip of Darius's sword nudged his back. When they were both out, Darius tied one end around Grick's wrists, then looped it about his neck, always careful to keep an eye out for Valessa in case she thought it an opportune moment to strike. When finished, he took the other end and held it while he replenished his store of food from the wagon.

"We're going to travel the way you came, Grick. You'll lead. We'll find those bodies, and if you and your bastard friend didn't bury them, then we'll do that, too. After that, we head to town, find someone who knew the people you killed, someone related. They'll decide your fate. But first..."

He nodded toward the wagon.

"Grab Gacy out of there. You have a body to bury."

Darius left him plenty of slack as Grick climbed inside and dragged out Gacy's body by a leg.

"In the field," Darius said when Grick paused.

"What am I going to dig with?" Grick asked.

"The gods gave you hands for a reason. Now start."

"What about the wagon? You just gonna leave it here? Someone will take it."

Darius chuckled. The irony was not lost on him.

"Then let's pray whoever finds it is much more deserving of it than you."

He watched Grick dig as the sun crawled across the sky. Progress was slow in the hard ground. Darius did his best to feel no compassion, no remorse, as the cuts grew across Grick's hands. He was a murderer, after all. Karak would have had him executed, the old ways even calling for his sacrifice upon an altar. Glancing down at the scratched off lion on his chest, Darius reminded himself he was slave to those ways no longer. Blood dripped across the shallow groove that was Gacy's grave.

"Slide over," Darius said as he jammed his sword into the dirt, still within arm's reach. "I killed him. This is my grave to dig, too."

Together they tore into the ground with their hands, until at last there was enough space for a body. Darius dragged Gacy into it, and then covered it with what dirt they had. It was not enough, and Darius knew wild animals would soon come to dig it up. Still, there was little else he could do. If not wild animals, then the worms would have him, but at least they'd done something.

"Come on," Darius said, grabbing his sword. "Walk."

Darius had no desire to chat, and thankfully Grick picked up on it. In silence they traveled down the dirt road, Grick ahead, Darius holding the rope like the other man was some sort of pet. The hours spent digging the grave had killed much of the day, and by the time they found a trio of trees growing beside the road, the sun had begun to set.

"There," Grick said, pointing toward the trees. "That's where we hid. Bodies should be around here someplace."

It wasn't difficult to find where they'd been dumped. Darius just followed the blood. There were three bodies. Two were husband and wife, lying side by side as if they would stay together even in death. At their feet, face down, was the body of a child. Darius rolled her over so he could see her face, see the bugs crawling across her pale skin, see the trickle of blood dripping from her nose to her mouth. The paladin swallowed hard, and he heard Velixar's voice in his head, mocking him.

What say you now, Darius? Is this man worth the time, the effort? Run your sword through him, and make this world a better place. Or do you still see compassion as a virtue, and not a weakness?

"Why?" Darius asked, turning to the thief. "Why did you kill the child, too? You had their things. You had their wagon."

Grick stepped back, reaching the extent of the rope. It tightened about his neck, and he winced.

"It was a mercy," he said.

"Mercy?" Darius felt his fury swell. "Mercy!"

He rushed the man, struck him with his fists. The heavy gauntlets smashed into Grick's nose and teeth. Darius flung him to the ground, kicked, and then fell upon him, his hands clutching the front of his shirt.

"Mercy?" he shouted. "You killed a child, and you call it mercy?"

"Gacy woulda kept her," Grick said, spitting out blood and a tooth so he could talk. "Woulda taken her, done...we didn't know she was in the wagon, and the parents died fighting back. She's just a little girl, no ma, no pa. It was mercy, please listen, either that or Gacy."

No warning this time, no certainty from Ashhur that he spoke a lie. Darius thought of the wounded man Velixar had brought him to, bleeding and in pain. Killing wasn't a punishment, Velixar had said. It was a mercy. Staring down at the thief, Darius saw pieces of himself, of what Velixar had sought to create, only in a far more terrible light.

"I made sure she felt nothing," Grick said when Darius said nothing. His words broke the silence, and Darius stood.

"We have no time for a burial," he said. "We'll burn them, just as you should have."

By the time the pyre was complete, night was upon them. Darius felt tired, his armor heavy on his body. The fire burned, and in it, Darius thought he saw a glimpse of the Abyss, and Velixar's mocking smile. This was the world he defended. These were the people Darius had sworn to defend, to save, when he sided with Jerico over Karak.

"How much farther is the town?" Darius asked Grick as the smell of burnt flesh and hair filled the air.

"Another four miles," Grick said.

"Too far, then. We'll stay here for the night."

They moved to the cluster of trees and built a small fire. Darius chewed on his lip, then removed the rope from around Grick's neck, leaving only the tight cords about his wrists.

"I won't leave you hog-tied through the night," Darius said, settling down opposite the fire and the trees. "You'll want to run, I'm sure, but know that I can track you. I've been trained for this, Grick. I know where you'd go, how you'd hide, and I can't promise to control myself the next time I find you."

"Then what do you want me for?" Grick asked, pressing his hands against his neck and rubbing the raw flesh.

"To deliver you to justice. Like I said, we'll let the townspeople decide your fate."

"Then just kill me now. You know that's what they'll do."

Darius rubbed his thumb and forefinger against his eyelids. Yes, he did know that. What in the gods' names was he doing? What did he hope to accomplish?

"You killed people," Darius said. "You know you must be punished."

"You killed Gacy. Don't see no one punishing you."

"Children," Darius said. "You killed children."

"Yeah, I did, and I did it to protect her. You saying you never done something like that?"

Darius opened his mouth, then closed it. The praying family flashed before his eyes, followed by Velixar's laughter echoing in his ears. Yes, he had. And Jerico had forgiven him for all of it. And now Ashhur placed his trust in him. Damn it, why couldn't things remain simple?

"Yes," Darius said quietly. "I have. And then I flung myself to my knees and demanded that my friend deliver justice."

Grick shifted against the tree he leaned against.

"Why didn't he kill you?" he asked.

Darius chuckled.

"Because he's a better man than I."

He rolled over, clutched the hilt of his sword. When he spoke, he did not look at Grick, did not want to see his reaction.

"Go if you wish, thief. I don't know what is right anymore. You deserve death, but then again, so do I. So go. Let someone who can sleep through the night decide your fate. Run away from your punishment. When the gods one day find you on your deathbed, may they possess greater wisdom than I."

He closed his eyes and tried to sleep. He heard rustling several times, but Ashhur cried no warning in his ear. At last sleep came for him, and he dreamt of a little girl running through a field, flowers in her hair, her face lit with a smile.

When Darius woke, Grick lay against the same tree, his head lolled to one side. His neck was slit, and blood soaked the front of his clothes. Valessa stood beside him, grinning. Darius grabbed his sword, but Valessa only laughed at him.

"Ashhur protected you from me," she said. "But not him. What does that mean, Darius? Can you answer?"

She stepped through the tree and vanished.

"What does it mean?" Darius asked, fighting away the lump in his throat. "It means I must bury him. That's what it means."

He spent the morning digging the grave and the afternoon filling it back up with dirt. He gave a quick prayer over it, for he knew not what else to say.

"I know nothing of him but his sins," Darius whispered to the cold evening air. "But he stayed. I pray that meant something."

The grave went unmarked, and traveling east, Darius did his best to think no more on it.

12

R obert awoke before dawn, as he often did, but this time
he felt unease the moment he opened his eyes.
Something was awry, but what? With Luther's departure,
along with the vast bulk of his private troops, he'd hoped
things would return to normal. Of course, the younger
priest had remained. The way Cyric looked at him when
they talked always put a queer twisting into his gut. As he
dressed, Robert felt certain the priest was to blame for his
current unease.

It felt foolish to fear anything in his own tower,
surrounded by his own troops, but he took his sword with
him anyway. Dressed, armed, and finished with his pre-
dawn rituals, he traveled down the stairs, feeling particularly
fat and old that morning. Two men guarded the doorway to
his tower, and by the way they saluted him, Robert knew
something bothered them as well.

"We weren't sure if we should wake you," one said
when pressed for an explanation.

"I'm awake now," Robert snapped. "Tell me."

"The priest..." said the other, then shrugged. "Best you
follow me, see for yourself."

Robert followed the guard to the northern side, toward
where Karak's followers had relocated their camp. The
cause of the guard's apprehension was immediately
apparent. Within the circular wall protecting the tower
they'd begun building a structure of impressive size. Its
center was of stone, though where they'd found it, Robert
couldn't begin to guess. What looked like stairs were on

either side, built of thick slabs of wood. Four pits marked the corners, each one already thick with flame.

"What in Karak's name is that?" Robert wondered aloud.

"It's an altar," said the guard.

"An altar? For what?"

He had no answer, and Robert dismissed him back to his post. The sun was just creeping above the horizon, and it cast a red hue across the clouds. Together with the fires, it gave a strange look to the altar that Robert liked not one bit. His eyes lingered on it as he approached, and his attention shifted from it only when stopped by Cyric himself.

"Welcome, knight," Cyric said, his smile ear to ear. Robert nodded, just a curt greeting, until he noticed the change that had overcome the priest. He looked healthier, stronger. Once he'd been nothing but a child with his nose in a book, but now...there was an aura, a glow. Now he appeared dangerous. His skin was darker, though perhaps that was just a trick of the poor light. His eyes were different too, he realized. Instead of a baby blue, they were a deep red, as if his irises had begun to bleed.

"Morning, priest," Robert said, not bothering to keep his tone civil. "What is this you've started building on my land?"

"You might rule this small patch of dirt, but all of Dezrel belongs to Karak," Cyric said, still smiling. "Surely you do not mind Karak taking such a tiny piece back for his own?"

"You're avoiding the damn question."

"I do not mean to," Cyric said. "We are building an altar, one worthy of such a momentous occasion. Come tonight, we will celebrate our god's glorious return."

"Return? Where? Speak some sense, or I'll have my men tear this thing down and haul that chunk of rock into the Gihon."

"I wouldn't do that, Robert." Cyric's smile grew wider. "Change comes upon the wind. Do you not feel it? You should rejoice to be witness to this miracle."

He felt it all right. It just wasn't inspiring any rejoicing.

"What miracle?" he asked. "Enough preaching. Tell me what you plan to do. Where has Karak returned, if that's even possible? And what does this have to do with your altar?"

"Karak has returned in me," Cyric said. "Tonight, upon that altar, I will show all your men, show all the world, proof of that fact. Do not interfere. It is no longer your place to stand in the way of gods and men."

Robert felt too old to deal with shit like this. The altar loomed before him, the flat stone as tall as him. Over twenty men worked on it, hauling in logs cut from distant trees. Others cut the logs into boards, ready to be hammered in by five men who worked non-stop, their muscular bodies slick with sweat. They all moved like men possessed, and he would have none of it.

"Tear it down," he said. "Karak has enough land as it is. Go build your altar elsewhere."

"No."

The word entered his ears and then sunk down into his stomach like a brick. Cyric said it so casually, so simply, that it showed he held no fear of Robert, no respect at all. Robert swallowed, and did his best to keep his temper in check.

"Pardon these old ears, priest, but I fear I heard you wrong."

"You did not. If you wish to destroy this altar, you are welcome to try. But you will fail. I'm stronger now, Robert, stronger than all of you. Don't throw away your men's lives, not when they are so close to seeing the coming glory unfold before them."

Robert's hand fell to the hilt of his sword, and he almost drew it then and there. He stared into the face of fanaticism, and he saw no reason in those red eyes. But he was surrounded by men loyal to Karak. Nearby, in particular, was a dark paladin, and he kept his axe ready at all times. If Robert struck at Cyric, the others would tear him to pieces long before any of his soldiers could protect him.

"You have one night," Robert said, releasing the hilt of his sword. Cyric's smile widened even more at the words. "But after tonight, you tear it down, you hear me?"

"Come tomorrow, you yourself will be kneeling before that altar," said the priest.

"Fuck all, I will," Robert muttered as he traveled back to his tower. Ignoring the guard's questioning looks, he returned to his room. He found little solitude there, for Daniel barged in moments later.

"Sir," he said, sounding immensely relieved. "I'm glad you're here. For a moment I feared..."

"Feared what?" Robert asked.

Daniel stood up straight, but it was clear he didn't want to answer. Robert shook his head, motioned for his lieutenant to relax.

"I feel it, too," he said, slumping into his chair. "I thought with Luther gone they'd be more obedient, but while their numbers have shrunk, their confidence has grown. Cyric outright refused an order of mine, and threatened me in return."

Daniel stood in the doorway, his jaw clenched tightly against his trembling anger.

"We need to strike," he said. "Before they're prepared. Before they have that altar built, whatever its purpose truly is. He's a threat. You know it, I know it, now let's do something about it."

"To what end?" asked Robert. "Losing half my men, all because I'm scared of a single priest? Their troops are well-armed, and you can tell by their scars alone they've seen more combat than most see in a lifetime. We cower and act like fools for no reason. King Baedan would never, ever allow an attack by the priests to go unpunished."

"If he hears," Daniel said. "If he believes it. The truth that reaches his ears will be what the priests make of it. We're the ones so far away. This is our land to protect, and I say we not give a fuck what those in Mordeina might think and just act."

"And what of my men?" asked Robert. "How many knelt in prayer yesterday before Luther's departure? Tell me that."

"Fifty," Daniel said.

Robert rubbed his forehead and swore. That was a quarter of their current standing forces in the Blood Tower.

"But they will surely not break their oaths to lord and king," Daniel said. "Not because of some priest."

"I've seen what men of faith will do," Robert said. "If Cyric has his claws in the hearts of our men, then any action we take risks defeat before the first swing. Whatever he plans, we'll wait, and we'll watch. He's a young man, foolish, proud. This may well bite him in the ass if things go awry."

"This is a mistake," Daniel insisted.

"Yeah? But it's my mistake to make. Dismissed, Lieutenant."

Daniel bowed and left without another word. Robert had plenty, all of them foul. He cursed, stormed about his room, and drank away the day waiting for nightfall. As the sun began its descent, one of his soldiers knocked on the door.

"What is it?" he asked, in no mood for courtesy. The door swung open, and the soldier stuck in his head.

"Sir, Cyric wishes me to give you a message. You're invited to join him at tonight's ceremony. He says you'll be given a place of honor."

Robert snorted.

"I'm sure I will. Tell him I'd rather fuck a goat."

The soldier blanched.

"I'll tell him you declined," he said, turning to leave.

"No, damn it," Robert said, flinging the door open. "I gave you an order, and I expect you to carry it out. Now what message are you to deliver?"

The soldier stood erect and saluted.

"That you'd rather fuck a goat, sir."

He made it sound so urgent, so important, Robert grinned.

"That's right. Now leave me be."

He slammed the door in the soldier's face and poured himself another glass of wine. Half an hour later, the door reopened, and Daniel stepped inside.

"What is it?" he asked.

"Cyric's extended an invitation to the rest of our soldiers," Daniel said. "Many want to go. What do I say?"

Robert scratched at his chin and looked out his window. He couldn't see the altar from there, but he could imagine it, grand in size and surrounded by a large crowd.

"Much as I hate that bastard, he's right. I won't stand in the way of a man and his god. Whoever wants to go can go, so long as their duties are completed."

Daniel clearly felt otherwise, but he held his tongue. Once he'd left, Robert peered down from his window. He might not be able to see the altar, but he could see the path there. He counted seventy men heading north. A third of his men.

"So much for king and country," Robert muttered.

He belted his sword to his waist, flung on a heavy cloak, and descended the stairs. Joining in the ceremony was out of the question, but he would not remain in the dark about whatever Cyric planned.

The altar was even more impressive than he'd expected. The stone slab had been painted a dark black, though how he did not know. Fires burned at the corners in the thick pits, while crisscrossing outward in seemingly random directions were tall torches whose fire gave off no smoke. Over a hundred men encircled the altar. Atop the stone were three men. Robert recognized Cyric, but the other two were unknown to him. They were naked from the waist up, their bodies covered with red paint. They knelt with their heads bowed, their eyes blindfolded, and their hands bound behind their backs. The crowd sang a song Robert vaguely recognized, though it lacked any joy, just the sound of a droning litany of faith toward Karak. The chant made his skin crawl.

Robert remained in the far back, as close as possible to his tower while still able to hear the words Cyric spoke. As the last light of the sun dipped below the horizon, Cyric called for silence.

"My friends. My soldiers. My faithful. Welcome to this glorious night. Beneath these stars, you will witness the might of Karak laid bare before you. Long have the gods fought over Dezrel, but at last we will find victory. The blood moon approaches. At last, the true god returns to these lands. At last, the Lion walks among us!"

"The Lion!" cheered the fifty soldiers who had remained with Cyric when Luther left. An ill feeling tightened Robert's throat, and he found his eyes drawn to the bound men. Who were they? What was to be done with them? Any normal day he would have forced an answer, but he was no fool. He felt the electricity in the air. If he protested, or came back with armed men, he'd have a battle on his hands.

"The Lion has returned!" Cyric cried, all smiles, all victory. "And he has returned in me. But I know there are many here who are doubtful, many who are not ready to believe. I pray that you come to wisdom, and quickly. We are owed nothing, not even our very next breath. 'A sign,' I'm sure you cry in your hearts. 'Give me a sign!' And so I will."

This was it, thought Robert. He couldn't imagine what sign Cyric would produce. He hoped it would be a meager one, born of smoke and visions. His men were better than that. Despite all the priest's words, they wanted action, wanted something firm. Cyric had made many promises. Now it was time to see if he could deliver.

A cold wind blew over them as Cyric motioned for someone to join him atop the altar. Robert recognized him as the dark paladin, though he did not know his name. The paladin knelt behind the first of the two bound men and lifted his axe.

"These two men have given their lives to Karak," Cyric told the crowd as a wave of unease stirred through them. "They are sinful, wretched beings. They stole. They killed. Perfection will never be possible for them in this life, but their faith is great. And so comes their reward."

The paladin swung. His axe tore through spine and flesh, and showered the altar with gore. Karak's soldiers cheered, and to Robert's horror, so did many of his men. Blood dripped across the stone and down its black sides.

"Praise be to Karak," cried the other bound man in a quivering voice. The paladin went to his side. No hesitation, no preaching, just another brutal chop, and down he went. More blood. More cheers.

"Their bodies are destroyed!" Cyric cried. "But they are not! Their souls burn in purifying fire, changing, becoming greater than ever before. Lift your voices! Lift your hearts! I am Karak. I am your god, now witness my power!"

The red markings on the two bodies flared, then suddenly burst into flame. High above, thunder rumbled. Wind blew. And then red lightning struck in rapid succession, hitting the center of the corpses. Cyric laughed as the altar split down its center. The corpses exploded, showering the crowd with blood. And then, from within those torn bodies, the lions emerged.

They were enormous creatures, easily the size of horses. Their skin cracked from the heat of their own bodies, which were made of a rough, dark stone. Along the cracks in their flesh shimmered the yellow glow of molten rock. One's neck was bare, the other with a thick mane of shadow, which billowed in the wind. Their obsidian claws glimmered. In unison they pulled back and roared, the force of it knocking many to their knees. Deep in their throats, Robert saw liquid fire.

The two lions circled about Cyric, eyeing him with their red eyes. Robert thought he would bow, show fear and respect to such amazing creatures, but instead it was the lions that lowered their heads. Cyric turned to the crowd and lifted his arms.

"Now is the time," said the priest. "Make your choice. Serve the true god, or be consumed by his fury. Kneel, or know death."

All but twelve kneeled, not counting Robert, who suddenly felt very exposed, and very alone. Before they could react, the lions leapt, moving with speed that seemed impossible for creatures of such size. They dove upon the men, slicing open flesh with a swipe of their obsidian claws and snapping necks with a single bite of their jaws. Those who knelt remained perfectly still, as if the slightest movement might bring the beasts bearing down upon them as well. Of the twelve, only one managed to run, and it was not far. His blood boiled across the tongue of a lion.

Robert had seen many horrors in his years as a soldier and a commander, but he'd never known such fear as when those lions turned their eyes to him. He felt his legs go weak, his stomach twist into his throat.

"Shit."

He ran as Cyric lifted his arms to the sky and cried out his worship.

"Glory and power to our beloved Karak! Arms, my brethren, take up your arms. We follow the old ways now, the way of sword and blood and faith. Kneel, or be made pure in death."

Robert heard a familiar sound, that of many swords being simultaneously drawn from their scabbards. His tower was not far, but he'd seen the speed of the lions. He did not expect to make it, but he didn't have to. The two men standing guard at the door rushed to meet him, their weapons ready.

"Inside!" they cried.

Robert did not slow, did not dare look back. He heard the brief sound of combat, and screams of pain. Then he was at the door, slamming into it at full speed. Once inside, he flung it closed, shut the locks, and leaned his forehead against the wood.

"Dear gods," he whispered. "What have I allowed?"

No time for that. The makings of a battle were upon him, and it was his task to lead his men. He could not be afraid, could not hesitate. Rushing up the stairs, he searched the barracks. Perhaps they could hold the tower, but how many were in there with him?

The second floor was empty, but on the third, he saw a dozen men gathered before the windows, bows in hand.

"Sir!" one said, seeing his entrance. "What word from Daniel?"

Robert didn't understand, so he pushed aside the archer and looked out at the battlefield below. Cyric's men had come pouring in from their camp, already within the outer wall. Near the tower and stables Daniel had formed a battle line. A hundred of his men stood firm, challenging the mercenaries sworn to Karak. Despite their inferior gear, the men seemed to be holding. The archers rained arrows down upon the enemy ranks, with perfect position from the windows.

"Daniel prepared for this," Robert said, realizing what he was seeing.

"He did," said one of the archers. "Forgive us, sir. We were told to say nothing in case he was wrong."

"We can hold them," Robert said, analyzing the fight. Karak's soldiers fought with religious fervor, but his own men defended their homes, their lives. They also had greater numbers, plus the advantage of the archers. Yes, they could hold...

"What the fuck is that?" asked the man at the northernmost window. Robert leaned out, and there he saw the lions approaching, flanking Cyric at either side. They seemed to be in no great hurry.

"Put every arrow you have into those things," Robert ordered. "And pray one pierces an eye."

The men changed their aim and let their arrows fly. Cyric stepped back, as if sensing he was in danger, but the lions continued on. Several struck true, but they bounced off the dark skin as if hitting stone. The archers showed no worry, unleashing a second and third volley. Still the arrows hit, and did nothing.

And then the lions burst forward, the sudden change in speed horrifying to see. They were too big to move that fast, they had to be. The lions crashed through their own ranks, then leapt upon Daniel's men. Swords could not pierce their flesh. Shields could not deflect their strikes. In seconds, the rout was on. Robert could not see Daniel, but he hoped he made it out somehow. Someone needed to tell the world what happened there.

The lions gave chase, but Karak's men did not. They turned their attention to the tower, and the locked doors. The archers continued firing at the men, but they were hesitant, and Robert caught many glancing his way. Worse, he saw Cyric lift his arms, darkness shimmering about his fingers.

"Get back," he ordered.

Two did not retreat in time. Arrows made of blood pierced their sides. One slumped by the window, the other fell through, his skull cracking on the ground below. Silence filled the room as the men stood there, looking to their leader. Robert knew they wanted hope, wanted victory, but he had none to offer them.

"Men, you have served me well, as you have your lords, and your country," he said. "I don't know how much your life is worth to you, or what gods you believe in. If any one of you wants to fall to your knees, I won't blame you. But as for me, I'll be in my room with my door barred. When they break through, I plan on killing as many as I can before tasting death. Any who still wish to fight, grab a sword and follow me."

Every man there took up arms, and Robert couldn't have been more proud.

At the top of the tower, they put his desk, chair, and chest of clothing against the door. Two men stood at the far side, bows in hand. The rest waited, swords drawn, listening to the cries of pain intermixed with worship outside.

"King Baedan won't allow this," said one, rubbing his sword with an oiled cloth. "When he finds out, he'll send his whole army. Wish I could see the look on that priest's face when he sees how doomed he is."

"He ain't going to hear shit," said another. "Who's going to tell the king what happened? You?"

"Daniel will. He escaped. I saw it."

"Enough," Robert said to them both. "Just...enough. I won't spend what little time I have left listening to you two bicker."

"Then how will we spend it?" asked a third. Footsteps echoed from the stairs beyond the door, and they heard scattered shouts.

"Like men," Robert said, drawing his sword. "Clear the door. I won't have them starve us out, and I won't wait for that priest to weaken us with his sorcery. Let those bastards in, and we'll give them a proper Blood Tower welcome."

Even facing death, none there would disobey their commander. They pushed away the barricade. So far nothing heavier than a man's shoulder pressed the door from the outside, so the locks still held. Robert held up his fingers, counting down for them to fling open the bolt. On three, he let out a cry and raised his sword.

The door burst open, and several men came barging in, their armor painted with a red lion. The first fell, two arrows in his throat. Another tried and failed to block a trio of attacks as Robert's men assaulted him from all sides. More soldiers poured inside, the archers abandoned their bows, and at last Robert joined in. He parried and twisted, but he felt none of the youth he had when he fought the wolf-men in Durham mere months ago. He felt old, tired. He was watching his men die before him, and for what? The whims of a mad priest?

They killed two for every one of their own, but still they fell. Robert plunged himself into the gap, drenching his sword with blood. Every time he watched the life fade out from those fanatical eyes, he felt a smile stretch across his face. A counter-riposte, and another died. They were down to four, but the mercenaries were beaten back to the door. Robert dared to think they'd hold, that they'd build a wall of the dead across the stairs.

Cyric stepped into the room.

Robert felt both fear and hope. Fear, for he knew the priest's power. Hope, because with one thrust he might end the entire conflict, maybe even send those blasted lions back to the Abyss where they belonged. The paladin was with him, but his attention was turned to the other men slashing and thrusting. The way was clear. Robert held the hilt of his sword with both hands and swung with every last remnant of his strength.

Cyric caught the blade with his bare hand. His skin shone a dull red. A few drops of blood trickled down his wrist.

"Hello, Robert," Cyric said, smiling.

The priest's other palm slammed against Robert's chestplate and flung him backward, as if he'd been kicked by a giant. Crashing against his desk, he rolled to one knee, gasping for air. His helmet had cracked, and he tossed it aside. Blood poured down his face; he didn't know the nature of the wound, only that he was blind in his right eye.

"Oh, have you finally found wisdom and kneeled?" Cyric asked as the rest of Robert's men died to the paladin.

Robert struggled to his feet, clutching his face with one hand.

"Go roast in the Abyss," he said.

Cyric stepped closer. He was smiling, but there was no joy in those red irises.

"I have. I came back."

A bolt of shadow leapt from his palm. Robert blocked it with his sword, only to find the power traveling up his blade and through his gloves. He shrieked as the skin of his hand erupted with pain. Cyric grabbed him by the throat, and with strength he couldn't possibly have, lifted him into the air.

"You won't die here, Robert," said the priest. "I won't have a rebellion on my hands, nor the king interfering. So you'll be a good little puppet, won't you? Write all the right letters, say all the right things?"

"Fuck...off," Robert gasped through his crushed windpipe.

Black electricity arced throughout his body. He'd have screamed if Cyric's hand hadn't denied him breath. The priest lowered him to his feet, so they could stare eye to eye.

"I'll burn every last shred of resistance from you if I must," he said, his voice a cold whisper. "I'll purify the chaos from your heart, through fire, through pain, just like our forefathers once did. Do you understand me, Robert? Is that what you desire? Or would you rather save yourself the torment, and kneel?"

Robert spat in his eye.

Cyric wiped his face, that smug smile finally gone from his lips.

"So be it," he said.

Robert felt pain, tremendous pain, and then darkness.

13

They stayed at the Williams' home for three days, letting Sandra fully recover. Jerico repaid their kindness as best he could by working in their fields. Truth be told, he enjoyed the simple work, knowing that in planting a few seeds and yanking out some weeds he wasn't making a mistake. He had no decisions to make. No lives to endanger.

By the third night, Sandra could walk without a limp, and she'd clearly grown restless remaining indoors. The air was fairly warm, and Jerico sat with her on their porch, looking at the stars.

"Feel like I'm constantly in the way," Sandra said, leaning her head back and sighing. "They're good people, but I'll be happy to leave."

Jerico chuckled.

"Well, that answers the question I was going to ask."

She glanced his way, raised an eyebrow.

"Which was what? If I wanted to stay with them?"

Jerico shrugged.

"It's a good life, calm, even if it is a bit meager. Cobb says he could find you a husband without too much trouble."

The way her eyes bugged out, Jerico realized he'd made a mistake, though he'd be damned to know what it was.

"Is *that* what you think I want?"

"You wanted a life away from your brother. Well, this is one, and Cobb has offered."

Sandra crossed her arms and sighed.

"You're ready to leave, aren't you?"

Jerico stared at the sky instead of meeting her gaze. Only a few clouds dotted the horizon, and they made the expanse of stars look that much larger.

"I must. Arthur needs my help."

"Do you want me to come with you?"

Jerico knew he could not lie, but what was he to say when the answer was both yes and no?

"Part of me does," he said. "But what I do...and with the dark paladins hunting me...you'll never be safe, Sandra. Not ever. I'm not sure you're ready for that life. And I know for certain you don't deserve it."

They fell silent. Inwardly, Jerico berated himself for broaching the subject so poorly.

"You said part of you," Sandra said, breaking the silence. "That means part of you wants me with you. Why?"

Jerico ran a hand through his hair. Battling wolves and dark paladins was easier. And made more sense.

"I enjoy your company," he said. "I feel happier around you."

"I barely know you, Jerico. What we have...I'm not sure it's what you think it is."

Jerico shifted, feeling increasingly uncomfortable.

"Then consider me a dreamer, as well as someone willing to find out. But I can't see you hurt again. I've lost nearly everyone dear to me. My friends, my teachers, they're all gone. Even Darius rushes to his death at the towers. I can't go back to Durham, —the closest place I've had to a home—for fear of Karak's paladins finding me there. I'll forever be on the run, forever alone. Except for you, and because of me, you nearly died."

"So for fear of losing me...you'd rather give me up willingly to a plain life, and then never see me again?"

He shot her a look.

"You make it sound so stupid."

"Maybe because it is?"

He laughed.

"Then I'm getting good at doing stupid things. Perhaps that's why I've survived where others have fallen. It's always the idiot that lasts the longest."

Sandra shifted over so their legs touched, then wrapped her arm around him and laid her head against his shoulder.

"You're not an idiot."

"Sure about that?"

She kissed his cheek.

"Absolutely. So what do we do now?"

He gestured northwest.

"Assuming the situation remains unchanged, Arthur's still besieged at the Castle of Caves. Other than myself and your brother, no one is coming to help him."

"Do you think you can really accomplish anything on your own, Jerico?"

"No," he said, smiling at her. "In fact, I expect to do little more than die while trying to get inside."

"Then why do we go?"

"Because I should. Because I think that's where Ashhur wants me to go. And because I can't let what happened to Stonahm go unpunished. Not after what they did to Beth..."

She ran a hand lovingly across his face, her touch like lightning.

"Well," she said. "It's a fool's errand then. Good thing that's what you do best."

"You're the one traveling with a fool. What does that make you?"

She kissed his lips.

"Figure it out," she said before going inside.

Darius was torn between apprehension and relief when he finally reached the Gihon River. His journey was almost over, and he would obtain an answer to his dilemma. Either they'd rescind the bounty, or remove his head. Obviously Darius preferred one over the other, but he had no intention of spending the rest of his life as an outlaw. If they decided to kill him, then so be it. They'd only perform the execution Jerico had stayed.

He set up camp by the riverside. Night fell as Darius waited for a boat patrol to pass. When the stars reached their fullest, he felt an itch in the back of his mind. He shifted and pointed his sword toward the tree line. Valessa stepped out, the smile on her face doing nothing to diminish the madness in her eyes.

"Where is it you go?" she asked as she paced before him. Darius kept ready in case she attacked. A shiver ran through him as she passed through the trees. He was haunted by a phantom, but her daggers were so very real.

"If I tell you, it'd ruin the surprise."

"You know you'll make a mistake eventually. Ashhur cannot protect you forever."

The paladin shrugged.

"Doing fine so far. Course, I'm not eager to wait forever. Strike at me, Valessa. Let's have another go. Or would you rather skulk and hide until I die with gray hair on my head? What will you then tell Karak when you return to the fires of the Abyss? That you thought your revenge best served when I was so feeble I couldn't lift my sword? At least you sent Grick to your god. I'm sure he'll be a very impressive sacrifice..."

Darius thought he'd finally goaded her into another fight, but then he heard the sound of men from the water. Glancing back, he saw torches burning in the hands of four men. They'd seen the light of his campfire, so far from civilization, and were crying out in greeting.

"You won't be safe with them," she said as the boat drifted closer to shore. "They'll put you in chains, without that damn sword of yours. Then I'll have all the time in the world, Darius. All the time I need to make you suffer for what you've done to me."

She fled back into the darkness of the forest.

"You flung yourself against my blade," he said sighing. "You, not me."

He walked to the water's edge and waved to the four men.

"Well met," he said, his voice carrying. "I hoped I might come across one of your boats. Which tower do you hail from?"

"Tower Silver," said the leader of the four, extending his torch so its light reached Darius. Tower Silver was the closest tower to the Blood Tower, which meant Darius would not have to travel far for his meeting with Sir Robert. He wasn't sure if this made him happier, or more nervous.

As the light shone upon him, the four men suddenly tensed.

"I see you are a paladin," said the leader. "But of what god? Things have not gone kindly between us and Karak lately."

"Ashhur," Darius said, wondering what business with Karak they referred to. He took a deep breath, pushing that aside in his mind. This was it. "But I have not always been. My name is Darius, and I once hailed from the Stronghold."

Silence filled the air, broken at last when one of the four looked to the others and muttered.

"Oh shit."

"I did not come here to fight," he said, jamming his sword into the soft earth before him. "Only to speak with Sir Robert Godley, so that I might tell my story, and have him remove the bounty placed upon my life."

"Begging your pardon, Darius," said their leader, "But there is no bounty for your life, not anymore. It's only for your capture, not execution. Robert changed it a few weeks back."

Darius grunted. Well, that was a pleasant surprise, though he dared not let himself feel hopeful. If it was still for capture, that meant they wanted to interrogate him, or even worse, send him to the Stronghold. Their torture rooms were the last place he wanted to be.

"Well," said Darius, "consider me captured."

The boat beached before him, and he offered his sword. The men held their weapons drawn, and they looked at one another.

"Climb on board," said the leader as he accepted the blade. "But don't get too eager about talking to Robert just yet. A lot's happened at the Blood Tower, and I think it best Daniel be the one to explain it."

Darius stepped into the boat, and he accepted a seat at its center. They pushed off, and one by one the men sheathed their weapons. With poles and paddles, they traveled upriver, toward the tower. Darius looked back many times, always for a glimpse of Valessa. He saw her once, standing at the water, watching. Then no more.

Hours later, they reached the tower. Once it might have been impressive, a great cylinder overlooking the savage lands beyond the river. But now he saw the disrepair, the moss growing on the stone, and the cracks across its foundations. Windows that might have given killing room to archers were instead boarded up to hold in heat for the winter. Of all the towers, it was the only one built across the Gihon, within the Vile Wedge. This had been when their cavalry numbered in the hundreds, and their lightning rides across the Wedge had been legendary. Now Darius hardly saw a single horse.

"Time hasn't been kind to the Silver," Darius remarked.

"Ain't nothing the wilderness is kind to," said a soldier. "Least of all those trying to keep order."

Two men at the docks threw them ropes. Once they were looped about the boat's front they pulled them in. Darius was led out first.

"Who's he?" asked one of the men on the dock.

"A guest," said the patrol leader. "Where's Daniel?"

The soldier jerked a thumb behind him to the tower.

"He's asleep in his room. Where else would he be?"

"Then go wake him. And don't ask me why, or how important it is. That's an order, now go."

The leader turned back to Darius.

"We have a small dungeon, fit for only a man or two. I plan on taking you there, where no one else but Daniel will know you've arrived. Will you come peacefully?"

Darius chuckled.

"Lead on. Just take care of my sword, will you?"

At the western side of the tower, dug into the earth like a cellar, was their dungeon. Darius stepped inside as the soldier locked him in. The only light came between the bars of the slender window in the door. The walls were cold stone, and he could touch every side from where he stood in the center. Man or two? No kidding. He shuddered to think of sharing such a small space with another.

Of course, such tight walls meant little to Valessa. Without his sword, he had nothing to fend her off, no light to burn her shadowed flesh. He could only hope and pray she did not show until after his business with Daniel was done. Time wore on, and though the night was deep, Darius had no desire to sleep. At last he heard a commotion on the other side of the door, and then it opened. Holding his hand to block the torchlight hurting his eyes, Darius smiled and stood.

"Welcome to my humble abode," he said, bowing. "I'm Darius, who once hailed from the Stronghold."

"Where do you hail from now?" asked the man. He was slender, but carried the scars of battle, and his eyes sparkled with wary intelligence.

"If the Citadel still stood, it might be from there," Darius said. "But for now, I guess I am without home or country."

The man leaned against the door and crossed his arms.

"I'm Daniel Coldmine, lieutenant for Sir Robert Godley. Do you remember me, Darius?"

Darius lowered his hand, his eyes finally adjusting. He better saw Daniel's face, and then nodded.

"You helped us fight the wolf-men at Durham."

"I did. Robert and I pushed our men night and day to reach you in time, to save the life of that little town. Yet all that's left now is ruin and graves. Tell me why, Darius. Why would you turn on those you once protected?"

Darius saw that Daniel held a knife, barely concealed between his arms. This was it, Darius realized. No court. No appearance before Robert. Looking into Daniel's eyes, he knew the man could not care less for the bounty. Either he gave Daniel a worthy answer, or kissed his life goodbye.

"I was a fool," Darius said softly. "I was desperate, and afraid. I feared I had lived my entire life as a lie to Karak, and then a prophet came to me, offering proof. Offering meaning. He brought me back to Durham, and demanded they kneel in faith to Karak, or perish. I was to execute all who refused."

Daniel shifted his arms. The blade glinted in the torchlight.

"Did you?"

Darius rubbed at his eyes as the horrible memories came back.

"No," he said. "I could not. I don't know who lived, who died, but ask them if you must. Ask Jeremy Hangfield. Ask Jacob Wheatley. I begged them to run. The prophet would return, and I couldn't stop him. At the time, I thought no one could..."

He shook his head.

"I see the anger in your eyes, and I will not deny it. Please, before you act, tell me how many survived. Let me go to eternity, be it fire or gold, knowing at least that."

Daniel remained silent for a very long time.

"Little over a hundred," he said at last. "And they've told me, same as you, that you begged them to run. That doesn't make you innocent, Darius. A boy who sets a house aflame, then yells for those inside to flee the fire, still deserves his lashes."

He moved to close the door, then stopped.

"That prophet," he asked. "Did anyone ever stop him?"

"I did," Darius said. He knew he should feel proud, but strangely did not. "I cut off his damn head."

Again Daniel fell silent. He was working something out, Darius could tell, but what?

"Things have changed since the battle at the Green Gulch," Daniel said, leaning against the door. "Two priests of Karak arrived at the Blood Tower, demanding that we hand you over to them. They want the North to worship their god forever. One of them, a pissant named Cyric, led a revolt against us. He sacrificed his own men to bring about strange creatures made of fire, and hurled arrows of shadow from his palms. Few of us escaped, and I don't know the fate of those we left behind."

Daniel struck the door with his fist.

"You say you killed this prophet," he said. "The one who many of Durham said wielded killing flame with his hands, and whose eyes shone red like the Abyss. Can you kill Cyric?"

"Release me, and I will try my best to end his threat."

"I don't need you to try. I need a fucking promise. Will you help me reclaim my tower, save Robert, and send that priest to the grave where he belongs?"

Darius fell to one knee and bowed his head.

"For what I have done, I've only begun to atone for. If Cyric wishes to continue what the prophet started, then I'll deliver him the same fate. You have no reason to fear my blade, Daniel. Karak is my god no longer."

"That'll do. I've set up a second room for you, which should be far more accommodating than this. My guard will show you the way. Sleep well. We have much to discuss come morning if we're to retake the tower."

14

They left the farm, the Williams refusing to accept any coin Jerico offered them.

"You've helped enough," Cobb said. "You worked the fields, and told my boys stories of lands they'll never, ever see. I just hope you think on what I told you. No reason for you to get yourself killed for any man other than yourself."

"My life's not worth much," Jerico said in return. "Not much need to be protective of it now. Safe days, farmer."

"You too, paladin."

They traveled northwest, following the road. Cobb had assured him it would lead to the Castle of Caves, so long as he took every northern fork. On his back, Jerico carried an impressive collection of provisions, and Sandra had a bag of traveling bread as well. That first night, they ate until both felt ready to burst, then lay down on their bedrolls. They camped in the open, in a field not far from the road.

"You don't have to do this," Sandra said as they stared up at the stars. "You don't owe Beth, nor my brother. We all owe you, if anything."

"Trying to convince me to turn tail, Sandra?"

"Trying to convince you to live. Surely you have something better to do with your life. Someone better to spend it with."

Jerico looked away, not wanting her to see the confusion and doubt on his face.

"It's what I must do," he whispered.

"Why?"

"Because if I run now, if I try to save myself instead of helping those who need it, then what was the point of me surviving when all others have fallen?"

He felt her hand brush against his arm. His entire body stiffened.

"I can think of several reasons."

Jerico rolled over to face her, and he took her hands in his.

"You won't change my mind, Sandra. The closer you get to me, the more likely you'll be hurt. I have no home, no place I will ever be safe. I...I don't think..."

"Stop thinking," she whispered as she slipped into his bedroll. "For tonight, at least."

She stopped his next sentence with a kiss, and despite his greater strength, she held his arms down with little difficulty.

"I just don't want you hurt," he said as she removed her clothes.

"Shut up, Jerico."

"I know, but..."

"Shut up, Jerico."

His clothes were next, and he helped her even as he protested.

"I'm just worried that..."

She kissed him, then held her hand over his mouth.

"Gods you're impossible," she said, then laughed despite herself. After her wounding, her many days of sickness, he could not resist the warmth of her body against his. She felt so vibrant, so alive. Her hair hung low across her face, lit by the moonlight as she hovered above him. Seeing her smile, her happiness, he gave in at last.

Come the next day, they traveled with a much brighter spring in their step. For once Jerico did not dwell on the fight that awaited him, and Sandra was in her best health since leaving her brother's camp. It seemed even the weather matched their brightness. They passed several couples, and a large family of twelve, heading toward the nearby villages to ply their trade. One couple sought a suitor for their daughter; another hoped his skills as a smith might be rewarded for a few weeks before moving on to the next town. Jerico wished them well, and prayed with those who were glad to see a man of Ashhur.

"Weather is fine," Jerico said on their fourth day. "Makes it almost possible to forget that every paladin and priest of Karak is trying to kill me."

"They're who knows where, and we're here," Sandra said. "Try not to worry."

"Easier said than done. It's my head they want on a pike, not yours."

"I'd join you on a pike, anyway. You think I'd let them take you without a fight?"

Jerico laughed.

"Indeed. And would you stop them?"

"I'm Kaide Goldflint's sister. Damn right I would."

The paladin looked her up and down while they walked.

"With what?"

She smirked at him.

"I keep a dagger on me at all times, Jerico. Well, perhaps not at *all* times."

He blushed, and she mocked him for it. From behind, they heard a distant shouting of orders. Jerico glanced back, saw a wagon train about a quarter of a mile behind.

"Caravan heading toward the castle?" he wondered.

"Sebastian would never let them through the siege lines," said Sandra. "Perhaps supplies for Sebastian's own men, instead?"

Jerico stopped so he could see better. The dirt path was mostly flat, with but the slightest of bumps from the gently rolling hills they traveled across. He saw groups of armed men, but their banners were of no mercenary troop he recognized.

"Reinforcements for Sebastian's army?" Sandra asked. "Jerico, I think we should get off the road."

Jerico nodded, starting to think she was right. But the banners, they almost looked like...

Lions.

"Oh no," Jerico muttered. "This is bad."

He looked about, seeing nothing but fields of grass in all directions.

"Very bad."

"What?" Sandra asked.

"They're pledged to Karak, which means they'll likely have priests or paladins with them."

All around were the flat fields of tall grass. They could hide within them, but if Jerico could see the caravan, then the caravan could see him. What would they think of the couple who suddenly rushed off the road to hide? And what if they recognized his armor, realized he was a paladin of Ashhur? If only there was a hill, a group of trees, that they could vanish behind to hide the direction in which they fled.

"Not good, not good, not good," Jerico muttered as his mind raced.

"Have you no ideas?" Sandra asked as she took his hand.

"None."

"Then we'll do mine. Walk into the field, slowly, as if nothing were the matter."

"What plan is this?" Jerico asked. Sandra led the way, pulling him along. Behind them, the wagons rolled closer.

"Why else would a man and woman wander off a path for a moment alone?"

Fifty yards out from the road, she turned so his back was to the road, and she could peer over his shoulder.

"Almost," she said, then grabbed his face in her hands and kissed. Jerico was too stunned to kiss back. When the kiss ended, she pulled him down into the grass, where they would not be seen.

"Will they believe it?" Jerico asked as he huddled on his knees.

"I don't know. You're a terrible troubadour."

"I'm no good at lying, nor playing pretend."

"A shame."

Despite their situation, she laughed, and he blushed again.

"Are you so certain they are a danger?" Sandra asked. She also crouched on her knees, ready to run at a moment's notice. Jerico wanted to look, but dared not for fear of revealing their farce for what it was.

"I know of no one else who might carry such a banner," he said.

"What will you do if they come for us?"

Jerico pulled free his mace.

"I'll do what is necessary. If they do come to inspect, you run like the wind, understand?"

"Worry about yourself." Sandra crept higher, peering through the slender stalks of grass. Whatever she saw startled her, and she ducked back down and spoke in a whisper.

"Two men, they're almost here."

"Are they armed?" Jerico asked.

"Yes, but they haven't drawn their blades yet."

"They might have seen my armor," Jerico whispered. "Get ready to run."

Sandra looked again, then shook her head.

"Jerico," she said. "Don't judge me for this."

His brow furrowed as he wondered what she meant, and then she began to moan. It started low at first, and quiet, but steadily grew louder. Jerico felt his neck flush, and his jaw dropped open. Her eyes were closed, and her face looked like she was in the midst of deep contemplation, but it did not match the noises coming from her mouth. Shaking away his shock, Jerico peered through the grass. Two soldiers were near, both with the symbol of a lion painted across their breastplates. Amused grins decorated their faces. They were talking, and Jerico did his best to ignore Sandra's performance in order to listen.

"Sounds like he's giving her a solid go," said the one on the right.

"Care to give 'em a startle?"

"Go ahead if you want, but I won't. Interrupting a king's knight while he's fucking is a good way to get yourself stabbed."

"I ain't scared of any knight," said the man on the left.

"Then go on, if you're so desperate to spy a tit. Or is it the man's dick you're after?"

They struck one another with their fists, then returned to the road, glancing behind only once. Sandra quieted, then stopped when Jerico motioned they were gone.

"Are we safe?" she asked.

"Seems like it," Jerico said, making sure one more time. When he knelt back down, Sandra caught him giving her a funny look.

"What?" she asked.

"Nothing."

"No, what?"

He shrugged.

"Some of that sounded familiar, that's all."

She punched him across the jaw. It bruised his lip, but he didn't complain. He definitely deserved it.

Once the wagons were far enough ahead, Jerico and Sandra emerged from the grass. Feeling safer, Jerico counted their numbers, and didn't like the estimate he came up with. At least four hundred, if not more. Given where they were, and the direction they were headed, there could only be one place they traveled.

"They're going to the Castle of Caves," Jerico said.

"If they join Sebastian's army, then Arthur will have no chance," Sandra said. "And Kaide...he'll still try to stop them. My brother is too stubborn to know reason. Whatever hope Arthur has is done."

"No," Jerico said, shaking his head. "Don't think like that. It isn't hopeless, not yet. We don't know the situation there. Perhaps a minor lord threw his lot in with Arthur. Your brother's band might already be on its way, ruining their supply lines and poisoning their water. We might not stop them, but at least we can try to stall."

"How?"

Jerico gave her a mischievous grin.

"Wagons are such fragile things..."

They stayed far back out of sight until nightfall, when the caravan set up camp. As the stars came out, Jerico and Sandra made up the lost distance, until at last they crouched at the far edges of the campfire light. Whoever ran the wagons showed no fear of bandits or marauders. Instead of circling them into a protective barrier, they remained set in the middle of the road, still in line. The oxen pulling them had been tethered in the fields, downwind from the camp. Sandra pointed to them, but Jerico shook his head.

"Perhaps after," he whispered. "They're tired, and might not scatter, plus I fear the noise."

"Noise?" asked Sandra. "For men of faith, they seem to share all the same noisy vices."

Jerico shrugged. While there were no camp followers, it appeared every other vice was welcome in the camp. The men drank, sang, and made a bawdy ruckus. Many brawled amongst themselves using only their fists, and others gambled on the winners. Jerico saw no sign of priests or paladins, and assumed them to be in the larger tents erected near the front of the wagon train.

"Fine. After I'm done, we'll go for the oxen, but I want to hit the wagons first. If I do this right, they won't notice a thing until morning."

Jerico removed his armor and the under-padding. He needed speed and stealth, not to rattle like a tin spatula in a kettlepot. Even his shield he left behind, bringing only his mace buckled at his waist—just to aid his sabotage, of course. He had no intention of fighting if he could help it.

"Stay beyond the fires," Jerico said as he placed the last of his armor in a pile, along with much of their supplies. "Follow me from wagon to wagon as best you can. If I'm spotted, you need to know immediately, and then run like Karak himself is at your heels."

"I'd rather you not get caught at all," she said, kissing him on the cheek for good luck. "But I'll keep an eye out on you just the same."

Swallowing his fear, Jerico approached the camp, always watchful for a patrol. The tall grass helped immensely, but the wagons were on the bare dirt road. Getting to them would be no easy task. He chose the one on the tail end first, crawling between two campfires the soldiers had built in the grass. They joked amongst themselves as they drank, talking of the many heathens they'd kill upon reaching Arthur's castle.

We'll see about that, thought Jerico as he reached the edge of the grass. To the far left and right he saw campfires, but no one patrolled the area. Too much arrogance, Jerico decided with a smile. Of course, who would rob or attack a patrol of armed men sworn to Karak? No one sane, but Darius had always insisted Jerico had a bit of madness in him. Or was it stupidity?

Either way, the path was clear, and Jerico ran with his body crouched as low as possible while still maintaining speed. Upon reaching the wagon, he rolled underneath and then paused, holding his breath for a long ten seconds while his heart hammered in his ears. No calls, no nearby footsteps. He let out his breath, then went to work. The dirty base of the wagon was inches above him, but the tight space was no bother. At the rear of the wagon, he stopped and unclipped his mace.

The cramped environment would limit his strength, but he prayed to Ashhur that it would be enough. Both hands grabbing the handle, he swung for the rear axle. His mace sank in with a heavy thunk, and a long crack ran along the wood. Jerico pulled it free, then waited. The wagon would muffle much of the noise, and the merriment would obscure it further. Once confident no one had heard, he struck again. The crack spread further.

All night, thought Jerico. *I've got all night, if that is what it takes.*

He waited another minute, then struck again. This time the wood split, and the entire wagon groaned above him. Jerico waited a good five minutes before moving, then slid toward the front axle to do the same. They would have spares, he knew, but how many? If he hit every single wagon, replacing all the broken axles would take a long time, longer if they ran out of spares. Without their food and supplies, the army would go nowhere. For all Jerico knew, that several day delay could make the difference at the siege further north.

The second axle taken care of, he rolled onto his stomach and then judged the gap between him and the next wagon. It, too, appeared unguarded, though there was a campfire about ten yards to the west that might overhear his sabotage. Glancing the other way, he looked for Sandra to see if she watched. The grass was thick, so he could only hope. Praying to Ashhur for safety, he crawled out and then sprinted for the next wagon. He nearly slid underneath, then realized the scraping dirt and gravel might alert the nearby men. Calmly he dropped to his side and rolled.

The men at the nearby camp, it turned out, were gloriously drunk. Jerico sighed with relief. There were twelve of them, and they were taking turns arm-wrestling with their elbows atop a log. From his low vantage point, Jerico watched, timing his strikes against the wagon with the start and end of every new competition, when the cheering was at its loudest. The rear axle broke with ease, appearing to have been well on its way toward doing so without his help. The front one took longer, but ten minutes later, he'd made a long enough crack that he trusted would break after a day or two of rough travel.

Reaching the third wagon looked to be far more difficult. This one had soldiers patrolling the area, looking bored and unhappy to be saddled with such duty while the rest drank and gambled the night away. A soldier watched each side, and a third circled, peering inside the wagon every other time. Watching for thieves, of course, but Jerico had no interest in swiping supplies. The men at the sides were just beyond the road, standing amid the grass. They feared an outside threat, not one from within. Hopefully the distance would be enough.

After the circling guard vanished around the wagon, Jerico crawled out and ran. His back ached, and a spasm struck his side halfway there because of his low crouch. Clenching his teeth, he stumbled the last few steps. No time to be graceful, he fell to his stomach and crawled. He heard rocks scatter and dirt kick out from below him, but did the guards hear it too? Holding his breath, he listened and waited.

A pair of boots walked along, then stopped at the rear of the wagon. Jerico slowly pulled his knees to his chest, for his feet were in danger of poking out below. He needed to get further underneath, but dared not move any more than he must. The boots shifted, and he wondered what the soldier could be doing.

Move on already, Jerico silently begged.

And then the guard knelt on one knee and peered underneath the wagon. His eyes must not have been fully adjusted to the darkness, for it took a full two seconds before he realized Jerico was there. The look on the soldier's face might have been amusing if not for Jerico knowing his chances of survival had just dropped to nil.

"What the..."

Jerico's heel smashed the soldier in the face, crushing his nose. He fell backwards, screaming through his hands as he tried to stem the blood. Jerico rolled out the side, toward the field where Sandra hid, and lurched to his feet. The man standing guard on that side turned, and Jerico took him down with a mace blow to the head. What little surprise he had, though, was spent by then. Two groups of men stood from their campfires and reached for their weapons. Speed was all Jerico could rely on now. He knew he could run for hours if need be, and Ashhur could grant him the strength to continue. But that involved getting out.

Men rushed into his way from all sides. Jerico ducked underneath a swing, rammed his shoulder into a guard to send him to the ground, then continued on. Another man raced along, then dove at his legs. Jerico leapt over him, wishing he could have turned around and kicked him for such stupidity. Two more soldiers had an angle on him from the right. He pumped his legs harder and shifted his direction. If he could only gain a bit more distance, get beyond the light of the campfires...

The men were fast, though, and their swords were long. Jerico parried the first swing, but when the other thrust, he had to fling himself to the left. His momentum sent him rolling to the ground, unable to keep his balance. The tall grass helped cushion the landing, but nothing cushioned the rock that cracked against his forehead. He tried to stand, but his stomach heaved, and his vision tripled and spun. The two men stood over him, and when he took a swing, they blocked it with ease.

"Still dumb enough to fight?" asked the one on the left. Jerico closed his eyes, opened them just in time to see a boot. It connected with his cheek, jarring his head hard to the side. Spitting blood, Jerico again pushed to his feet. He would not die without a fight. One of the men grabbed his wrist, preventing a swing of his mace, and then the other held him by the throat, choking him. Jerico kneed him in the groin, and gasped in air as the man's hand released.

"Damn fool," said the other, striking Jerico across the head with the hilt of his sword. Jerico dropped to his knees, and he wished more than anything to have his shield in hand. But he had no armor, no shield, and then the tip of a blade pressed against his throat.

"Stand up, and die like a man," said the soldier.

Jerico had no time to obey. The soldier jerked forward, and the sword fell limply from his hand. Sandra shoved him aside, a bloody dagger in her hand. Before the other man could recover, she cut his throat as well.

"Sandra," Jerico murmured as warm blood ran down the side of his face.

He wanted to go to her, but the rest of the camp was upon them. Sandra swung her dagger at one, but her target parried it aside, then returned the favor with the flat of his blade against her face. Another struck her from behind, knocking her to the ground beside Jerico.

"You were supposed to run," Jerico told her as his hands were bound behind him with thick rope. His voice sounded drunk in his ears.

"You'll forgive me," Sandra said, her own hands bound the same.

"Quiet, both of you," said an older man, who appeared to be in charge of the soldiers.

"Or you'll what?" Jerico asked, giving him a half-cocked grin.

In answer, the man struck him with his gauntlet hard enough to rattle his teeth.

Fair enough, thought Jerico as his consciousness faded.

15

Darius saw more familiar faces than he expected when he joined the meeting in Daniel Coldmine's room. Two chairs had been pushed together to form a table, a crinkled map unfurled across it and held down with rocks. Daniel stood over it, arms crossed and looking miserable. Beside him was the young but sharp-witted soldier, Gregory. Darius and Gregory had met in Durham, guarding what few survivors remained in the ruins of a mansion. Together they'd held a doorway until Sir Robert arrived with reinforcements, chasing away the last of the wolf-men attackers. Darius had nodded in greeting, but Gregory gave him the cold shoulder. It seemed he was not yet willing to forgive him for his part in Velixar's attack on the town.

In the corner, making up the last of the group, was an older man, his face covered with a wispy, gray beard. His eyes were hard, and he still bore enough muscle to show how dangerous he might have been in his youth. His name was Porter Grayson, and Daniel introduced him as the man in charge of Tower Silver. Together, the four planned the assault against the Blood Tower.

"How many does that bastard have fighting for him?" asked Porter, leaning against the wall of the cramped room.

"Luther left him with fifty of their personal guard," answered Daniel. "I don't know how many we killed during our retreat, but there's also another seventy of our own men that joined his betrayal."

"Surely they won't fight against you," Darius said. "Not after killing Robert."

"Robert's not dead," Gregory said. He pointed toward Daniel's bed, where several letters lay in a pile. "Cyric's been sending orders down the Gihon, claiming he's merely advising Robert. Every letter bears Robert's signature, and I don't believe it a forgery, either. Cyric is keeping him alive, using him to prevent the king from interfering. If we're to have any help from the capital, we need to rescue him."

Darius shook his head and looked at the parchment on the chairs. It was an excellent replica of the Blood Tower, drawn that morning by Gregory. The defenses were simple, but effective. An outer wall surrounded the tower, thrice the height of any man. Within that was the tower itself, and in between nothing but flat killing ground. On the opposite side of the river was a single entrance through the wall, its doors made of thick wood and reinforced with steel. The only other entrance was the river itself. A hundred men could easily hold the fortifications against a far larger group than what he and Daniel had.

"We don't have the supplies for a lengthy siege," Daniel said, shaking his head. "And I helped build those doors. We don't have the time to build a sufficient battering ram, nor enough men to endure the archers as we try to pound through. Right now there's only a hundred or so, and we need to retake it before reinforcements arrive."

"Are you sure they will?" asked Porter. "What if the priests in Mordeina deny any involvement for fear of angering King Baedan?"

"They'll still send men, even while they deny it," Darius said, staring at the map as if he could bore a solution out of it with his eyes. "The priests always protect their own. Daniel's right. We have to retake it now, before any more of Karak's followers arrive."

"If we can't retake the walls, why not go around them?" Gregory asked. He tapped where the outer wall met the river. "If all our boats beach at once, we might overwhelm them."

"How many men are at your disposal?" asked Darius.

"We've got soldiers coming from the nearby towers, and if we leave a skeleton crew in the rest, that gives us about two hundred. I'm not sure it is enough."

"Two hundred against one?" Darius shrugged. "If we can get them on anything like open ground, how could we not win?"

"The lions," Daniel said. "You didn't see them. They tore through our ranks like we were children. Robert shot them with a hundred arrows from his tower, and not one pierced their skin. We try to push in with brute force, they'll eat us alive."

"No exaggeration there, either," Gregory added.

Darius frowned, and thought of his teachings at the Stronghold. He'd heard the occasional story of a priest summoning lions of the Abyss, but always it had been in the earliest days of history, during the anarchy that had followed the Gods' War. No mortal blade was supposed to be able to kill them, no mere human fast or strong enough to defeat them. If even a third of the stories were true, two beasts guarding the river would be difficult to overcome.

And what did it mean that Cyric could summon them? How great was the power given to him by Karak?

"What keeps men from walking into the river and around the wall?" he asked, pointing to the same spot on the diagram as Gregory.

"That wall goes out deep into the river," Daniel said. "We rake the bottom every year, and add rocks when needed. Anyone trying to wade through will be in over their head, and risk drowning. Even if they make it around, they'd still be easy pickings for archers when they try to reach the shore."

"Again, it looks like boats are the best way," Darius said.

"You didn't see what I saw, Darius," Daniel insisted. "That priest wielded fire and lightning in his hands like it was nothing. If they spot us coming, and they will, then what happens if he destroys our boats before we ever reach them? And that's ignoring the *regular* arrows the men on the walls will bury us with on the passage over. I won't have my retaking of the Blood Tower end with half my men drowning, and the other half eaten by lions."

"You three are too focused on the tower," Porter said, turning and spitting out the window. "Remember the man who rules it. What does Cyric hope to achieve? What's he gain by owning some boats and a wall that guards nothing but empty fields and farmland?"

Gregory and Daniel looked to each other, and they both shrugged.

"He spoke of the old ways," Gregory said. "I'm not sure what else, or what that even means. We were both preparing for battle when he performed his ritual that brought about the lions." He turned his attention to Darius. "Do you know what he means by the old ways?"

Darius rubbed his forehead with his fingers and tried to remember.

"Study of such things is generally left to the priests," he reminded them. "Our lectures on the faith were more practical, and devoted to winning over the hearts of the people. But I've heard enough stories that I think I know what he means. There's a lot of old practices that the priests have deemed...no longer relevant. Too violent, really. They lasted as long as they did because the kings had not yet solidified their power over Dezrel."

"What type of practices are we talking about?" Gregory asked.

Darius shrugged.

"Ritual execution of murderers and thieves. Punishment of those who speak out against Karak. Conversion by the sword. That sort of thing."

"Shit!"

All eyes turned to Daniel, who stood with his fists clenched.

"The people of Durham," he said. "Cyric wished to meet with them. He insisted he only meant to talk, but he was damn persistent. He must want to get back at them for taking witness against the prophet of Karak who attacked their village."

Gregory's face paled, and Darius didn't like the way the men-at-arms looked at one another.

"Where are the survivors of Durham?" he asked, dreading the answer.

"Robert gave them land a few miles east of the tower," Daniel said. "There's a town there, Willshire. We thought it best the people go there until we could be certain of Durham's safety."

Darius's blood ran cold.

"Someone will talk," he said. "One of the converted soldiers, or maybe even Robert himself. And when he finds them..."

The old ways, the paladin kept thinking as the others stared him. Something nagged at the edge of his consciousness, some tiny detail. What would Cyric do when he found them? Make them kneel, or be put to the sword? Sacrifice them? If he was so smitten with the old ways, wanted them resurrected...

"A calendar," Darius said, startling them. "Do any of you have a lunar calendar?"

They looked at him as if he were crazy.

"Of course not," Daniel said. "We're lucky enough to have food to feed our men."

"I have the blood of farmers in me, paladin," Porter said. "What is it you wish to know?"

"The blood moon," Darius said, feeling feverish. "It happens once every four years. Do you know of it?"

"Aye, I do," Porter said. "It's said to never lay with your lady on that night, for nothing good ever comes of a child conceived during the blood moon."

"It is this year, isn't it? How long until then?"

Porter scratched at his beard.

"Five days, I believe."

"Then that's how much time we have," Darius said, turning his attention back to the diagram of the tower. "Even now, Karak's paladins will sacrifice a man guilty of murder at the steps of the Stronghold. That is how sacred the blood moon is to our...their god. If Cyric wishes to return to the old ways, I can only imagine the tribute he has devised for that night."

"I'm not sure I want to imagine it," Gregory said. "What do we do? How do we stop him?"

"Well," Darius said, nodding toward Porter. "Now we know the man, and I do know him, or at least men like him. Young, stubborn, seeing history through diamond eyes, yet seeing the lives of those around them through mud and contempt. Karak's gift of the lions will only increase his pride, his certainty of his ways. If he succeeds, he'll move on, slowly increasing his numbers. He'll bring the old ways of faith to the North until someone stops him."

"No one will," Daniel said. His whole body trembled with rage at the thought. "Arthur and Sebastian are too busy killing each other to pay attention to the lands they're sworn to protect."

"Then that leaves us," Darius said. "The tower might cause us problems, but we know where Cyric will be five days from now, don't we?"

"We do," Porter said, pushing off the wall and slowly walking over to the diagram. "And that means a far smaller guard at the tower, too. I've learned a few tricks in my time, and my gut says if we're to save Robert's life, we'll do it quick, do it quiet, and most importantly, do it my way."

"And what way is that?" Darius asked him.

The old man grinned.

"The least honorable way possible, so long as it works."

Jerico knew he'd only been out a moment or two, given that they were still dragging him toward the tents and wagons. A man held each arm, hoisting him from his armpits. His toes dragged across the ground.

"Morning," he told them, still feeling groggy. They ignored his remark. Jerico wondered why they didn't make him walk on his own, then realized his ankles were also bound with rope. Not much likelihood for escape. He looked to either side, but the soldiers holding him blocked his view. Where was Sandra? He thought to call out to her, but worried the guards might strike him again. His head already felt like it had split in half. Adding another few bruises sounded like a terrible idea.

But he called out for her anyway. Since when did he let a little unconsciousness get in his way?

"You still alive, Sandra?" he asked.

Sure enough, they beat him, but he heard a muffled 'yes' to his right, and he smiled through the pain.

They took him to the blank space between the third and fourth wagon, then looped another rope through his bindings and tied it to a wheel. The soldiers guarding

Sandra placed her opposite him and bound her to the
fourth wagon, this one by the gate across the back. A man
slapped her face after she was tied, and she spat at him in
return. Jerico saw the fear in her eyes, lurking behind the
defiance, and tried to comfort her best he could.

"Such kind hosts," he said, smiling at her, knowing
with his bleeding lip and bruised face he must have looked
a wreck. "Why'd you stay?"

She smiled back, and her lips trembled.

"I didn't want to be alone."

The revelry resumed about them, with even greater
cheer. They'd caught a paladin of Ashhur, perhaps the last
of their kind. Seemed a rather pathetic end to his order.
He'd rather have gone out in a blaze of glory, slaughtering
paladins of Karak by the dozens while the common folk
cheered his name. Dying without his armor in empty
wilderness after failing his heroic task of breaking a few
wagons felt a little too far from that for his tastes. Not that
he had a choice in the matter.

Jerico leaned against the wagon and closed his eyes.

"Good thing there's room for failures in the Golden
Eternity," he muttered to himself.

"Will they kill us?" Sandra asked, having heard him.

Jerico started to answer when a dark paladin arrived.
His weapon remained sheathed, but Jerico could see his
desire to draw it.

"I thought we would have to scour all the dark corners
of the world to find the last of your cowardly kind," he
said. "To think you came to us, instead."

"Hate to be an inconvenience."

The paladin smirked, then turned his attention to
Sandra. He released her from the wagon, then dragged her
to her feet.

"Luther will speak with you once he is done," said the dark paladin. "We'll see if your tongue is still so glib then."

Sandra remained proud and said nothing, even though she was clearly frightened. Jerico wanted to comfort her, to prevent anything from harming her. But his arms were bound, and he had nothing but words.

"We are here only a little while," he told her as the paladin cut the cords about her ankles so she could walk. "Close your eyes and pray. The pain will pass, I promise, it'll pass..."

The dark paladin struck Jerico across the face, then grabbed Sandra's arm.

"Save your words for when you have something useful to say," he said to Jerico, then led Sandra away.

Jerico spat a glob of blood, leaned back against the wagon, and looked up at the stars.

"I messed up, didn't I?" he asked them. He didn't need Ashhur's voice in his ears to know the answer to that one. Time crawled on, and he prayed that Sandra escaped torture and pain. She'd killed two of their soldiers, though, and traveled at his side. Whatever fate awaited her, he did not trust it to be kind.

When she returned, he sighed with relief. He saw no marks across her hands or face, and no blood on her clothes other than from the men she had killed. Death might await her still, but at least she was not yet tortured.

"On your feet, paladin," said the man escorting her. "Luther would speak with you, and if you have any sense, you'll treat him with respect."

Jerico shifted onto his heels, then pushed himself to a stand. The dark paladin cut his ankles free, then led him to a large tent at the front of the caravan. Luther sat atop several cushions in the center. A small meal lay beside him on a plate.

"Hello Jerico," Luther said, smiling as the dark paladin cut the ropes around Jerico's wrists. "Yes, I know your name, for Sandra has told me much. Would you care for something to eat?"

"Not much in the mood for poisons," he said.

"I'd ask if you truly thought I would stoop so low as to poison my own prisoner," said Luther, setting aside the plate. "But then again, I am the vile, evil servant of Karak. I sacrifice infants and have sex with the dead. Is that not what you've been told your whole life?"

Jerico shrugged.

"Everything but the sex. Common knowledge at the Citadel was that all your priests have their testicles removed the first time they say an ill word about Karak."

Luther dismissed the dark paladin and then gestured for Jerico to have a seat.

"Indeed, and at the Stronghold, the dark paladins talk often of the games your elders play with the orphans taken under their wing. But surely you can understand the lack of truth in these insults, the childish desire to turn a man with an opposing view into an inhuman enemy?"

Jerico sat, trying to keep his guard up. It felt odd having a priest of Karak treat him so...humanely.

"You're unlike most priests I have met," Jerico said. "And I think I will accept that plate."

Luther handed it over. On it was a potato, already chopped into pieces and smothered with butter, along with a small assortment of boiled vegetables.

"No knife?" Jerico asked.

"Try not to insult my intelligence, paladin. Our meeting will progress better that way."

"Had to ask."

He popped a piece of potato in his mouth, licked the butter off his fingers, and then closed his eyes. It tasted so good, his hunger awoke with a fury.

"You say I am unlike the priests you have known," Luther said as Jerico wolfed down the food. "But how many is that?"

Jerico paused a moment to think. The only priest of Karak he had actually known, for however brief a time, was Pheus.

"Just one," he said. "I know that's not a lot, but to be fair, he did try to kill me."

"One man, yet you judge hundreds by him. That is your way, I suppose. But yes, there is a large portion of my sect that wishes nothing more than to eliminate your kind. I feel it largely unnecessary, for we were already taking the hearts and minds of Dezrel away from you. Sadly, I am in the minority."

"You're not helping your argument much," Jerico said, finishing the plate.

Luther gave him a patronizing smile.

"Perhaps. But I say this so you know I do not lie, nor try to hide the failings of my order. The North is ours now, Jerico, and I will do everything in my power to keep it so. Lord Sebastian will prevail over Lord Arthur. You know this as well as I. Your presence here is simply...irrelevant."

"Then why capture me?" Jerico asked. "Why speak to me, instead of putting a blade through my brain?"

Luther leaned closer, his hands together as if he were to pray.

"Because I am one who lives by what he believes. Did I not just say I thought our hunting of you unnecessary? I have no desire to create martyrs, Jerico. It is a funny thing, trying to eliminate any people or race. No matter how weak as a whole they are, the strong will emerge. There comes the rare survivor who cannot stop even unto death, and he is the most dangerous. Men who might have accomplished nothing in life are suddenly declared precious and heroic in death. I have no desire to kill you, nor do I fear for myself if I let you live."

"Perhaps you're right," Jerico said, the tent suddenly feeling far colder. "But how do you know I'm not the strong that endures, the rare survivor who cannot stop even unto death? Because my friends often tell me how stubborn I am..."

Luther shook his head, just a little. Jerico sensed the mockery in it, the superiority. To the priest, Jerico was a child, foolish and rash, nothing more.

"I think you just might be, Jerico. But I also know I captured you with hardly a thought, and only a few casualties to my men. If you are the greatest threat Ashhur poses to us, then our war is already won. Like I said, Jerico...you are irrelevant. You can stop nothing. Destroy nothing. You hold faith in a dead god, and that faith blinds you to what this world has become."

He stood, and Jerico did the same.

"And what is that?" he asked. "What has this world become?"

"Ours."

Guards stepped in and took Jerico by the arm.

"Stay away from Arthur Hemman," Luther said. "Go anywhere else, and try in vain to find meaning in the last years of your life. The damage you've done to our wagons will delay us for a few days at most. If you interfere again, I will not be so kind as I am tonight."

"A priest of Karak, threatening to kill me?" asked Jerico. "Will wonders never cease?"

"Take him to the road," Luther told the guards. "Kill him if he tries to return."

"Wait," Jerico said, pushing against the guards as they tried to remove him from the tent. "What about Sandra?"

Luther lifted an eyebrow.

"She stays with us. I know her full name, Jerico, who she is. Kaide Goldflint is the last player in this farce, and with his sister's life on the line, it should be easy to manipulate him as I so desire."

"If you lay a finger on her, I'll.."

"You'll what?" asked Luther, tilting his head to one side.

The corner of Jerico's mouth twitched into a dangerous smile.

"I'll be far less kind than tonight."

Jerico flung aside the guards, sliding free of their grasps with ease. His fists struck one in the jaw, the other in the kidney. As they staggered back, Jerico turned to the priest, lunging with all his speed. It was not enough. Luther outstretched his fingers. Dark lightning shot from them, spiking through Jerico's nerves. His body arched, his jaw clenched tight, and every muscle stretched to its limit. When the power faded, he dropped to his knees, completely exhausted.

"Get rid of him," Luther said to his guards. "And Jerico, should I see you again, even hear rumors of your approach, I will sacrifice that whore to Karak. She'll die naked, alone, and screaming in pain. Think on that the next time you would play the hero."

More lightning arced across his body. Jerico endured as best he could. When the guards reached underneath his arms and lifted, he could not resist. Jerico glared at the priest, and there was no amusement anymore, no sarcasm.

"I'll kill you," he said as he was led from the room.

"A paladin of Ashhur, refusing to see reason?" asked Luther as the tent flap closed between them. "Will wonders never cease?"

16

When Darius flagged down the men in the boat, Valessa thought her moment of victory was finally at hand. The paladin handed over his blade, leaving him defenseless as he sat amid the soldiers. Valessa crept closer, watching, waiting. She could pass through solid trees as if they were smoke, so what protection could a boat be against her, especially when she did not even need to breathe? Submerged beneath the water's surface, the men would have no warning of her approach.

And then she tried to enter the river.

When moving, when fighting, Valessa had to concentrate to become firm, corporeal. It came naturally with her feet, for she'd spent her whole life walking. It wasn't much harder keeping her hands solid, but the rest of her body was another matter. Wearing clothes, or using her knee as a weapon, was far more difficult. But when her right foot dipped into the water, her mind recoiled with a horrible sensation of cold emptiness. The water was shifting, swirling, threatening to pull her away. She was shadow and smoke, she knew, and while the wind was something she could resist, the river was not.

Pulling free, she saw a shriveled stump where her leg should have been. Slowly, feeling returned, and while it hurt, at least it was not as terrible as enduring Ashhur's light. Fighting down her panic, she told herself she still had all the time in the world. Darius would be their prisoner, yet those walls would mean nothing to her. Racing along the water's edge, she followed the boat as it traveled upstream, toward one of their towers.

Except the tower was on the wrong side. They pulled their boat to shore and exited into the Wedge, while she remained in the opposite forest. There was no bridge.

"Damn you," she whispered, trying to think. Perhaps she could not pass through water like she could wall or tree, but what about atop it? Closing her eyes, she gathered her concentration, then stepped again. Her foot remained firm when pressed against the water, which for the moment, held.

Light as air, she thought. *I am as light as air. Light as a moth's wing. Calm as a crow's feather.*

She stepped out, now both feet atop the water. Her balance shifted, and her concentration wavered. No good. The water was always in motion, the surface never the same. Her ankle sank, and as the water poured across her, she screamed. Flinging herself to the shore, she crawled free. On her stomach, she closed her eyes and waited for her body to heal. Again she wondered if her form were a blessing, or a curse. Rolling onto her back, she stared at the tower. Darius was inside, she knew, but how to get to him?

Looking to the skies, she saw the bright red star, wafts of its light shining down on the tower. Yet there was something more, and though she did not know why, she trembled. She had known its presence before, just a subtle kiss in the back of her mind, but now it was closer. A black star shone in the sky, darker than the night itself. Others might not see it, but she could. It pulsed in her mind, swallowing all other light.

Karak's presence was upon Dezrel; it was strong, and it was near. Could she even go to it amid her failure?

When at last she could stand, she knew she had no other choice. It called to her, even stronger than the red.

"What is it you desire from me, my god?" she asked. "Who is it I am to meet that is so dear to you?"

She ran, careful not to stray too close to the water. Her eyes remained on the black star, and she passed through tree and rock without thought. Her daggers itched in her hands. If only she could give them blood to drink, and life to take. The moon dipped, the sun rose, yet even in the daylight the black star still shone, a pockmark on the blue sky. Who might it be? Whose presence left her enslaved to its call? She told herself it did not matter, that she trusted Karak fully...but the doubt still remained.

The day passed, and she saw no signs of life. Even though she made not a sound, the wild creatures sensed her approach and fled. The sunlight burned, but the trees were plentiful, and mostly guarded her from it. At last, as sunset came again, she reached where the black star shone down its darkness: the garrison of the Blood Tower. She thought to hide, but decided it was unnecessary. She could *feel* the presence of whomever the black star beckoned her to. If he was truly so powerful, she would not need to hide her allegiance.

Assuming her normal form, she approached the gate to the wall surrounding the tower. It was shut, and three soldiers stood above it on the wall, calling for her to halt.

"What is your name," one asked, "and why do you come here?"

"I am to speak with he who is most faithful to Karak," Valessa said.

This seemed to surprise them, for no doubt it was far from the answer they expected.

"Cyric is the embodiment of Karak's will here," said another of the men. "His duties are many, though, and I must ask the reason you would speak with him."

Cyric...the very name gave her chills.

"I am Valessa of the gray sisters. I answer to none but the priests of Karak. Let me through, so I may speak to Cyric."

The three debated with one another, then gave her their answer.

"Wait here, Valessa. We will find Cyric, and see if he will allow you to enter."

Valessa rolled her eyes. She didn't have the patience for this nonsense. She walked right through the outer gate, emerging on the other side. As the men stared down at her, their mouths agape, she blew them a kiss.

"Escort me, if you wish," she told them. "But I will not be stopped."

One of them grabbed his bow and loosed an arrow, which flew through her breast as if she were but an illusion. Another rushed down the steps, his sword drawn. Growling like a feral animal, she blocked the sword strike with a dagger, then stepped forward and clutched the soldier's throat with her other hand.

"I do not mean him harm," she said. "But I will harm you, if I so desire. Take me to Cyric."

The soldier nodded, his eyes wide with fear.

"As you wish, milady," he said.

"Good." She let him go, and sent a glare to the man with the bow. "Lead on."

They crossed the empty space to the tower, then walked around it to the other side. Two soldiers with pikes guarded the door, and they saluted at their arrival.

"Lady Valessa of the gray sisters wishes a word with our master," the soldier told them. The guards exchanged a glance, then opened the door for her. Valessa followed her guide inside. They traversed the steps that wound along the inner walls, until stopping at a room near the top. The guard moved to knock, but Valessa pushed him aside and walked straight through the door.

The sight of Cyric immediately sent her to her knees. Outwardly he was but a simple looking man, wearing the garb of a priest. He was only a pupil, she realized, given the chains he wore about his neck. But her sight was not like that of mortals, and as Cyric turned to greet her, a smile on his face, she saw the ethereal fire. It was a dark gray, flickering violently across his clothes and skin. It made no noise, and gave forth no heat, but the power within it would have taken her breath away, if she had breath to take.

"I...I am Valessa," she said, lowering her head. She wasn't sure what else to say. "Karak has guided me to your presence, and I am but your humble servant."

"Servant?" asked Cyric. His voice was deep, commanding. "I do not want servants. I desire followers. A servant obeys without thought or choice. A follower obeys all the same, but with a loyal heart. You do not strike me as a slave, gray sister."

"I am a slave to our god," she said. "For I would be a fool to think I could ever exist without his mercy."

"Then you are as wise as you are beautiful," Cyric said, gesturing for her to stand. As she did, her body swirled with shadow, and she knew he saw it. His eyes widened for a moment, and his smile thinned.

"You have a gift about you, Valessa. What is it?"

Valessa knew not how to answer, so she closed her eyes and let the image of herself fade. She became darkness, then bowed as her skin returned along with her clothing. When she looked into Cyric's eyes, his smile was gone.

"I have read of your kind," he said. No charm remained in his voice. No bemusement. "That is no blessing upon you. How did you fail Karak, gray sister?

What is it you have done that would anger our god so greatly?"

To hear her spoken of so poorly, to hear her blessing from Karak denied, filled her with fear.

"I was to kill a traitor to our order, a paladin named Darius," she said. "I failed, and died by his blade. Karak showed me mercy, and gave me this form that I might bring his vengeance upon the traitor."

"Darius?" asked Cyric. "How...interesting. I am aware of him, for his bounty was a disgrace against our faith. If Karak has given you a second chance at removing him, then I will aid you, if I can. Do you know where Darius is now?"

"South along the river," she said, feeling shame at letting him slip away. "He was taken into the nearest tower, but I could not cross the river to follow. My...form...does not allow it."

"That close? Then he is with Daniel and the rest of Robert's unfaithful lot."

Cyric turned to the large map against a wall, which showed much of the North, and the many towers along the Gihon River. He rubbed at his smooth chin.

"If he joins with that rabble, then you will yet have your chance. Have patience, Valessa. From what I have read of your curse, none have ever failed Karak in killing their target. For now, I would have you accompany me as I travel. There is a village nearby, and I think your talents might have use for me."

"As you wish," Valessa said, dipping her head. The sight of that fire was so unearthly, so unnatural, that she wished for any chance to not look upon him. He was a man most faithful to Karak, she knew. She should feel comfortable in his presence, but for some reason, did not.

"Where is it we go?" she asked as he opened the door for her. Prudence kept her from mocking the unnecessary, chivalrous act.

"A small place of little importance, other than who I believe hides there. It's called Willshire, and is not far."

Exiting the tower, Cyric nodded to the guards, but dismissed them when they tried to follow.

"I will be safe with Valessa at my side," he said. "And I trust Lilah to be close behind as well."

"Lilah?" Valessa asked as he led her toward the gate.

"You will see."

His smile only unnerved her further. They crossed the compound, exited the gate, and then turned north. Waiting along the path, fur bristling with embers, was a creature Valessa had never believed existed. It was a lioness of the Abyss, fire burning deep within her throat, her yellow eyes watching with frightening intelligence.

"What dream is this?" Valessa asked as Cyric rubbed the creature across its back. It turned and nipped at him once, but he did not flinch.

"No dream. This is Lilah. Karak sent her to me, along with her brother, Kayne."

"You named them?"

"I would never dishonor them so. Lilah is her name, for she told me herself."

"If you say so," Valessa said, walking past the lioness, who continued to watch her.

"Do you question me?" Lilah asked, her voice a deep, feline growl. The sound sent shivers down Valessa's nonexistent spine. The force of it was like wind pushing against her being. The lioness padded alongside her, eyes never leaving hers. Valessa's mind spun. The creatures could *talk?*

"Of...of course not," Valessa stammered. "I only...forgive me, Lilah. You are truly a wondrous gift to this world."

The lioness growled, and Valessa feared she had somehow offended her further. But then Lilah stepped aside, allowing her to pass. Cyric's eyes sparkled with amusement at her discomfort.

"Karak is power and fury," he said. "These lions represent his strength, and they serve me now, for I am Karak in this world, his physical incarnation. We shall bring the truth to this hollow wasteland."

Valessa looked at him, saw the fire burning hidden on his skin, the black star shining down upon him, and could not deny the possibility that he spoke truth. Could Karak truly have found a way to break free of his prison and assume mortal form? But why Cyric? Why a young priest in the relatively empty North? But the lion served him, and Lilah did not dispute his claim.

"I will listen and learn, so long as I may bring vengeance upon Darius," she said, dipping her head in respect.

Again that smile from Cyric. She tried to see wisdom in it, to revel in his presence, but only saw madness instead.

"Lilah, we go to Willshire," the priest told the lioness. "Do you know the way?"

"I have watched these lands bloom and fade over the centuries," Lilah said. "There are few corners of this dark earth that I have not looked upon. Yes, I know the way."

Lilah leapt ahead, and Cyric and Valessa followed. While there was no road, Valessa soon saw signs of wear along their path. Perhaps a farmer or two traveled from Willshire to the tower every week, just enough to beat down the grass. Ahead, the cracks in Lilah's skin burned deep, like red embers. Every graceful step sent ripples through her muscular body. Valessa yearned to see the creature in combat, yet feared it as well.

"Why do we go at night?" she asked as they passed over the gentle hills.

"I am most comfortable at night," Cyric said. "As is Lilah. Ashhur is slave to the sun. Let us find solace in the stars and moon."

"The people of Willshire will be asleep."

"Then we will wake them."

Soon they reached worked fields. In the distance, she saw hints of smoke, and tiny flickers of torches. Valessa kept silent as she wondered why they came. Had the village done something to earn Karak's ire? Did they come as messengers, or executioners?

At the edge of the village, the lioness stopped. Cyric turned to her, and he rubbed his chin as he thought.

"I once read that the unfinished can change their appearance at will. Is that true?"

Unfinished, thought Valessa. Was that what she was? Unfinished? Was it because of her failed task, or did the term refer to her faith, her very form?

"I can," she said. "Is my form...unpleasing to you?"

"You are beautiful, Valessa, but I do not ask for myself. It is you. You cloak yourself as if you were still a gray sister, but you are not. You have been granted a rare second chance. Accept it, and be glad. Your very presence should inspire fear and awe. You are not meant to hide in a crowd, not anymore. Let the crowds bow to you. I am Karak, come to this village. Let them see a mighty queen at my side."

Valessa nodded, and tried to picture herself as a queen. Why did Cyric always make her so uncertain? Was it Karak's presence? She did not know, and tried not to think on it, instead thinking on how she should appear. She'd been in the presence of Queen Annabelle in Mordeina once before, and she thought of her regal dress, her crimson cloak, and the gold crown upon her head. A bit garish for the wilderness, but Cyric demanded a queen. Opening her eyes, she saw herself clothed in similar flowing robes and cloak. Turning to the priest for approval, she instead saw disappointment.

"A mortal queen," he said, shaking his head. "I ask for the bride of Karak, a mighty warrior for order. Is that how you would picture her?"

No, it wasn't. Valessa knew how she pictured a woman equal to her god, but feared it might be blasphemous. Cyric demanded it of her, though, so she obeyed. This time, when she opened her eyes, she wore dark platemail, full of sharp edges and painted with the red lion across her chest. A thin silver circlet rested upon her brow, a single ruby in its center. Her cloak had shrunk, and was now a deep violet. Her skin was the color of milk, her eyes like sapphires. She was a woman dressed for battle, yet still bearing the trappings of a queen. She crossed her daggers and curtseyed to Cyric, who, to her relief, was greatly pleased.

"Magnificent," he said, smiling. "Right now you are but an illusion, a form without substance. Serve me well, and I will make you whole. Make you real. Do you understand me, Valessa? Never doubt, never question, only serve."

"And Darius?"

His smile grew.

"We'll sacrifice him together, both our hands upon the dagger that pierces his heart. His blood will flow, and it will make you complete."

Instead of unfinished.

The unspoken fact took whatever joy she might have felt at his words. Suddenly feeling foolish in her farcical armor, protecting flesh that would not bleed, she gestured to the rows of wood and straw homes full of sleeping villagers.

"We are here, and I am as you desire. What are we to do?"

"Bring them out from their homes. The people of Durham are here, hiding. I want to see them for myself, to look upon those who would dare speak against Karak's greatness."

"They will run in fear," Lilah said, glancing at them. Valessa tried not to shudder at the sound of her voice. Every time, it startled her, made her afraid.

"Let none escape," said Cyric. "But kill as few as possible. I have greater plans for them than a quick death at your claws."

"Any mortal should feel blessed to suffer death by my claws," Lilah growled, but did not object to his request. Cyric walked toward the village center, and Valessa kept at his side. Closing his eyes, he whispered the words of a prayer, then spoke aloud. His voice thundered across the village, magically enhanced.

"People of Willshire, I am Cyric, the Lion made flesh. Come to me, for I await you. Do not run, and do not be afraid. Those who give in to fear will die. Come to me."

For several long moments, they heard little. Children cried from several of the scattered homes, waking frightened at the sound of the priest's voice. Valessa watched, waited, trying to harden her heart against their fear. The faithful should show no fear in the presence of Karak, was not that what she'd always been taught? Then why did she feel fear when Lilah looked upon her, as if she were one wrong word away from being a meal? Why did she shiver when Cyric cast his smile upon her? Was he not Karak? Were they not his most trusted servants?

Doors opened, and the first of many stepped out into the night.

Don't run, she thought, unsure of the reason for her sympathy. The lioness lurked at the village edge, and despite Cyric's request, people would still die. A creature of that size, that strength, could only do so much to subdue without killing. The way Lilah looked upon her, she knew the idea of bloodless subjugation was nowhere in the lioness's nature.

"The priests say they should kneel by choice," Cyric said as he waited for the villagers to gather. "My teacher, Luther, always taught me that the common folk would resist if they felt otherwise. Little more than children, he would say. But I have read the words of the prophet. I know Karak's true desire. For what reason does it benefit a man to let him burn in fire through his choice, when he might be saved through the strength of others? Let them see the strength of Karak; let them cower in fear. That fear will strip away their pride, their selfishness, and their delusion that somehow they have worth apart from Karak."

The crowd was gathering about them now. A few asked questions, but Cyric ignored them as if they were not there. Valessa stood tall, trying to feel regal, beautiful, dangerous...instead of little more than an imposter. Her daggers yearned for blood. She wanted to descend upon the crowd in a slaughter, to lose herself in the flow of combat, to rely on instinct. In battle, she could feel no doubts. In life, she had never known them, either. What was happening to her? What cruel sort of penance led her to doubt her faith, instead of reaffirming it as she rectified her failure?

In the distance, Lilah roared, and Valessa heard screams.

"Go to the priest, or suffer my claws," she heard the lioness say, that terrifying voice booming throughout the village.

Men and women cowered, and children cried. Grief and terror all around her, Valessa realized, and in the center Cyric smiled and lifted his arms as if they were his beloved children.

"I have come," he said. "I hear your questions. Hush your babies, listen, and you shall hear your answers. Valessa, my queen...is it not right that you should introduce me?"

Valessa felt so many eyes upon her. She tilted her head and spoke what was expected of her.

"You stand in the presence of Karak," she said. "All with faith shall kneel."

Only a scattered few did so. Valessa was last, and she bowed her head, unwilling to look at the accusing faces.

"I see so many without faith," Cyric said, sadly shaking his head. Of the several hundred gathered, hardly more than twenty knelt. "A shame, but this world is a shameful place. People of Willshire, I come not for you, but those whom you harbor. The people of Durham, brought to you by Sir Robert at the Blood Tower. Let them come forth. I wish to look upon their faces."

"You'll kill them," a brave man said from amid the crowd.

"I will kill you all if you do not obey," said Lilah, stalking in from the outer edge of the village. Blood sizzled across her muzzle and jaw. "And do not presume to know the will of Karak."

"I will commit no murder," Cyric said. "No one will die tonight, that I promise you. As I said...I wish to look upon their faces."

Still the gathered villagers did not move. Valessa glanced at Cyric, wondering how he would react. Would he unleash Lilah upon them, or would he expect his 'queen' to do his bloody work? Perhaps neither. Perhaps she would see a display of the raw power that burned within him and consumed his soul with gray fire.

"Is this how you treat your god?" Cyric asked as the painful silence stretched on.

"You ain't our god!"

A different man. Valessa caught sight of him, just a young redhead no older than twenty. The crowd murmured along with him. She looked to the priest, waiting for the order to punish him for his insolence. But instead, Cyric breathed in deep, then let it out. His shoulders sagged as if he were greatly disappointed.

"Yes," he said, his deep voice eerily quiet. "I am."

He lifted his arms.

"And I said *kneel!*"

The word rolled off his tongue like a shockwave. Men and women flung themselves to the ground. It didn't matter if there was no room, or if they held babes in their arms. Children, even the elderly, lurched to their hands and knees. Valessa was no exception. As she quivered, unable to resist the compulsion, she listened to the sounds of the crowd. Abandoned babes sobbed, the elderly cried out from broken bones, and many whimpered from strained and torn muscles. All throughout, she smelled the stench of fear, so palpable it was as if she could reach out and pluck strands of it from the air. With great effort, she forced her head up to look. The only one in the entire village without knee bent to Cyric was Lilah.

"I promised safety if obeyed," Cyric told them. "But I make no such promise to the disloyal. Karak's fire will burn the weak, the foolish, and the disobedient. I would ask for those from Durham to come forth, but I know they hold no faith to Karak. So I ask the rest of you, lift your fingers, and reveal to me the outsiders to your village."

"I can tell you who they are," a ragged man offered. Cyric turned to him, then beckoned him to rise. He looked wafer-thin, an uneven growth of beard on his face.

"Your name?"

"Billy," said the man. "Lived here all my life. I can show you who don't belong." He turned to the rest of the village, and he snapped at them, as if he could sense their disdain. "And they don't belong! They ain't us! No reason for us to die for them."

"Walk among them," Cyric said, all emotion gone from his face. "Touch them, so I may know. As for the rest of you...are there any here who would serve their god? The Lion stands before you, and your reward will be great."

Eleven men lifted their arms, and with a wave of Cyric's hand, they stood. Valessa knew she should view them as faithful converts, but instead saw them as traitors to their village. Cyric bade them come to the front, where he put his thumb against each of their foreheads. It burned there for a moment, then faded, leaving only a black scar.

"If any harm you, or resist you, I will know," he told them. "Now find me the people of Durham, and bring them here."

No doubt they knew as well as Billy who the traitors were, but they did not scatter amid the crowd. Instead, they followed him as he walked, and grabbed every man, woman, and child he touched. Some struggled, only to be beaten by the eleven. Others burst into tears, but most remained stoic, saying not a word as they walked toward the front. The minutes crawled along. Valessa felt the villagers grow restless and angry, but Lilah's presence was more than enough to keep them in check. The lioness prowled around the perimeter of the crowd, softly growling.

When nearly a hundred stood before them, Billy looped through the crowd a few more times, then shrugged.

"I think that's it," he said.

"Very good," Cyric said. "Kneel at my right hand, as is your reward."

Billy did so, and Valessa hated how pleased he looked. Cyric would give him no reward, other than perhaps rule over the pathetic little village. What he'd done, he'd done out of fear, not faith. There was little to cherish in that.

Cyric looked over the people of Durham, and Valessa did the same. There was nothing special about them; they were just tired and frightened farmers, herders, mothers and their children. They had a defiance to them that impressed her, though it was foolish, as she knew it would be.

"Who will speak for you?" Cyric asked.

"I will," said a man, stepping forward. He was tall but heavyset, and dressed in finer clothing than the others. "My name is Jeremy Hangfield. I am the one who came to Sir Robert and told of the destruction Karak brought to our village. Strike me down, and get this over with."

"You say Karak brought destruction upon your village," Cyric said, approaching Jeremy. "But it wasn't Karak, was it?"

Jeremy shook his head.

"A priest of his, then. He wore your robes, and his eyes shone like fire. Darius told us to kneel, or suffer. And we suffered, unjustly, unfairly."

Cyric laughed in his face.

"Unjustly? Unfairly? You deserve nothing, not even the breath that fills your lungs. You were commanded to kneel, and warned of the punishment that would ensue if you did not. How is that unfair? You spat in the face of your god, the god who created you, who demanded worship lest he revoke your gift of life. Did you think you might resist without consequence? You are a spoiled child, angry at the punishment after willfully committing the misdeed."

"Even so," said Jeremy, "we did nothing but tell Sir Robert the truth of what happened."

"Truth? What truth is that?"

"Karak destroyed our village. We all know it."

Cyric shook his head.

"Karak did not destroy your village," he said.

"Prove it."

"You were asked to kneel, and you did not. But I commanded the same. Tell me, Jeremy, what did you then do?"

Jeremy glared but said nothing. Cyric knelt closer, as if he were sharing a secret. His voice was soft, like a whisper, but somehow the entire village still heard.

"You knelt, because while you refused a prophet, and one of his paladins, you cannot refuse me. I am no paladin, no priest, no prophet. I *am* Karak, and you will worship my might by the rise of the blood moon. I was not there in Durham, but I am here now."

Lilah roared, and her power rolled over the villagers.

"Kneel!" cried the lioness. Those from Willshire obeyed, though the people of Durham did not.

"Valessa, my queen." Cyric's words startled Valessa. She felt like she'd been lost in a dream, unable to interfere.

"Yes, Cyric?" she asked.

"Go to the Blood Tower. Fetch me twenty of my guard, and send them here. I will need them to help keep order while we await the blood moon."

"I am a stranger to them," she said. "They may not listen."

"Go as you are," he said. "No one will refuse you. But for your peace of mind, Lilah will also accompany you, and her presence will prove you speak my will."

Valessa bowed her head, then put her back to the spectacle. She thought to ask him if he would be safe on his own, but knew it a foolish question. The power of Karak was with him, even if he wasn't Karak made flesh.

"Must I lead the way?" Lilah asked as they put the village behind them.

"If you could," Valessa said. In truth, she knew the path, but preferred to have the lioness farther ahead instead of traveling beside her. At least then she might be alone with her thoughts.

She glanced back toward Willshire, and suppressed a shudder.

At least then she might not be afraid.

"I will serve," she whispered. "I will obey. I am faithful. I am faithful."

And all the while, a soft voice in her head cried, *liar, liar, liar.*

17

Sandra's wrists bled from struggling against her bonds, yet she did not stop. The blood only made them slicker, gave her hope to pull free. Jerico had not returned from his meeting with Luther, and despite Luther's act of kindness, she still feared for her friend's life. Or was he her lover now? She didn't know, didn't want to think about it. Morning was rapidly approaching, and come daylight, she knew escape would be nearly impossible.

"Come on," she whispered as she pulled. Her hands were on fire now, and she felt more skin scrape away as she worked her right arm. No guard remained to watch her between the two wagons. If only she could...if only...

She stopped for a moment, biting her tongue to hold down her sobs. Her hands shook, whether from pain, blood loss, or fear, she didn't know. She wanted to believe she was brave. She wanted to believe that no matter how expertly tied her bonds were (and make no mistake, they were very expertly tied) she would still be strong and escape.

But Luther had only looked at her, brushed away her hair from her face, and asked for her full name. That was all, yet she had given it. But it wasn't because she was afraid, she told herself. It wasn't because she saw a horrible evil lurking in those eyes. It wasn't because she felt like little more than meat in his presence, and that his touch had swirled with shadows most unnatural. No, she'd just been foolish, made a mistake and forgotten he might use her against her brother. That was it. Better a fool than afraid.

Tears running down her face, she pulled once more against the ropes. Better bleeding and maimed than that man's prisoner. He'd told her he meant her no harm. He'd whispered that she was beautiful, and he would protect her from his men so long as she told him what he wanted. Just her name, that was all he'd wanted. What did it matter that she gave him her name? Jerico was the one they wanted. Jerico was the one they hunted, and he might still be in there, suffering at the hands of that...

"Sandra?"

She screamed. Her right hand slipped free, and she stood. Luther caught her fist with his hand and held it firm. He said nothing, only stared into her eyes. She felt her stomach heave at the look.

"Do not strike at me again," he said. He glanced at the rope, and her bloodied hands. "I must commend you, despite this foolishness. You are not in danger, Sandra. I have use for you."

"I won't help you," she said. "Where is Jerico?"

"I sent him away," Luther said. He still held her fist, and her blood trickled across his fingers as he forced her hand downward. "I told him I would sacrifice you to Karak if he interfered any further with Karak's work in the North."

"You said I was not in any..."

"I told him what he needed to hear," Luther interrupted. "I know him, as much as he might try to deny it. He loves you greatly, and will be reluctant to put your life in danger."

"You think you know him?" she asked. She pulled her hand free, then slipped out of the rope. The two stood alone between the wagons, in a darkness away from the light of any fire. In the starlight, Luther looked healthier, more alive than he had in the tent. Worse, he looked far more dangerous.

"I think I know him rather well," he said. "Do I not?"

"He won't run, Luther. He knows me, too. He knows I'd rather he kill every single one of you than give in to your demands, even if it costs me my life."

She expected him to argue, or be angry, but instead he let out a tired chuckle.

"I know, Sandra. Right now, I expect him to be running toward the Castle of Caves with every shred of strength left in his body. He'll hate himself, yet still believe he honors your...feisty spirit in refusing to give in to my threats. Foolish, really, but that stubbornness and sense of honor are why he has survived as long as he has. I want him at the castle, especially after the damage done to our wagons, which has given us a delay we can ill afford. As for you..."

He took her bleeding wrists in his hands. She told herself to run, but again she saw the danger lurking in his eyes. If she tried that, she'd be dead, and that death would not be quick, or painless.

"I have a request involving your brother. I wish you to take him a message."

"I don't know where he is," she insisted.

"Then you'll find him. There are many villages nearby, and I'm sure all of them are loyal to the bandit. He marches to Lord Arthur's aid, if he is not there already. Can you carry my words to him? And not just repeat them, Sandra, but make him believe? Make him listen?"

"What is it?" she asked, daring to hope.

"Tell him to pull back his men from the Castle of Caves, and avoid any battle with Lord Sebastian. Do this if he wants to spare the lives of his men, and ensure his safety. I know of his rebellious desires, and the grudge he bears against Sebastian...but make him listen. Make him *understand.* I ask this in his best interest. Should he listen, well..."

He grinned.

"Karak's mercy will smile down upon him for it."

The very notion of Karak's mercy made Sandra want to spit in the priest's face, but she did not. He was letting her go, quietly in the night. He didn't want the rest of his men to know, but why? What game was he playing?

"I'll do it," she said. "But I won't promise any more than that. Kaide will do as he desires, regardless of what I say."

"Of course," Luther said, releasing her wrists. When she looked down, the bleeding had stopped, and the pain was gone. "If he did as he was told, he'd never have resisted Sebastian in the first place. But for the sake of his men, for your sake, too, convince him. Now go, to the east, quickly. There are no guards watching, I made sure of that."

She glanced behind her, fearing a trap. But it didn't seem like it, and furthermore, it made no sense. Games, she thought. The priest was playing games, and she didn't know the rules. She looked at him, almost thanked him, then bit her tongue. What insanity was that, that he should have her thanks? Without a word, she ran east, off the road and into the fields. The grass resisted, but she pushed on. Her heart pounded, and her lungs burned, but still she ran, until the fires of the wagons were out of sight. Falling to her knees, she finally allowed herself to cry, to tremble in fear.

"Please keep him safe," she begged Ashhur as her fingers clawed the earth. "He's done everything you asked, now keep him safe, damn you."

She didn't know if Ashhur was even listening, but she felt better for the demand. Sleep pulled at her limbs, but she rose to her feet. Her back to the caravan, she ran until dawn's first light met her eyes. Then she found a flat space in the field, curled her knees to her chest, and slept.

They'd left Darius free to roam the grounds of the tower, and he took advantage of it as often as he could to find some privacy. At night he slept in the barracks with the rest of the men, and though he had plenty of blankets, nothing could keep away the chill that pervaded the air. He felt it with every glare his way, every shoulder turned when he dared speak. No one struck him. No one lifted a sword, or even mentioned the word Durham. But he knew it was in their minds.

More men came north upon the Gihon, soldiers pulled in from the other towers. The newcomers tended to treat him better, at least for a while. Then the whispers would begin, the conversations in the corners, and the welcome smiles would become clenched teeth. Darius stopped trying by the end of the first day. Wandering beside the river, he enjoyed the solace of the nighttime sky and the gentle mumble of the water across the rocks. At least the fish wouldn't judge him.

"What in the world am I doing?" he wondered aloud as he squatted beside the shore and tossed a rock at his reflection.

"Running away, perhaps?"

Darius startled, even though he knew it was only Gregory, patrolling around the grounds. He must have spotted him at the water's edge. When Darius first heard his voice, he'd feared it was Valessa, come to make another attempt at removing his head from his shoulders.

"I flagged down your boat willingly enough," Darius said, slowly standing. "What makes you think I'd run now?"

Gregory gave a dismissive grunt and crossed his arms. Darius did not fail to notice the way his hand rested on the hilt of his sword. The man was young, and intelligent. A dangerous combination, Darius knew, especially if she should become emotional.

"You'd run if you'd done everything you needed to do here," Gregory said, a hard look in his eyes. Darius frowned, and it took him a moment to realize what exactly the man was accusing him of.

"You think...you think I'm leading us into a trap?" he asked. He couldn't decide if he wanted to laugh, cry, or wallop the soldier upside the head.

"We'll be split up," Gregory said. "Our entire plan relies on surprise, and if either Willshire or the Blood Tower is ready..."

"Daniel trusts me. Perhaps you should listen to your superior. I'm tired of the cold looks I get from you and your men."

Gregory stepped closer, and his hand was a clenched fist, the hilt firmly in his grasp. He was an inch away from drawing, Darius knew. His greatsword was strapped to his back, but there was no way he could pull it free faster than Gregory's longsword.

"What sort of welcome does a traitor deserve then, Darius? Tell me."

"Traitor?" he asked. "Who have I betrayed? Karak?"

"The people you swore to protect! You protected them from the wolf-men. You and me, side by side, we held when all seemed lost. But then some priest or prophet of Karak arrives, and you stand by and let him kill?"

"I told you," Darius said, feeling his temper rise. The waters of the Gihon were growing awfully tempting, as if their mumble begged for him to toss Gregory in headfirst. "I was confused, I was lost. I thought I was doing what was right by my faith, don't you get it?"

"No!" Gregory shouted. "No, I don't get it. Don't you see? Every damn fool could tell that prophet had you twisted around inside and out. How could you be so blind, so stupid, as to fall for any of that nonsense? To think that killing simple farmers and their families could somehow be justified? I know you, have fought with you, and know you're strong, and wise. It makes no sense to me. You can't have been that foolish. You're lying to us, hiding something, and I want to know what."

"Or what, you'll run me through?"

The night turned deadly silent.

"I will protect my friends, my family," Gregory said. "But I guess you wouldn't understand that either, would you?"

Darius felt his anger and pride rising, but he closed his eyes and shook his head to force it away. It would be too easy to get defensive, to attack Gregory for doubting him. But he was right, and Darius would give the young man an honest answer, not unearned ire.

"I'm not sure you could ever understand," he said, looking away from the soldier and to the water. "Imagine knowing something, knowing it so well that it is burned deep into your gut. You'd question your own name before you questioned this. And then...one day...the whole world changes, and you know nothing. Every friend you've known since childhood has lied to you, every mentor and teacher was nothing but a monster in a mask. Think of the wolf-men you slew, and imagine pulling off their faces to find human children underneath. What would you do to put the masks back on?"

He breathed in deep, then sighed. If only Gregory could hear Velixar's words, feel the way they burrowed into the mind, sounding so terrible, so true.

"I was a dying man in a desert, Gregory. A man offered me poison and told me it was wine, and gods help me, I drank it. He handed me a sword, and bade me to save people with its blade. And I did. If you don't understand it, don't see how I could have been so foolish, then I am happy for you. No one should walk in a valley so low."

Darius looked back and his eyes met Gregory's. The disappointment was still there, but the fury had abated. His hand no longer clutched the hilt of his sword.

"Daniel says you pray to Ashhur now. Are you so certain he is better than Karak?"

Darius shrugged, and he shifted, feeling uncomfortable.

"I did what I did to earn back the love of my god. Yet now, Jerico says I have the love of Ashhur, and will never need to earn it, nor fear losing it. I never knew my parents, but I'd like to think that is how they should be, how they would look upon one of their children. And right now, I feel I am little more than a child."

Silence stretched between them, until at last Gregory picked up a stone and tossed it into the river.

"I watched Cyric slaughter my friends with a simple wave of his hand. While I ran like a coward, his lions tore apart armor and flesh like we were nothing. I'm scared, Darius. I look north, and my stomach twists just thinking of him waiting there for us. No matter what, we'll have to face him. If we hide here, he'll come for us. I see no way out, no real chance for victory. As much as I hate to admit it, you're the one hope we have. We don't need a child. We need a warrior. For all our sakes, I hope Ashhur's paying attention."

With that said, he returned to the tower, leaving Darius alone with his thoughts.

"Are you paying attention?" Darius asked, glancing up at the stars. He drew his sword, and the blue-white glow shone across the blade. He stared into it, let it cast away his fear. He'd already given himself up to death once, and Jerico had denied him. This time, he'd be doing it for others, not for selfish, cowardly reasons. Win or lose, by gods, he planned on giving it a damn good attempt.

"Good enough," he told the cold night air. Still weak, still just a fledgling faith. But it'd been enough to kill Velixar, and it'd be enough for Cyric.

He put his sword on his back and trudged to the tower. When he entered the barracks, he found a waterskin lying on his bed. Uncorking it, he put it to his lips and drank.

Wine, he thought, and despite the others sleeping about him, he laughed until he cried. *Wine for a man in the desert.*

He drank it all, and for the first time in what felt like months, slept peacefully.

18

Every step was painful, but Jerico pressed on, for he did not have much farther to go. Blisters covered his feet, everywhere that wasn't already callused. His armor was heavy on his back, but he refused to remove it. Luther's men had caught him unarmored, and without his shield, but he would not risk that again. After the priest had let him go, he'd found where he'd stashed his armor, dressed, and then flung his shield upon his back. He'd been tempted to go crashing back into the camp to rescue Sandra. They'd been so confident, they'd even given him his mace. But that wasn't what she'd want. He knew that. A heroic but pointless death would not impress her.

No matter what Luther had said, he knew she would want him to go on to the Castle of Caves, to help save Arthur from Sebastian's men. And so he ran along the path, every aching step pulling him away from where he thought Sandra remained imprisoned, and one step closer to the next battle at hand. He'd run all through the night, and then the day. His mind was in a fog, his stomach empty. It hurt at times, but he kept his legs moving, kept his lungs filled with air. He prayed Ashhur would give him the strength to continue, and, despite the pain, he never stopped.

Come nightfall, he could go no further. It didn't even matter that he was in the center of the dirt road. A nighttime rider might have clomped right over him, but moving was no longer an option. Collapsing, Jerico hit the ground and passed out. His dreams were of Sandra lying in the dirt. A great hole was in her chest, where her heart had been. Black blood circled through her veins and spilled across his hands. When he woke, his eyes were red, and his stomach heaved, though he had nothing but bile to spit onto the dirt beside him.

"Not far," he told himself. "Not far. Not far at all."

Of course, getting to the castle was just the half of it. Getting inside would be an interesting endeavor. Much as he might like it, he doubted whoever was in charge of Sebastian's troops would just let him walk right through their siege lines.

Jerico resumed his trek toward the castle, but this time at a walk. He kept his eyes peeled, and when he saw a small collection of bushes with overripe berries on them, he nearly burst into tears. He ate until he threw up, the red berries sickly sweet on his tongue, and then ate some more. Belly full, he resumed his walk, crossing the final few miles to the Castle of Caves. It was midday when he first saw the smoke of the enemy encampment surrounding the walls. Deciding he could no longer be so careless, he veered off the path and slowly wound through the hills, eyes open for any scouts who might be watching.

Atop the first hill, he lay flat and scanned the area. The castle was built upon a tall hill, and surrounding it on all sides were tents with the yellow rose waving from their banners. From what he could tell, only a limited amount of siege works had been built. It seemed Sebastian was confident of starving Arthur out...or that their commander was hesitant to sacrifice so many lives on such an assault.

"Soldiers, tents, and more soldiers," Jerico muttered as he scratched his chin. "Of course things couldn't be easy. That'd be crazy."

The only time he'd been at the castle before was with Kaide, and they'd not entered through the main gates. Instead, they'd traveled through a tunnel built into the network of caves beneath the castle. Jerico wondered if he might use that same tunnel to bypass the army. He had only a vague idea where the entrance was, but he believed it to be outside the siege lines. Desperately praying he didn't go from being one man's prisoner to another's, he hurried down the hill and farther away from the path.

Finding the entrance turned out to be easier than expected. Where it had once been carefully concealed, now he found the entire ground worked over, with dirt caved in and then covered with heavy rocks. Jerico stood before it and frowned. It seemed Sebastian's men had discovered the tunnel, and when they couldn't gain entrance to the castle that way, they sealed it over. Jerico thought of the traps he'd been shown, including the narrow bridge across the chasm he and Kaide had crossed. Kaide insisted it had been rigged to collapse. He wondered how many had fallen to their deaths before they gave up and just sealed it.

Jerico glanced about, and saw another worked entrance a hundred yards to his south. Kaide had said there were about twenty tunnels dug throughout the area. Was it possible Sebastian had found them all? More importantly, could he expect to find one that all the soldiers had missed?

"Oh no," he muttered. "It just couldn't be easy, could it?"

An idea came to him, and he sighed. It might work, but it could just as easily get him killed. But really, what else did he have to lose? At least if he died, Sandra might be spared. He'd tried not to think of her often, or of what continuing his fight might mean. Usually, he failed.

Jerico spent much of the day resting in the far hills, having moved away from the siege lines. He searched a bit for more berries, but sadly found none. He did find a stream, and drank until his stomach hurt. Crawling along, the day finally reached its end, and night came. Jerico returned to the hill overlooking the siege. He could see the faint outlines of men marching along the walls carrying torches, looking like miniscule lightning bugs. Still, tiny as they might be, he could see them. And that meant, just maybe...

He stood, took his shield in hand, and lifted it high. The front lit up, and as he prayed, it shone a strong blue-white. And then he waited to see who noticed him first. The eyes of the enemy should have been on the castle, while Arthur's men looked out. All it would take would be one of them to realize what it was, and just one tunnel still intact.

A lot of 'if's. A lot of luck. Jerico tried not to think about that either.

"Come on," he muttered, watching the men patrol the walls. "Come on, come on, see the big blue dot? Not a bug, not a fire, now turn and look!"

He held it for ten more minutes, then decided it was enough. If they hadn't noticed his shield yet, then they might never. Holding it aloft any longer just increased the odds of the wrong party spotting him. Sitting down, he waited. And waited.

When someone tapped him on the shoulder, he nearly screamed.

"Jerico?" asked the man, caked with dirt. His hair was cut short, and his clothes were ragged.

"Damn it, man, can't you make some noise when you walk?" Jerico asked.

The man looked about, clearly worried. If he noticed Jerico's embarrassment, he didn't show it.

"Follow me," he said. "I saw a rider this way, and we have little time. Now hurry!"

The paladin thought he'd been far enough from the castle that no cave entrance might be beyond him, but he was wrong. His guide beckoned him to follow, and together they put their backs to Sebastian's army and ran. There seemed to be nothing but hills and tall grass, but it was dark, and Jerico knew firsthand how well Arthur's men could hide both themselves and the cave entrances. The man introduced himself as Jerek Wallace, talking in hurried, hush tones as they traveled.

"I fought alongside you at the Green Gulch," he said, his furtive eyes always checking behind them. "Not with the bandit's men, though. Arthur's. It was our line you helped at the end, before the call to withdraw. Never forgot that shield of yours. A man swung at you with his sword, and it hit that light..." He slapped his hands together, then winced at the sound. "Sword shattered like it was made of glass. When Degan saw that blue light out here in the hills, I just knew it was you. Had to be."

"Flattered," Jerico said, and he was, though he also felt uncomfortable. All that adulation...did Jerek forget they actually lost that fight? "How far is the tunnel?"

"Not far," Jerek said, guiding him through a minor valley between two hills. They all looked the same to him, and the castle was growing disturbingly far away. It certainly explained why no one had located the entrance like the others. His guide glanced back, then swore.

"Get down," he said, grabbing Jerico's shoulder. The two fell to their bellies. Jerico shifted about so he could look. Two men on horses rode perpendicular to their path, torches held aloft. They looked like strange phantoms, just black shapes outlined by fire.

"Can they track us?" Jerico asked.

"Depends on how good they are," Jerek whispered. "It's dark, but you're not too light on your feet."

"It's the armor."

"If you say so."

Jerico's hand drifted to the hilt of his mace for reassurance.

"Don't worry too much if we're spotted," he said. "Two against me? They'd need a lot more men."

"Like that many?" Jerek asked, pointing. Seven more riders joined with them, and they crisscrossed the spaces between the hills.

"Yeah, that'd do it."

"Looks like Sebastian's men remember you as well as I do," Jerek said, getting to his feet. He kept his back hunched and his body low. "We stay here, they'll find us eventually. Follow me, and for the love of the gods, don't put so much weight on your heels when you step."

"You an elven scoutmaster now?" Jerico grumbled, doing his best to stay low and follow the man. Jerek tapped the slender bow slung over his shoulder.

"Best hunter Arthur's ever known. Said so himself. Now hurry!"

They rushed on, and this time Jerico joined Jerek in taking worried glances backward. But true to his word, they were not far, though Jerico could hardly believe it when they arrived.

"Here we go," Jerek said, stopping at a strange circle of yellow mayflowers.

"Where's the tunnel?"

Jerek gave him an amused grin.

"Right here," he said, standing in the flowers' center. *"By Karak's bearded ghost!"*

The man dropped right through the ground and vanished. Jerico blinked and lifted an eyebrow.

"You've got to be kidding me," he said. He stepped into the flowers and stomped a few times. No give. Nothing loose. Sighing, he shook his head and repeated the words, foolish as they were.

"By Karak's bearded ghost?"

He went from standing on grass to air, and he dropped with a surprised yelp. Dirt passed over his eyes, and then he was in pure darkness. His feet hit ground, and the landing jarred his knees. He started to fall, then his body halted as it struck stone. A thousand curses ran through his mind, and he wanted to yell all of them.

"What was that?" he asked instead.

"Arthur had all our tunnels dug and worked by us," Jerek said, his voice a few feet ahead of him. "All but this one."

Jerico pulled his shield off his back. At his touch it lit up, revealing his surroundings. He and Jerek were in a cramped space cut out of dirt and stone. Before them was a small tunnel, so long that his light could not reach its end. A foot above his head were planks of wood, and he pressed against them with his hand, still surprised by their solidity.

"Magic?" he asked.

"Believe so. This was back when he and his brother first had their fallout. Brought a wizard all the way over from Veldaren, if you'd believe it, some queer looking man in yellow. Arthur wanted someone not associated with the council."

"The activation phrase?"

Jerek shrugged.

"Wizard's idea. Most of the other tunnels have been found, but not this one." He frowned. "Going to be a tight fit with all that armor."

"I'm not taking it off."

"You might get stuck."

Jerico looked at the cramped tunnel ahead. While he could currently stand, going on ahead would involve crawling on his hands and knees. He thought about what it might be like to be stuck in such a claustrophobic space.

"I'll manage," he said, trying not to sound worried. He was the hero of the Gulch, after all. Hate to disappoint the hunter.

Jerek shrugged, then fell to his hands and knees and began crawling. Jerico swallowed, took a deep breath, then wondered where the air was coming from. Reminding himself others had used the tunnel plenty of times before, he slung his shield onto his back, returning them to darkness. Using his hands to feel ahead, he crawled into the tunnel after Jerek.

His armor scratched and creaked, and he didn't want to imagine the damage he was doing to it. Probably take all day to bang out and polish the dents. In the tight space, the noise was tremendous.

"Hey, Jerek?"

"Yeah?"

He stopped a moment to catch his breath.

"Can anyone hear us above ground?"

"Normally I'd say no, but damn you're making a ruckus."

Jerico laughed.

"Let's hope they have no shovels, then."

Progress was slow, one hand after the other. So far there seemed to be no turns, but he feared banging his head against one when they reached it. The tunnel had a very steady slope downward, which helped a little. Often he had to shift his weight one way or the other as a piece of his armor or an edge of his shield caught a rock. The ground itself was wet and cold, which explained Jerek's appearance when they had first met. As the minutes wore on, Jerico felt the weight of the earth above him growing more present in his mind, and it seemed he could not catch his breath.

"One of these days," he muttered. "One of these days, I'm going to enter your lord's castle through the front door, just to say I did."

"What's that?" Jerek called out. His voice was disturbingly far away, and Jerico pushed himself along faster.

"I asked how long does it normally take to get to the castle?"

"An hour, but at your rate, I'm thinking three."

Jerico pressed his forehead against the back of his hands as he took another deep breath.

"It would've been easier to fight my way through Sebastian's army. More exciting, too."

Jerek's laughter echoed from up ahead, urging Jerico on. After what felt like an eternity, his fingers brushed against the first turn. Following it, his stomach lurched as the path downward steepened tremendously.

"If you're covered with enough mud, you can just push yourself down and slide," Jerek told him, having waited there for his arrival. Jerico jumped at the sound of his voice so close, and was glad the darkness hid the descent.

"I don't think I'll be doing much sliding," he said.

"I think you'll be surprised."

He heard the sound of skittering rocks, and then silence. Jerico followed, crawling along. His blood rushed to his head, but movement was certainly easier. He pulled himself along for ten more feet or so, then found himself at an even steeper decline. Deciding to give it a shot, he dug his fingers into the dirt and flung himself forward. The following sensation of speeding down a drop in pitch black was something he never, ever wanted to endure again.

At the bottom he heard steps, and then an arm grabbed his. To his surprise, he was able to stand, and removing his shield, he lit the space up with its light.

"Welcome to the deepest cave," Jerek said, gesturing. It was about thrice their height, though the stalactites were long enough that Jerico could reach up and brush them with his fingers. The walls, floors, and ceiling were wet, and water dripped constantly from above.

"I thought it'd take an hour," Jerico said as he glanced behind him, seeing that they'd emerged from a manmade tunnel into the natural cave.

"It will. Never said we'd be crawling the whole way, though."

Jerico clenched his teeth together.

"There's many, many things I want to call you right now," he told his guide, who only laughed.

"Come on," he said. "And step lightly. The ground is slick, and with all that weight, you might take a nasty tumble."

Slick floor or not, Jerico was just glad to stand, and have the light of his shield once more. Jerek led the way, and he followed, once more admiring the beauty of the cave. He had no idea whether or not it connected to the others that he and Kaide had used, but it wouldn't have surprised him. The minutes passed as they made their way carefully through the cave. Many times they encountered sections where the floor had been carved into steps, or passageways had been widened. The ugly marks of pickaxes and hammers ruined the beauty, but at the same time, after his weary crawl, Jerico felt glad to not have to do it again.

At last they reached the end. Above them was a tall ladder, at least twenty feet high, and above that, a trapdoor.

"Guests first," Jerek said, gesturing.

Jerico put his shield on his back, returning them to darkness. Grabbing the rungs of the ladder, he tested their strength and found them thankfully strong, without an ounce of give. Climbing until his head bumped against the top, he felt against it with a free hand.

"There a latch?" he asked.

"The side closest to you. You'll find it. Push up."

Jerico finally did, and when cool, fresh air blew against his face, he felt happy enough to cry. Crawling out, he found himself in the center of Arthur's courtyard, emerging from a hole. Rubbing his eyes, he looked to his left and saw a bench and realized he and Arthur had sat and talked mere feet from the tunnel exit.

"If a siege ever went sour, this is where Arthur would flee, isn't it?" he asked as he helped Jerek up.

"That's the idea," Jerek said, closing the trapdoor behind him. The top was covered with sod and grass, and Jerek did his best to smooth it out. The two looked at one another, both covered with mud. Jerek gave him a grin.

"I think you look fit to meet a lord, don't you?"

Jerico pointed at him, his finger an inch from his nose.

"One day," he said. "Just...one day."

Jerek smirked, then led him into the castle. He didn't make it far. Men in armor Jerico had never met before waited in the next room, and they slapped his back and congratulated him. Jerico couldn't tell if it was for surviving the Green Gulch, or just the travel through the damn tunnel. All of them looked tired, their strength sapped by the controlled rations and constant stress. His presence buoyed them, and Jerico did his best to smile and accept their greeting graciously.

At the door to Arthur's room, Jerek knocked several times, then stepped aside. As it opened, Jerico knelt in respect and dipped his head. His knee smeared mud across the floor, and a chunk of dirt fell from his red hair and onto the carpet.

"Milord," Jerico said, grinning up at Arthur's stunned expression. "I heard you could use an extra shield on your walls, and I've come to offer mine."

Arthur embraced him, either not noticing or not caring that he dirtied his expensive bedrobes and left his hands wet with mud.

"That I could, paladin," Arthur said. "That I could."

David Dalglish

19

Valessa walked through the walls surrounding the Blood Tower to the empty land beyond. The silence was blessed to her. With a sigh, she let her armor and cloak vanish, adopting the image of how she had always been, plain clothes and all. With Cyric remaining in Willshire, along with half his men, she'd assumed his mantle of leadership. Not that the lions didn't have their say. Kayne and Lilah were always about, patrolling, watching. They spoke little, but when they did, they were obeyed without question.

Night had fallen, and while most guards slept, Valessa would not. She looked to the clear sky and tried to ignore the burning red star shining in the distance, mocking her, always reminding her of her failure, her unfinished mission.

Soft footsteps padded behind her. She looked back, saw one of the lions there. She held back her grimace. Over time she should have grown more comfortable in their presence, but so far she had not. Her nocturnal visitor was Kayne, the male, slightly larger and with a fiery mane about his neck.

"You are troubled," Kayne said, resting on his haunches beside her.

"I am tired. I was trained for stealth and assassination, not preparing defenses and managing supplies."

Kayne breathed out heavily through his nose.

"You know that is not what I speak of. I am of a world you do not know, and my eyes glimpse what mortal eyes cannot. I see the uncertainty of your faith. I smell your

225

doubt. The rest sleep, and we have solitude here. Tell me your fear."

Valessa looked to the distance, imagining the people of Willshire watching Cyric's preparations. What would they think? What would they believe?

"He says he is Karak," she said to the lion. "Not that he works his will, or hears his voice, but that he *is* Karak, returned in mortal flesh. In my training to be a gray sister, we heard of Karak's return, of his freedom from the elven whore's prison...but it was always a day of glory, an ultimate defeat of chaos and false gods. The world was to shake, and a million voices cry out in triumph."

"You doubt him?" Kayne asked, his voice even deeper than Lilah's. Heat wafted over her from his mouth. It felt like an inferno rumbled in the lion's belly.

"Of course I doubt him. How is what he says not blasphemy? Shouldn't Karak strike him down for such claims?"

Kayne shook his head, an odd motion to see from a creature so large and magnificent.

"In many ways, Cyric is Karak made flesh. His power embodies him, his presence fills him, and he does speak our god's words in all matters of faith."

Valessa frowned. That wasn't good enough. Kayne was avoiding the question, giving her excuses and explanations instead of real answers.

"Then he's wrong," she said. "He isn't Karak, not in the way our prophets have foretold."

Kayne looked at her, and the intelligence in his eyes frightened her in a way no mortal weapon ever could.

"No," the lion said at last. "He is not."

"Then it is blasphemy."

"It is a mere reflection of the truth."

"There is only one truth! Karak cannot let this go on!"

Kayne leapt toward her. His eyes met hers, his teeth were bared and stopped just inches from her breasts.

"Would you tell a god what he can and cannot do?" asked the lion. "Cyric will accomplish what none have done in ages. He will bring back the old and true ways to the North, and beyond. The faithful will grow numerous, honed with fire and blade. So long as the priest serves, and furthers the cause of our god, then I am to protect him. As should you."

She refused to back down, to let the creature see her fear.

"I will listen," she told Kayne. "And I will obey, but I will not call him god, nor call him Karak."

"Tread carefully," Kayne said, snarling. "My teeth can consume more than flesh. You are not safe, not from me. Do not think yourself forgiven for your failure."

"I would never," she said. It took all her strength to walk past his bared teeth. She had thought herself unable to feel worldly sensations, but the creature was not of their world. The heat of his body radiated across her, made her feel alive for the first time since Darius killed her. But that only heightened the awareness of her pain, made her realize how much had been taken from her.

At the entrance to the Blood Tower, she stopped and looked up at the high window, which was lit with a candle.

"Your home is overrun by a madman," she whispered, thinking of Robert locked inside, helpless as Cyric as filled the heads of his men with promises of eternity. When Cyric spread his influence south, when he conquered the priesthood in Mordeina and began to travel east, might she one day feel the same?

Icy fear stung her non-beating heart. Dangerous thoughts, she realized, far more dangerous than she'd believed herself capable of. Cyric did Karak's will. She had to trust that. She had to believe.

Because the alternative was so much worse.

In the first village Sandra had come to, walking on bleeding feet and with an empty stomach, they'd fed her, repaired her clothes, and sent her on her way. They'd known her, supported her brother, but did not know where he'd been. Tombrook, they told her. Go to Tombrook, and someone there would know. And so she did, carrying her dagger in one hand and a satchel of dried food in the other.

At Tombrook, when she mentioned Kaide's name, they hushed her and took her to their village elder, who summoned one of his grandsons.

"He's a fast lad, and knows many paths," the old man said, his eyes milky white and his teeth black. "I trust he might take you somewhere you want to go."

The grandson was a boy of fourteen, and he carried a large sack of loaves over his shoulder.

"Will we need that much food?" she asked him.

"Food ain't for you," had been his reply.

And so she followed him out to the hills. Arthur's castle was close, she knew, and for much of the time they walked along the only road toward it. After a time, the boy veered off, into a heavy patch of brush and thorns that seemed to stretch for miles. Briars pulled at her clothes, and her skin bled from many cuts, but the boy endured without complaint, and so would she. Then they reached the camp, a large clearing painstakingly cut into the brush. They hadn't built any fires that might reveal their presence as they sat hidden, yet so close to the road.

"You're a godsend," the first guard said to the boy, grabbing the sack. His eyes had swept over her without seeing her, and she smiled at him with her arms crossed.

"Hello, Adam," she said.

He froze as if hit by lightning. The big man's grin grew, and then he wrapped her in a bear hug.

"Sandra!" he cried, and with that, many hurried her way. She greeted the men as best she could, then pushed them away.

"I must see my brother," she said.

"And I seek my sister," Kaide said, pushing Adam aside. A smile was on his face, and Sandra immediately felt relief at seeing it. He bore her no ill will, no anger, only an embrace she gladly returned.

"Is there somewhere we can talk?" she asked as the men returned to their posts. Kaide gestured to the sprawling camp.

"No walls, no tents, no homes," he said. "Though there's a stream a bit farther in. We can walk there, and talk along the way."

The brush had been carefully cleared, creating a pathway that weaved and curled so as to be unnoticeable from afar. Kaide led the way, and Sandra followed a step behind him.

"So what has my little sister been up to?" he asked her. She could tell he was dying to know, but kept his tone gentle, uninterested.

"Not near as much as you," she said. "How goes the siege?"

"We've not been here long, but we've assaulted nearly every supply wagon that's tried to slip past. Twice now we've even sneaked into Greg's camp and stolen food."

"Greg?"

"Sir Gregane," Kaide said, glancing back at her. "He's in charge of the troops. You think Sebastian would be brave enough to leave his castle?" Her brother laughed. "Not likely. He won't venture out until both mine and

Arthur's heads are on stakes. But it won't happen. We'll only get bolder. A hungry army poses little threat, and if we're lucky, I can assault..."

"Kaide," Sandra said, grabbing his arm and stopping him. "I...Jerico and I were captured by a man named Luther. He leads an army to aid in the siege."

Kaide's jaw clenched tight, and she could see the anger her words brought. Not at her, but at the thought of all his plans crumbling in an instant.

"How many?" he asked.

"I don't know," she said. "But at least four hundred, maybe five. He has paladins with him, too. Whatever chance we had, it's gone now. We must withdraw."

Kaide nodded, but she knew he was only thinking, not necessarily agreeing with her. Her brother's hands clenched into fists, then loosened.

"You said you were captured. How did you escape?"

"They let me go," she said. "I was to bring you a message. Luther said for you to not interfere, and if you left now, we'd be rewarded."

"Rewarded?" Kaide snapped. "Rewarded? How? Will he give me Sebastian's head? Will he give us vengeance for Ashvale? Of course not. They'll keep their puppet lord alive, and when Arthur's hanging in a gibbet, they'll come for me. For us." Kaide shook his head. "If he wants me gone, that means his victory is not so certain as you might think. I will not run now, not when Gregane's army is so close to breaking. If Arthur would just ride out..."

"Jerico's alive, too," she said. "I thought you might like to know, being his friend and all."

Kaide crossed his arms.

"Don't look at me like that. Of course he is my friend, and I'm glad he lives. Where is he now?"

"I think he's with Arthur."

"How? They have the castle surrounded."

"Do you think that'd stop him?"

Kaide laughed.

"No, I don't. Then let us hope we meet him on the field of battle as we crush Sir Gregane from both sides. We're not leaving, Sandra. I fear no man, no army. When we break this siege, Arthur will rally the rest of his host, and we'll march south to the Castle of the Yellow Rose. We'll hang Luther's head next to Sebastian's, how does that sound?"

"Sounds like a fool's hope," Sandra said, and she did her best to smile.

"A fool's hope," Kaide agreed. "We've lived on that for years. Perhaps, just once, we might find something more. If you're thirsty, follow the path. I must return to camp and send a rider to discover how much time we have before this Luther fellow arrives."

Sandra kissed his cheek, then let him go. Amid the thorns and brush, she watched him, and thought of Luther's words.

Should he listen, well...Karak's mercy will smile down upon him for it.

She would have to pray he was wrong.

20

Sir Gregane stood at the entrance of his tent and stared at the castle. The sun was starting to set, and from the high walls, he watched one of Arthur's men wave a loaf of bread then duck below the ramparts before someone shot him with an arrow. Gregane rolled his eyes and stepped back into his tent.

"They're still getting food," he told his trusted advisor, a seasoned knight named Nicholls. "Damned if I know how, though. How many of their tunnels have we collapsed?"

"Eighteen, if I remember correctly," Nicholls said. "Though to be honest, we've dug in so many I've lost track. Are you sure they aren't waving the same loaf over and over again? It might be tough as stone by now, and they're down to eating rats."

"We'll be there soon ourselves," Gregane said, walking over to his desk and glancing over his most recent tally of their supplies. "Three wagons, all raided and burned to the ground. No survivors. Our private stores dwindle, yet our guards see nothing. What does it sound like to you?"

Nicholls sighed.

"It sounds like Kaide finally made his way here."

"That's what I think, too, and it hasn't been for long, either. Four days, five at most. Yet look at what he's done with so little time. I've already had to cut our rations in half. Morale wasn't great to begin with, and now the men grumble behind my back when they think me too far to hear."

Nicholls cleared his throat and clasped his hands behind his back. Gregane knew he was about to hear something he wouldn't like, but demanded that his friend spit it out anyway.

"What if we break siege?" Nicholls asked. "We've already beaten Arthur in the open field, and he was damn lucky to escape then. Why not fall back, resupply, and catch him on the road south? If we cannot deny them food, and it is our men dying in the night instead of theirs, what good is it if we stay?"

Gregane put his hand on the parchment before him and stared at the numbers as if he could make them grow through sheer force of will.

"We cannot," he said. "Our lord gave us our orders, and we must follow them. The siege continues until victory, or our deaths. We have numbers, supplies, and time."

"Forgive me, sir, but time is not on our side, and it seems everyone but our lord knows it."

Gregane struck his desk with his fist.

"Do you think *I* don't know that?" he asked. Embarrassed by his outburst, he looked away and took in a deep breath. "Kaide's only gotten better at this...dishonorable way of combat. If we sit here, he'll starve us of supplies. If I send out escorts, he'll pick off my men one by one, and if I send too many, I risk leaving us vulnerable to an attack from Arthur. No, only one option remains. Is the battering ram finished?"

Nicholls blanched.

"It is, but we've yet to reinforce the top. Arthur's archers..."

"Will not stop us," Gregane said. "Is that understood? Come first light, we smash open his gates and hang his soldiers from the ramparts, along with their loaves of bread. If they want to flee through those caves of theirs, then so be it. We'll claim the castle, and Arthur will have his second defeat. The common folk will not consider him their savior after that."

"If you say so, sir."

"I do. Now go."

Nicholls left, and in the following silence, Gregane felt his frustration boil over.

"Damn you, Sebastian," he said, scattering his reports to the dirt. Come morning, he would end it all, one way or another. And if he failed, then so be it. At least then the better lord had a chance of victory.

"First light," he whispered. "First light, Arthur, we settle this. I pray you have the wisdom to surrender."

Arthur wouldn't, though. Not to him, and not to his brother. Much as it saddened him, their conflict was to the death, and they all knew it. Buckling his sword to his waist, he stepped out to observe the final preparations, and ensure every last detail was set. Next morning, hundreds of his men would die. The best he could do now was minimize the loss.

"**A**re you sure you're still up to this?" Daniel asked him.

"No," Darius said as he adjusted his plain shirt and slacks. "But we don't have much choice, do we? The blood moon's tomorrow, and I'm not expecting any knights to come riding in to the rescue."

They stood by the bank of the river, on the opposite side of Tower Silver, with Darius and six other men dressed as common villagers. The only things uncommon about them were the swords they held, and Darius's greatsword strapped to his back.

"The people of Durham will recognize you, even if Cyric doesn't," Gregory said softly, standing beside him in similar plain clothes. "Are you so certain they will protect us?"

"No, I'm not," Darius said. "But I have to trust them. Whatever fear they have of me, I think they'll fear Cyric more."

Daniel paced before the men after shaking their hands.

"You make me proud," he told them. "Every one of you deserves a song sung in your praise."

"And we'll sing it nice and loud when we come back with that bastard's head," one of the seven said, and the others laughed. Daniel smiled, and clapped the man on the shoulder.

"Damn right," he said. "And no one will be singing it louder than I. My men will arrive on time, don't you ever doubt it. Try not to die before then."

"No promises," Darius said, bowing low. "Have fun at the Blood Tower."

He looked at the rest of men, and the way they looked back, he knew he was their leader now, the one they put their faith in. He prayed he wouldn't disappoint.

"Let's go," he told them. "We have a village to save."

They traveled north, keeping the Gihon to their right at all times. Darius's hand often reached for his sword, and he kept expecting Valessa to be behind every tree, or lurking in every shadow. Each time, nothing, but his nerves remained on edge nonetheless. The rest of the men said little, even Gregory falling silent as they marched. They had many miles to cover, so they saved their breath. An hour in, Gregory spotted a road, and they followed it away from the river. It wound through the flatlands and fields of wild grass. Darius felt naked without his armor, but was glad for the lack of weight as the miles passed.

"Don't look like there's any patrols," said the oldest of the seven, a long-haired man named Zeke.

"Why would there be?" Gregory asked. "Why would Cyric think we knew his plans? He was an overconfident bastard the few times I met him, and I doubt he's gotten any better now he thinks he's a god."

"He ain't a god," said Zeke. "He ain't even much of a man. Just wait. I'll shove my sword in his gut, and we'll see how proud he is then."

The rest laughed, all nervous chuckles and sideways glances. Darius made sure to grin wide, and let none know of his private fears. A priest claiming he was Karak returned in human form? The rest of the priesthood would flay the flesh from his skin when they learned of such blasphemy. So why hadn't Karak denied him his power? Why send lions of the Abyss? Was there a grain of truth to it? Darius had killed a prophet with his blade, but could he kill a god?

The road widened as they neared the village, and the ground was markedly flatter. By now they could see torches, mostly gathered around the village center.

"Close enough," Darius said. "Time we split up."

"Darius with me," Gregory said. Darius could sense the young man assuming leadership, and was glad to let him do it. He knew the men better. "Zeke, go with Reb and Thomas. Stay at the farthest edge of town, close to the road. I want us to always know who leaves and who goes from Willshire."

The three men saluted, lowered their backs, and ran toward one of the homes. Gregory turned to the final two, lowborn brothers who'd enlisted at the same time, and been considered unworthy of anything other than a station at the towers. Darius had rarely spoken to them, learning little more than their names. They both had short red beards, making them even more identical.

"Something's going on in the center," Gregory said. "Think you two can find a home close enough to see?"

"Finding one's the easy part," said Gavin, grinning. "It's sneaking in unnoticed that'll be tricky."

"Can you?"

"We can," said Kris, the younger. "And no tiny village door is going to be locked or barred, not well enough to stop us."

"You certain?" Darius asked.

"There's a reason Daniel picked us for this," Gavin said. "We might have been a bit ... troublesome before being sent to the towers. Come on, Kris. I promise, come tomorrow night, we'll be ready for Cyric's little game."

"Stay low, and don't do anything stupid," Gregory told them.

"You mean besides our whole damn mission?" Kris asked, grinning.

Darius looked at Gregory and shrugged.

"He's got a point."

"Thanks for the confidence," Gregory said, gesturing to the quiet village. "Where are we to go?"

Darius analyzed the homes, then shook his head.

"To the other side," he said. "Maybe we will see something from a new angle."

He led the way, his body crouched and his head low. So far they had yet to see soldiers, or any sign of Cyric, but he refused to believe the priest had not begun preparations for the blood moon. Someone watched over the city, and kept them in line. As they circled Willshire, they reached a space where they could see through a gap of homes to the center. Both stopped, and Darius felt his heart stutter.

"What is that?" Gregory whispered.

"It's an altar," Darius whispered back.

"It can't be. It's too big to be one."

The paladin shook his head.

"Blood will spill there," he said. "Trust me."

Surrounded by torches and watched by soldiers bearing the standard of Karak was a massive table, built of five carved slabs of stone. Tied to the stone were twenty men and women. They sat with their backs to it, their heads sagging as they slept. Darius felt fury burn in his gut, and time slowed as he saw the man lording over it all: a priest dressed in black, standing atop the stone with his head bowed and eyes closed.

"We can attack them now," he said. "We have surprise, and I count only thirty or so guards."

"No," Gregory said. "We follow the plan."

"But the people..."

"...will die if we fail." Gregory put a hand on his shoulder. "They will endure. Now come, I think I see a place for us to stay."

He pointed to a large barn, far from any torchlight. The two of them could stay the night there, and come the morning, they'd just be two more villagers native to Willshire, eager to work the fields and participate in whatever ceremony Cyric had planned. Darius gave one last look at the priest, let his face burn into his memory, and then followed.

The barn itself was not quite as empty as they had expected. Instead of silence, they heard snores, and shuffling. Peeking inside through a crack, Darius saw at least thirty people sleeping amid the hay. Gregory snuck around to the front, then hurried back.

"Six men guard the entrance," he said, keeping his voice low. "Those from Durham must be inside."

"Cyric fears they'll flee. I can't imagine why."

"What do we do?"

Darius looked up, saw a high window. Too tall to climb. Other than that, there was the front entrance. The paladin scratched his chin, thinking. He looked at Gregory and frowned.

"How good a liar are you?" he asked.

"No one will play dice with me anymore. That good enough?"

Darius pulled the sword off his back and lay on his stomach. The wood on the barn was old, and carefully he checked board after board until he found one that was loose. It didn't have much give, but when he pulled, it opened up enough of a crack that they could slide their weapons inside. Gregory looked unhappy doing so, but he trusted him. That done, Darius stood, wiped a bit of dirt into the sweat of his face, then did the same to Gregory.

"The men at the front are just mercenaries," Darius explained in hurried whispers. "We at the Stronghold never liked them, nor respected their faith. They're in it for the money and power. While they praise Karak, they think like men, not priests. And like men, they assume other men are just like them."

"What are you getting at?"

"Just stay with me, and say as little as possible. We're going to get ourselves some women."

"*What?*"

Darius ignored him, and stepped around the corner of the barn and into the light of the guards' torches, pretending to have come from further inside the village.

"Stay where you are," one of them said upon seeing him. Several drew their blades, and Darius let a heavy drawl enter his voice, as if he'd downed too much liquor. Gregory stood behind him, looking nervous, which was exactly how Darius wanted him to look.

"Them people in there," he said, pointing at the door. "They're nothing but trouble. No good, that's what they are."

"You should be in bed, farmer," said the man directly before the entrance. Darius saw the markings on his armor and knew him the highest ranked of the six, so he focused his attention on him.

"Sun'll rise no matter whether I sleep or not," Darius said, and he grinned as if what he'd said was the most brilliant thing ever. "But my friend here, Greg, you see, Greg ain't never been with a gal, and that's a damn shame. Damn shame. But I'm thinking some of them women in there, well, they ain't too proud, know what I'm saying? Durham girls, they're loose..."

The guards shared a look, and it took all of Darius's self-control to hide his anger. The soldiers knew what he asked, and it amused them, for they had done the same. They'd taken the women inside, no doubt while their husbands watched. The question was...would they let them in?

"Those whores in there won't be much for a first time," said the guard, and he laughed. "What's wrong with your friend? Why ain't he porked one of the local gals, instead of harassing us in the dead of night?"

Darius tried to think of a reason, but Gregory beat him to it. He opened his mouth, closed it, then made a slashing motion over his throat. Darius bit his tongue to prevent a reaction. He'd told the man to talk as little as possible. Leave it to him to pretend to be a mute.

"Can't sweet talk a lady when you got no tongue to do it," said one of the other guards, and they chuckled.

"Lots of things you can't do to a lady with no tongue," said another.

"Least if the lady's got a tongue, she can still be of use."

Darius's sword was inside that barn, and it was probably a good thing, too. Fantasies of cutting off all six of their heads turned his vision red. But he smiled, shifted side to side as if he were still drunk out of his mind.

"So you fine men understand," he said. "Care to let us in? Anyone asks, we're just there to talk. Right?"

"Talk?" said their leader, grinning at mute Gregory. This sent him to laughing again. "Aye, we'll tell Cyric we let a mute fucker inside to talk."

Darius stretched his grin, and acted as if he didn't understand why it was so funny.

"Let 'em in," said the guard. "Worth it for the damn laugh."

They stepped aside, and Darius grabbed Gregory by the shirt and pulled him into the dark barn.

"Greg don't know what he's doing," he said just before they shut it. "So we'll be 'ere all night."

"Fine by me," said the guard. "But if they cut off your balls while you're asleep, don't expect us to do shit about it."

The door closed, sealing them in darkness. The two stood there, letting their eyes adjust to what little light streamed in through the cracks of the walls. Darius could hear people shuffling, and knew their conversation had awakened many. They might have overheard why they were there, or deduced the reason, so caution was of the utmost importance. As his sight improved, he saw many lying in piles of hay or under blankets, staring at them with wary looks. Two thirds appeared to be women, and many of the men looked old or frail. One man looked healthy, and Darius recognized him all too well.

"I don't see no sword," said Jacob Wheatley, standing before two young girls huddled behind him. "No armor, neither. You think you'll have fun just like the others?"

"No, I don't, Jacob," Darius said. "I expect to hide, and pray, and hope that come tomorrow night I cut off Cyric's head and present it to you all in penance."

Jacob's jaw dropped. He took a step closer, and squinted in the darkness.

"Darius?" he wondered aloud. Before Darius could answer, Jacob clocked him across the face with his fist. As Darius dropped to his knees, Gregory flung himself in the way, just barely keeping the farmer from latching about his throat.

"Enough," Gregory hissed, trying to keep his voice down. "We're Sir Robert's men, and we've come to help!"

"Help?" asked Jacob. He pushed Gregory away, then pulled at his shirt to fix it. "You got a lot of nerve coming here, Darius. Thought you'd be out there with that fucking priest, singing praises and sharpening your sword."

Darius took a deep breath and rubbed his sore jaw. He deserved worse, he knew, and did his best to keep his temper in check.

"I'm not asking you to forgive me," he said, walking around him while giving him a wide berth. "I'm not going to explain myself, for I'm getting tired of finding a thousand different ways to say I'm sorry I was a fool."

He reached the far wall, found his greatsword, and lifted it into the air. Soft light enveloped the blade, and it shone upon the people of Durham, all of whom were now awake.

"But I'm here to protect you," Darius said, his voice falling. "Will you let me?"

Jacob grunted, and he sat down next to one of the women.

"Don't mean we're even," he said. "But if you can kill Cyric, I think it might be a damn fine way to start."

21

Before they came for him that morning, Jerico already knew the battle had begun. He stood before the bed Arthur had given him, wearing his armor. On the bed lay his armaments. His fingers ran along the symbol of the golden mountain painted across the front of his shield, but his god was far from his mind at that point. All he could think of was Sandra held captive by the priest, Luther, and what his promise had been.

...should I see you again, even hear rumors of your approach, I will sacrifice that whore to Karak.

He had no reason to doubt him, no reason to believe he lied. There'd been such intensity in his eyes, such loathing...

The door opened. Jerico kept his back to it, his head low.

"Jerico?" asked a soldier he did not know.

"Yes?"

"They're...they're rushing the gates. We need you."

She'll die naked, alone, and screaming in pain.

"I know," he said, glancing back. The soldier opened his mouth, then closed it.

"Right. Arthur wished you to know, that is all."

He closed the door as Jerico picked up his mace. The weight felt reassuring in his hands.

Think on that the next time you would play the hero.

By aiding Arthur, he was killing Sandra. He picked up his shield, slung it over his back. By fighting Sebastian, he ended the life of the first woman he'd ever loved. Closing his eyes, he thought of her face, her stubborn smile. But this was what she'd want. He knew that. She could have run, but instead she killed the two men that had threatened him. Cowering to threats, giving in to cruel demands...that wasn't her, wasn't something she'd ever do.

But that didn't make it any easier.

He left his room and made his way to the courtyard. Soldiers lined the walls and formed rows before the rumbling gates. From what he'd learned, there were a hundred stationed within, and approximately six hundred outside the walls. Should they break through, they couldn't hold. He also knew that. They'd die, without hope of victory. As the wood groaned, and the battering ram slammed again and again, he took up a position at the front of the defense, where the tired men stood, quiet, nervous, watching.

"They'll hold," one said to him as he stood at his side.

"If not, then we will," Jerico said, and he smiled a smile he knew they all needed to see.

Screams filled the air. Glancing up, he saw the men on the walls pouring boiling oil on the attackers. Others shoved stones through murder holes, the sharp rocks plentiful because of the caves. Arthur's archers were few, but they loosed arrow after arrow while ducking behind the ramparts when Sebastian's men returned fire. More oil, and for a brief moment, the slamming against the gates stopped.

Jerico dared to hope. Perhaps something had broken the wheels of the battering ram, or Sebastian's general had lost his taste for bloodshed facing such casualties. It was a false hope, and he knew it, but the respite from constant hammering was still welcome. He took a step forward, and looked to the men when the battering ram resumed its work, despite the oil, the arrows, and the killing stones.

"The archway is tight," he told them. "Two men abreast, that is all they can send. When it breaks, I'll be there. My shield will block the way, and unlike wood, unlike stone, *I will not break*. Stand with me, at my side. Let our enemies see no fear, see no doubt. Let them see a wall of swords!"

Silence greeted him, but he saw the resolve hardening in their eyes. As he turned to the gate, he heard a single sarcastic clap from Jerek upon the walls.

"Good show," he shouted. "Hope you meant it, because they're coming through!"

Jerico felt his own terror crawl up his throat, and he choked it down.

"Play the hero," he whispered.

The thickest of the boards snapped, one half twisting and falling free to the ground. The gates flung open violently upon the next smash, revealing the carnage on the other side. Dead men lay slumped, arrows in their bodies. Others were horribly burned by oil, flesh charred and bubbling. Some were still alive, moaning softly or shaking. So many dead, maybe fifty, maybe a hundred, but it didn't matter. The gates had fallen.

Time to play the hero.

"With me!" he cried, rushing forward as Sebastian's men poured into the archway. Jerico's shield led the way, and it shone with a vicious light. He threw all his weight into the charge, his head ducked low and his legs pumping. A handful of men made it out of the archway as his charge met them, smashing aside one as if he were a child. Jerico's mace swung, punching through chainmail to crack ribs and puncture lungs, and then he spun, striking down a third trying to rush past him.

Without thinking, he pushed his shield forward in the air, though nothing pressed against it. A sound filled the courtyard, like that of a thunderclap. The closest attackers jolted backward as if struck. Their weapons flailing, their feet out of position, Jerico rushed ahead, the flanged edges of his mace tearing flesh and splattering blood across the stone archway. He stopped just before it, so the men above could continue to hurl their stones and fire their arrows.

For a moment it seemed that time slowed, and there was a pause in the attacks as the next wave of men prepared. Behind him, the rest of Arthur's soldiers cut down Sebastian's men, who were scattered and few. They took up positions beside him, and they cheered at the victory. Jerico breathed in heavily, knowing it was just a start.

But the delay in the attack wasn't a figment of his imagination, or a quirk of battle. He heard shouting, and from what he could see through the gate, the attackers were redirecting men away from the castle.

"What's going on?" he asked.

Jerek peered through the defenses, then spun, a grin on his face.

"It's Kaide!"

Whatever effect the bandit leader had, it wasn't enough. Jerico tried not to think of what he'd say if he met the man. Odds were high neither would live, and he found that comforting enough. The next wave of men gathered, shields raised to protect them from Arthur's arrows. They were nearly a hundred in number, fresh in strength, and with many reinforcements.

But Jerico stood against them, and as they charged, he lifted his shield high and cried out the name of Ashhur.

They'd crept among the hills, avoiding the road as much as possible. They were only a hundred, without armor or significant training. But Sandra knew her brother would steal every bit of advantage he could find. Their scouts had alerted them to the start of a frontal assault on the castle, and within minutes they were out and ready. A hundred men, plus Sandra, traveling with an unnerving silence.

"Their leaders will be in the back, watching the siege," Kaide had told them as they exited the camp. "If we're lucky, we'll smash their skulls in before they know we're there. Might even get Greg, too, if we're lucky. And Bellok has a fine surprise for them, as well."

The men had cheered, the last bit of noise, really, before heading out. Bellok was their wizard, his power minor compared to those trained and belonging to the Council of Mages. But Bellok had aided them before, at the Green Gulch, and the way he grumbled, they all thought he had another trick up his long sleeves.

All of them held their weapons ready, and Sandra was no exception. Kaide, realizing she would not stay away from the combat, had given her a spear, the tip freshly sharpened.

"It isn't an easy thing, killing," he'd told her, handing it over.

"I've seen people die," she said in return. "And with Jerico, I also killed. Don't lecture me."

Now she walked amid their meager army of rebels, bandits, farmers, and criminals. But they moved silently, and toward an army unaware of their approach.

"Stay with me," Adam said, keeping his deep voice low so it was no louder than the general sound of their movement.

"Fuck that," Griff said, sliding up beside her. "You'll be safer with me."

"I'll stay with you both," she said, smiling to hide her nervousness. "And I'll stab anyone who tries at your backs. Sound like a plan?"

The twins grinned at her.

"The little Goldflint's got some teeth," Adam said, and they both laughed far, far too loud.

They crossed the final hill to see the army encampment at the bottom. Before Kaide could give the order to charge, a cry went up from a distant hill. A combination of fear and swearing went through the army as they realized they'd been spotted by a scout.

"Charge!" Kaide screamed. "Surprise is lost, so hit them now or die!"

He turned to the wizard. "Bellok!"

Bellok lifted his arms, and as the bandit army charged downhill, the wizard cast the strongest spell he could muster. He was no expert at fire, could not conjure boulders of ice or arrows of shadow, but he could manipulate time. Sandra felt a strange tingling in her skin, and then realized the whole world had come to a standstill. It did not last for long, maybe a heartbeat. Sebastian's men turned, trying to shift aside lines and pull in troops from the castle to guard their rear flank, but they did so as if moving through molasses. With each passing moment they moved faster, closer to their original speed, but that brief delay was all that mattered.

Sandra followed Adam and Griff, both wielding enormous clubs. The spell was just starting to end when they met resistance, the soldiers moving far too slow to avoid their attacks. Two clubs smashed either side of a man's head, and Sandra felt shock at how his face crumpled and blood shot from his mouth. Only sheer momentum kept her moving, and when Adam hit another hard enough in the stomach to double him over, Sandra thrust her spear through the exposed gap at his shoulder. The tip pierced below his neck and into his lungs. His limbs flailed as he died. Sandra pulled, trying to free it, as Kaide's men blasted through tents and leapt against disorganized lines.

"Stay calm," Adam said, turning to see her struggling. He yanked the spear out and kicked aside the body. He grabbed her chin, pulled her face up. "Stay focused."

The two rushed to aid Griff, who was raging like a maniac at a group of knights. His club swung with wild abandon. One had been foolish enough to block it with his shield, and it had popped his collarbone in half. Adam bellowed like a bull, and he bowled into the group, Griff right at his heels. In the chaos, Sandra stabbed another from behind, wondering what Jerico might say to that. As she twisted it free, she looked about, saw that Sebastian's men were finally gathering together, twice their number coming to face them.

"We can't hold them off," she shouted to the twins. They glanced about, saw what she saw, then pointed toward the castle archway.

"Kaide's pulling back," Adam shouted. "We've done what we can, now get your ass out!"

Just as quick and unexpected as their attack had begun, they turned and fled, leaving a camp full of bodies in their wake. Halfway up the hill they stopped, for a large number had given chase. Kaide led the counterattack, his dirks moving with blinding speed. Sandra managed to link up with him as Sebastian's men fled back down the hill.

"How did we do?" she asked. Kaide sheathed his blades and wiped a bit of blood from her cheek with his thumb.

"Killed far more than we lost," he said. "Maybe a hundred to our thirty."

She looked down the hill, saw over a hundred soldiers organizing into defensive lines in case they made another charge. Unarmored and outnumbered, they would shatter against that shield wall if they tried.

"Any last tricks?" Kaide asked Bellok as they met the wizard at the top of the hill.

"That is the last I have," the wizard said. He pointed to the castle entrance. "They might hold, though only the gods know how. They have some good archers, and whoever fights at the gate must be Karak himself."

"Or Ashhur," Sandra said, glancing at her brother.

"If Jerico's there, and still not dead, then Gregane's going to need..."

He stopped, for that was when they heard the drums.

Lost in the battle, Jerico let his primal sense take over, let his body fight on instinct and training, without doubts, without fears. There would be no consequences save death should his shield falter, or his mace fail to block a sword strike in time. There was no Sandra with her life in a mad priest's hands. There was no Citadel, no war against his kind by the order of Karak. Just him, his foes, and the glowing white of his shield. His muscles ached, and a wicked gash bled across his arm from a stab he'd noticed too late.

But he stood before the archway's exit, and Arthur's men stood with him. Kill by kill, they built a wall of the dead, and they gave no reprieve for it to be cleared away. Their foes had charged with renewed vigor when Kaide's attack began, as if they knew victory needed to be soon. But Jerico would not let them have it. He flung his shield forward, again and again, slamming aside soldiers as if they were nothing but hollow toys. Others died around him, and it seemed Sebastian's army did its best to ignore him and take down the soldiers at his side, as if they would bury him once they broke through. The thought amused him darkly.

Any who slipped past, who tried to act as if his shield were his only threat, found a mace eager and ready.

Exhaustion threatened to overcome him, but he fought on, begging Ashhur for strength. Sebastian's men pulled back several times, trying to drag away bodies so they had a clear path, but the archers continued to fire their arrows, and the stones rained down from the murder holes.

"Still breathing?" Jerico asked the rest as their foes prepared for another charge. "Still with me?"

"We'll be here to the end," said one.

"Damn right," Jerek shouted from the wall.

"To the end," said a deep voice behind him. Jerico turned to see Arthur there, wearing his armor and brandishing a finely polished sword.

"I won't be my brother, hiding in hope of victory," he said, nodding toward the paladin. "Give me a place to stand. I still have the strength to swing a blade."

"At my back," Jerico said, and he grinned. "I'll need you to take my place when I fall."

He turned, lifted his shield. That next wave was the worst, heavily armored men charging at full speed. They tripped and stumbled over the dead, but still they came. Jerico smashed his mace through their armor, and his shield flared, its light a physical force that struck down his opponents and left them blind. After a time, he could not swing, could not attack; he only clutched his shield and braced his legs as he held against the attackers. At either side, he saw Arthur's men come running with their own shields. They pushed and yelled, and all the while Arthur thrust his sword over the top, taking life after life.

At last the assault broke, unable to maintain pressure with so many casualties. Frightened men fled, and Jerico fell to one knee, gasping for air.

"I hope I never have to do that again," he said.

Throughout the castle, morale was growing. Arthur cheered his men on, and they cheered back at their lord and his bloodied blade.

And then they heard the drums.

"What is that?" Arthur asked.

Jerico's heart sank. He knew what it was, but he looked to Jerek anyway, praying for any other news.

"I see an army," Jerek said, looking down at them with the defeat evident in his eyes. "Their banners show the Lion."

"Karak's men," Arthur said, and it was a curse on his lips. "How many?"

"Four hundred at the least."

Whatever morale they had, died. Jerico walked toward the bloody archway and peered through. Sebastian's men had pulled back, more than eager to wait for reinforcements before resuming the attack. Looking to the distance, he saw Kaide's bandits were atop the far hill, watching the proceedings. Would this loss be the end of Kaide's rebellion? Of course not. Even down to his dying days, the man would resist.

"Now is the time to flee," Jerico said, turning to Arthur. "We will not survive, not this. Take the secret ways."

"I'm not fleeing," Arthur said. "I have already lost on the field of battle. To lose my home, my castle..."

"*Look!*"

All the archers were shouting, not just Jerek. Jerico turned back, and his jaw dropped. He couldn't believe what he saw. His eyes were lying to him, he thought. They had to be. Like in a dream, he walked through the archway and to the oil-soaked dirt beyond.

Luther's army, upon reaching Sebastian's, had drawn their swords, lifted their shields, and attacked. Caught unaware, they died like flies. Even those who had the presence of mind to fight dropped quickly, for they lacked both the training and numbers to resist. Worse were the dark paladins, their blades wreathed in black flame as they tore through the ranks. But nothing came close to Luther, who walked amid the battle like a dark god. Shadows and fire leapt from his hands, consuming all. At last he reached the leaders' tents. Jerico waited, expecting more death, but it seemed those there were allowed to live.

"What's going on?" Arthur asked, calling from inside the castle.

Jerico shook his head.

"I don't know," he said.

"Are they friendly?"

Jerico had no answer to that either. It made no sense, none at all. Sebastian was Karak's friend, and Luther had made his intentions clear...hadn't he?

The battle ended as abruptly as it had begun. Sebastian's men flung down their blades and surrendered, only a hundred in number from the original six. They fled along the streets, and even Kaide was so stunned that he did not order his men to chase. Instead, they tentatively descended the hill, as if expecting an ambush at every step. None came. Luther's army was already putting away weapons and preparing to leave.

"Jerico!" a voice cried out, and he saw Sandra rushing to him through the remnants of Sebastian's camp. He couldn't believe it. He laughed, and his mace hung limp in his hand. His legs went weak, and he fell to his knees. Sandra flung her arms about him, and he felt her lips kiss his forehead.

"You lived," she said, all smiles.

"But...how? Why?"

"Just shut up," she said, kissing him again.

Jerico forced himself to a stand. He saw Luther approaching, surrounded by four dark paladins. His insides turned. Would they still want his life, given their war against his order? But why let him go before, just to kill him now?

"I told you to stay away," Luther said, just out of reach of their bows. "I told you to flee, and not play the hero. And you!" He looked at Kaide, who approached the entrance with his men, watching Luther's army. "I told you the same. Did I not warn you? Did I not say you would be denied Karak's mercy?"

Jerico did not understand. His actions, his words, they didn't connect, didn't make sense. And then Luther lifted his arm, pointed his finger at Sandra, and whispered. The tip flared black. Lightning shot forward, dark as midnight. Thunder roared. Sandra screamed, and Jerico screamed with her as she collapsed in his arms. Her eyes were wide, and her mouth open. Her chest did not move. Clutching her, Jerico could only look at her body in shock. He thought to heal her, but she was dead already, her heart burst by the spell. Her soul was gone. With a shaking hand, he touched her cheek, brushed her lips with his fingers. He heard shouting, cries of rage and sorrow, but they were distant, muffled in his ears.

He looked at Luther, rage in his eyes.

"You monster."

He gently put her down, lifted his mace. It didn't matter that he was outnumbered. Didn't matter all that Luther had just done. Didn't matter what was right or wrong, or if he died trying. He would kill the priest.

The dark paladins leapt in the way. He blocked their strikes with his shield, but each one sent a jolt of pain through his arm. His mace struck the armor of one, but it could not penetrate. Fury gave him strength, but he was still tired, and vastly outnumbered. Swords hit his armor, and the bruises swelled. Jerico continued on, enduring them, fighting them away. He would reach Luther, would look upon Sandra's cruel murderer.

And then he was through, beaten and weary. Luther lifted a hand, and before Jerico could strike, a bolt of shadow struck him in the chest. He gasped, fighting for breath. A second bolt followed, this one hitting his throat. The muscles in his neck tightened, and spots swam before his eyes as his lungs threatened to burst. Unable to stand, he collapsed to his knees once more. Luther stood over him, and he leaned down so he could put a hand on Jerico's head and whisper.

"At least you are wise enough to kneel," he said. "Now do you understand, Jerico? You have done all that I wished, and little more. You are insignificant, just a puppet to my desires. Go off into the wilderness and die. There is no longer a place for you in this world."

Luther pushed him onto his back. When he hit, it knocked the air from his chest. Fighting through the agonizing pain, Jerico drew a breath, then another. A heavy ringing filled his ears, and he heard the priest call for the others to prepare for their march south. Rolling onto his stomach, he tried to stand, but could not. Tears blurring his vision, he looked back to the castle, saw Kaide on his knees, his little sister's body in his arms. The bandit leader cried out wordlessly, whatever rage that dwelt in his heart now magnified tenfold.

What little strength Jerico had left drained away. His fingers clawing the dirt, he pressed his face into the grass and sobbed, a broken man.

22

They pulled their boat off the Gihon so they might walk the final mile. Porter led the way, looking strangely spry and alive in the growing light of the blood moon. Daniel followed him, content to let the man lead. It was his plan, after all.

"Stay low," Porter told them. "A single alarm, and we'll all be dining in the Abyss before the night's over."

There were only five of them, a small enough force to slip in and out of the fortification without notice. Their true force marched for Willshire, where battle might be fought without towers and high walls. If they took Cyric's head, most of their problems vanished, but just in case, they needed Robert. No matter how much the King might hate his family, he couldn't sit idly by if the knight knelt before his throne and told of the usurpation of his tower. Treason was still treason, even when committed by priests.

The trees thinned out the closer they came to the tower. Daniel felt his nerves rise, and his heart quicken. This was it, the first major obstacle. It all depended upon how numerous the guards were, and how alert. When they saw the torches, and the handful of men upon the walls, Daniel let out a sigh of relief.

"A skeleton crew," he said. "Cyric must be gone after all."

"I'd be pissed to know if my tower were as lightly guarded in my absence," Porter said. "Laziness and lack of discipline is what that is."

"What it is, is a lucky break," said one of the other soldiers. "We ready to swim?"

"Aye," Daniel said. "Let's go."

The walls surrounding the tower went deep into the river, but once around it, the way was clear. From their inspection of the defenses, the few men guarding the walls were all stationed along the southern end. They did not watch the opposite shore, or the north. They no longer guarded against the creatures of the Wedge, as was their purpose. They watched for a human army. Daniel and his men were all smeared with mud, wore no armor, and brandished only short swords, light and small enough for them to swim without difficulty, plus a few extra supplies just in case things went terribly wrong.

Beyond the reach of the tower's torches, the five circled around to the north, nothing but black and brown shapes in the far distance. When they reached the other side, they slipped into the Gihon, submerging all but their heads.

"Damn that's cold," muttered one.

"No words," Porter said. "We're too close now."

Going limp, they floated, aiming for the wall within the river. Normal circumstances would have had a guard atop it, and as they neared, they saw a man sitting there, his back to them. His armor was that of Karak's mercenaries. *Watching the courtyard*, Daniel realized, and he pointed to make sure the other four saw.

Boisterous sounds of cheers and song met their ears as they floated closer. Daniel clenched his jaw tight to keep his teeth from chattering. Carefully, he swam toward the wall, then went limp again, letting the water bump him against it. He lay flat, until all five were gathered. Glancing up, Daniel waited for the light of a torch, or even a single glance downward to show them as odd shapes in the reflected moonlight. This was it, the most vulnerable part of their

David Dalglish

plan. Porter lifted three fingers, then counted down. At one, he alone pushed off and floated around the wall.

All they could do was wait and listen. After several minutes, they heard a soft gasp, then the sound of armor hitting stone. Another minute later, Porter leaned over from atop the wall and beckoned them to come. Pushing off, Daniel led the others around and onto dry ground. They kept their backs to the wall, in the deep shadows cast by the scattered torches. He could see the men on the opposite wall, and he tried not to panic, and convince himself he could not be seen.

One of the soldiers with him, a young dark-haired man named Slint, tapped him on the shoulder.

Lion? the man mouthed, lifting his shoulders to accentuate the question. Daniel shook his head. They saw no sign of it yet. If they were blessed, the two horrible creatures would be in Willshire, or even better, back in the Abyss from whence they came. Daniel pointed to his eyes, telling them to stay alert. On the far side, many tents filled the killing field. They could all hear the ruckus. It was a time of celebration, just as Darius had insisted. They were gathered about bonfires, roasting meat and drinking themselves stupid. No wonder the few men on guard were inattentive, and kept their attention focused toward the interior. The fires would also ruin their vision, something Daniel was plenty thankful for.

Besides the men on the walls, the only other guards were two stationed at the doors of the tower, both looking tired and leaning against the building. Daniel kept his anger in check when he saw they were both recruits of theirs, men who had bowed the knee to Karak and turned against their commander.

There'd be no mercy, not for them. Daniel drew his sword, pressed his back to the wall, and crept along. Above them, Porter did the same, tracking their progress. When they reached another guard, they stopped and waited. Porter snuck behind him, for the man watched the north. Daniel winced as he heard the man's body hit the ground on the opposite side of the wall. Too much noise, but it seemed no one heard. They continued on after Porter gave them the go ahead. Once they'd crossed beyond the two guards' line of sight, they ensured no eyes watched and then made a break for the tower.

No time to waste, Daniel knew. He hurried to the tower door. No hesitation, no commands, he trusted his men to follow. The closest of the two guards died before ever realizing he was under attack. As Daniel held his hand over the man's mouth and twisted the blade he'd stuck in his back, the other let out a soft yelp before two of his soldiers thrust their swords through his throat and belly. The dying cry went unnoticed amidst the songs of the mercenaries. Testing the door, Daniel found it unlocked. Throwing it open, he gestured for the other three to hurry. They dragged the bodies inside, and Daniel quickly followed, slamming the door shut behind him.

The sounds of revelry quieted once within. Knowing whatever time they had was dwindling fast, Daniel led the way toward the stairs. The second anyone noticed the missing guards, and was sober enough to look into the matter, they'd be caught. They needed to have rescued Robert and vanished long before then.

"I hear snores," Slint whispered into Daniel's ear. Daniel paused a moment, then nodded. Men were sleeping in the adjacent rooms. The three looked to him, and he could tell they wanted orders.

"Kill them," he whispered back. "I'll get Robert."

The three opened the door, and like wraiths in the night, they slipped inside with swords drawn. As Daniel climbed the circular steps leading to Robert's chambers, he heard a sound that made his heart freeze. It was the roar of a lion, and it was furious. Racing up the steps, he found a window overlooking the wall Porter hid upon. There, atop the stone, was one of the lions of Karak, Porter's body flopping as the creature shook it in its jaws. Daniel forced himself to look away.

At the top of the steps, Daniel found a mercenary rushing down to investigate. A quick stab underneath the ridge of his breastplate sent him toppling. Daniel yanked free the iron key attached to his belt, then continued on. Stopping at Robert's door, he unlocked it and thrust it open.

"Time to go, sir," he said, then froze. His jaw dropped, and his hands trembled.

"No," he whispered. "Gods, no."

Robert sat in a chair, his waist and legs strapped to it with chains. Before him was a table, rows of parchment, and a single candle. He held a quill in his gray, lifeless hand. His eyes were open, and his mouth hung limp. His flesh was already rotting, his tongue cut from his throat, but he still lived...if living was what it could be called. A wicked cut remained open across his throat, his clothes and skin below it stained red, but the wound itself did not bleed.

"What have they done to you?" Daniel asked as he heard the lion roar once more.

Robert dipped the quill into an inkwell, then carefully wrote a message on the parchment before him. Daniel stepped forward, and he read it with tears in his eyes.

Kill me. Last order.

Daniel swallowed.

"Are you sure?" he asked.

The undead mockery of his commander nodded. Daniel clenched his jaw and wiped away his tears, so he might strong, might be proud.

"I understand," he said. "It was an honor to serve you, Robert. A true honor."

He cut off Robert's head. It fell to the floor, rolled once, then lay still. The rest of the body sagged in the chair, all strength vanishing from it. Daniel stared, holding back his grief, but not his anger.

"Sir?"

Daniel turned to see the other three gathered there, looking at the corpse with wide eyes.

"Cyric's doing," Daniel said, his voice croaking. "May the bastard suffer for an eternity when we find him."

"We barred the door downstairs," Slint said. "The rest of the traitors are dead, but..."

"The lion," Daniel said, knowing what they feared. Porter had been found, and the lion stalked the tower. He looked out the window, saw men hurrying to investigate. Whatever hope they had of escape was gone.

"Forgive me," he told them. "I led you to your deaths."

"Save the apologies," Slint said, pulling some rope off his back, one of their emergency provisions. He thrust it into Daniel's hands. "You're lord of the Blood Tower now, and our commander. Any hope of honoring Robert is now in your hands."

Daniel looked to the rope, then the window, and shook his head.

"I won't. They'll find me before I ever set foot on the ground."

"Not if we distract them."

The three saluted him with their swords. They were willing to die, and appeared ready to carry out their plan whether he agreed with it or not. Taking a deep breath, he saluted back.

"I couldn't be more proud of you," he told them. "Take as many with you as you can."

"Damn right."

Daniel tied the rope to Robert's desk, which he shifted closer to the window. When the tower was built, the entrance had faced the river, but Robert's window faced the gate to the walls, so he might always see the arrival of any guests. Looking down, he saw no one watching, everyone gathering at the other side. From down below, he heard a loud banging as something smashed into the barred doors. Holding the rope in his hands, he waited to throw it, listening for what he also feared.

Loud cracking, then screams. They were through. Daniel offered a prayer for his men, then tossed the rope. He climbed down fast as possible, the rope burning his hands as he slid at a reckless pace. Hitting the ground, he looked about, knowing he had no time. He wanted to run to the dark side they'd entered, but his gut told him otherwise. Sprinting for the side with the tents, he kept his head low. Whatever celebrations had been going on had clearly halted, with nearly every armed man making their way to the walls and tower, letting out confused cries and shouting questions about a surprise attack. As he weaved through them, he heard shouts from up top. An arrow struck the ground beside him, another just ahead. Daniel said another word of thanks, this time for intoxicated archers.

A roar behind him curdled his blood. He was almost to the river, but he dared a glance back. The lion chased, far ahead of any soldiers still on the ground. It barreled through the tents, which burst into flame upon contact.

Shit, thought Daniel. *Shit, shit, shit.*

He cast aside his sword, every bit of his strength going into his pumping legs. Another roar, this time closer. The ground seemed to shake with every leap the lion took, and it was so close, so close...

Something slashed at his back. It tore through his clothes, and his skin burned with fire, but he continued on, leaping into the river. The pain in his back eased with the cool water, and like a madman he swam toward the far side. He glanced behind only once to see the lion snarling furiously as it thrashed about. Massive amounts of steam curled into the air from its skin, and when it roared again, it was clearly with pain.

The river might stop the lion, but the rest would be in boats in no time. Reaching the other side, Daniel paused a moment to catch his breath, then ran. He knew well the lands of the Wedge, which grounds were safe and which were occupied by various monsters. Wishing he'd kept his sword, he ran deeper into the Wedge, his back to the tower. Let them chase, but he would not be caught. He couldn't be. Death would not take him—not yet.

Not until he found vengeance for what they'd done to Robert.

23

Cyric's men brought food and water into the barn only once, just after dawn. Darius reluctantly took his share. The people of Durham were clearly malnourished, but if he were to protect them in battle, it wouldn't help to do so on an empty stomach.

"Is there a way up to that window?" he asked Jacob when he noticed the light streaming in through it. The window was up in the loft, and in answer, Jacob pointed to where a ladder had been.

"They broke it when they locked us in here," he said.

"Where are the rest?" Gregory asked.

Jacob shrugged.

"They've got plenty at whatever they're building in the center. Don't know where the rest are. Maybe in a home or two, locked up like we are."

Time crawled, and Darius spent much of it pacing and wondering what was going on outside.

"I trust my men to do their job," Gregory said, relaxing in a pile of hay.

"And if they're noticed? Interrogated?"

Gregory shrugged.

"Least we have our weapons. We'll get to die fighting."

Darius chuckled, and he leaned against a wall of the barn, wishing he could see out.

"You're right, Gregory. That makes it so much better."

"You whine like a child."

Slowly, so slowly, but the day continued to pass. As night approached, a cold tension filled the air. Even locked away, the two could sense it, could hear it in the way the guards outside the barn talked, and in how the noise of the village dwindled. The many people around them started to fidget, murmur, or cry silently. Darius paced before the door, eager for the night to start, yet dreading it as well.

"What if they don't come for us?" Jacob asked as the sun began to set.

"They will," Darius said.

"And if they don't?"

The paladin shrugged.

"I'll break the damn door down."

Jacob gestured to where Darius's greatsword lay on the ground.

"Time's running out. If you want to hide it, better get started."

Darius looked about the men and women. He'd told them his plan, but he still did not like it.

"Who would be best?" he asked.

"I'll do it," said an elderly woman. Darius tried to remember her name. Ezre Reed—that was it. Gary's mother.

"Are you sure?" he asked.

"I already walk with a limp," she said. "No one will question an old woman hiding from the chill."

Darius and Gregory exchanged a look.

"Your decision," said the soldier.

Using some twine, they tied his sword to her side, the tip at her feet, the hilt tucked underneath her armpit. She took a few awkward steps. A smile lit up her wrinkled face.

"Not so heavy as I feared. Carrying my children was worse."

Darius smiled back.

"Good. Now let's get you protected from that cold, cold wind."

Another couple handed over their blanket, and they wrapped her from head to toe. Her elbow hiding the bulge of the handle, she clutched the two edges of it and walked again. No sign of a weapon.

"Excellent," Gregory said. "But next time, just bring a dagger."

"Stay with me, near the very back, if you can," Darius told her as she leaned against a wall, unable to sit because of the sword. "When I draw it, I might be in a hurry. My apologies in advance if I hurt you."

"My son died when that evil man came," she told him. "You could never hurt me more than you did then."

Her bitter words stung, but whether that was her intent or not, he didn't know. Looking to Gregory, he saw the man had hidden his shortsword by tying it against his inner thigh.

"Step carefully," Darius told him, earning himself a rude gesture.

The door was flung open, startling them all. Six soldiers stood there, half holding torches. The light stung their eyes, and several let out cries.

"On your feet, all of you," said one. "You all should be proud to bear witness to tonight's miracle."

Darius bit his tongue, and offered his hand to Ezre. She took it, then began limping along. Unable to bend her right knee, she hobbled forward, and put more and more weight against Darius. He helped her, always careful that the blanket did not pull back to reveal the blade.

"Hurry it up," one of Cyric's mercenaries told him.

Darius started to retort, but Ezre beat him to it.

"Hush you. I'll get there when I get there."

The soldier blinked for a moment, stunned by the outburst, then laughed.

"Remind me of my own ma," he said, then struck her across the face. "Hated my ma."

Darius caught her, and his heart skipped as he felt the handle of his sword press against him. Ezre straightened herself out, moaning only a little. The blanket fell loose, covering the blade again. The guard did not notice, instead turning his back to them and ushering others along.

"I'm sorry," Darius whispered to her.

"I'll be fine," Ezre said. "Took worse from my husband for saying less."

"Stay near the back. When we take our place, start untying the twine."

She lifted a curled hand as they walked toward the center of the village, far behind the other people of Durham.

"My hands can't thread a needle like they used to," she said. "You'll have to do it."

He nodded, not sure how he would do it, but knowing he had little choice in the matter. Trying to fight his nerves, he brought his attention to the spectacle at hand. A great altar waited in the clearing, and it looked like something out of his old lessons at the Stronghold. Stone slabs joined together to form an enormous altar, propped up by wood where necessary. At least four men could lie flat on top of it, but Darius felt certain that Cyric would do just one at a time. He wanted this to last. He wanted to revel in his return to the old ways.

Darius hoped to ruin all his fun.

They stopped at the back of the crowd. Soldiers kept them separated from the original inhabitants of Willshire, who were lined up on the opposite side of the altar. Tied to it were the twenty he'd seen the night before. They looked haggard and tired, and he knew many of them. They'd endured the wolf-men, survived Velixar's assault, and now this. It was amazing that any still clung to life, given the horrors they'd faced. If Ashhur were kind, he'd make sure this was the last.

Standing at the center of the altar was Cyric. The very sight of him twisted Darius's stomach. His eyes were a deep red. They weren't the burning fire of Velixar's, but his smile, his robes, were all eerily similar. Most remarkable was how young he was, and how overwhelmed he was by his faith. Beside him was a paladin of Karak, steadfast and quiet as he protected his master, an enormous ax strapped to his back. Darius vaguely recognized him from his time training in the Stronghold, an old veteran named Salaul.

"A joyous night!" Cyric kept repeating. "Such a joyous night!"

Gregory slipped through the crowd and took up a spot beside him.

"See the others?" Darius asked, speaking low, as if he were just muttering to himself.

"Behind Cyric, the house with two windows."

Darius saw the building, but the windows looked empty to him.

"Gavin and Kris?"

"Believe so. Let's pray their arrows are accurate."

"The other three?"

Gregory nodded toward the large group of people from Willshire.

"He's in there. Spoke to him for a moment. No one came in or out. We should have them...shit."

Cyric had been speaking, and then he gestured grandly toward the road. Marching in was a small group of mercenaries, about fifteen in number. In the center walked a woman wearing a silver crown upon her forehead, a long violet cloak, and armor that was both regal and deadly with its sleek lines and dark silver hue.

"Valessa," Darius whispered.

The crowd parted as if they were royalty. Cyric beckoned her to join him upon the altar, and she did, accepting his hand reluctantly. Her face was an emotionless mask, and Darius could not read it. Something about it didn't feel right, though. Where was her smile? Where was that same triumphant faith that Cyric exuberated with every movement he made?

And then came the lion. Fire burned across its molten skin, and Darius felt terror grip his heart. It was like something out of the tales he used to listen to as a child, when his teachers would lay them down to bed in the Stronghold. The ancient times, when Karak walked the land, his armies of wolf, bird, and lion at his side.

"Welcome, Valessa, my queen," Cyric said to her before turning his attention to the lion. "Welcome, Kayne. You two are my most honored guests."

"Let it all be done in the name of Karak," Kayne said, sending fear rippling through the gathered crowds.

"Indeed," Cyric said, smiling. "In Karak's name."

Darius took in their numbers. He counted about sixty in total, not including the more dangerous players, like Valessa or the dark paladin. The numbers would be in their favor, for the most part. But how many might Kayne kill? How great was Cyric's power? As for Valessa...

She would have to be his first target, he realized. No one else could harm her, and she would tear through their ranks.

"Welcome, all of you!" Cyric cried, and as his voice thundered over them, suddenly many times louder than before, the crowd quieted, but for the soft sobs of a few tied to the altar. "This night, this most sacred night, will be one for all of Dezrel to remember. Consider yourselves blessed to bear witness. Consider yourselves beloved. Few look upon their god while still walking this world, but you shall. All of you shall!"

He gestured to those at the altar.

"These here spoke out against Karak. They spoke out against me! They dared believe themselves wiser than gods. They dared believe they could turn the worldly law to their side, could ally with the imperfect structures of man to bring down the divine constructs of our priesthood. They will atone for this, for I am not here to destroy, but to save! The old ways will reignite true faith in Dezrel. That faith will preserve them, purify them, instead of eternal condemnation burning them away in Karak's fire. True Order! Let it be known!"

He reached his hand to Valessa, and she gave him one of her crimson daggers. With a nod from Cyric, the dark paladin went to the first of the many tied to the altar. He was a man Darius knew well: Jeremy Hangfield, the wealthiest and most influential man in Durham. He'd lost a lot of weight, leaving him haggard and thin. He didn't resist as they cut him free and dragged him to the wood steps. The dark paladin held him down, but Cyric would not be satisfied.

"His daughter, too," he said.

A stabbing pain hit Darius's gut. All around him people stood frozen, as if unwilling to believe it. Ezre turned away, and she pressed herself against Darius as if crying.

"Hurry now," she whispered. "Take your sword, damn you."

Darius reached his hand underneath her blanket and clutched the hilt. There would be no time to untie the twine. Their walk over had loosened the ties enough that he could lift the sword straight up. His fingers tightened, and he stared at the altar. Drawing now would risk ruining their plan, but how could he wait?

Valessa was the one to get her, slicing Jessie Hangfield free from the altar and tugging on her wrist. Jeremy struggled, but the dark paladin kept him pinned, the edge of his axe pressed against his neck.

"A glorious night!" Cyric cried. "A night to remember! Do not weep, do not know fear. Let the blood spill upon the altar, and with it, cleanse away their failures, their transgressions against the most holy and true. We abide by the highest law."

"What are you waiting for?" Ezre asked him as Darius watched. "Are you a coward?"

"Not yet, Darius," Gregory said beside him, no longer needing to whisper because of the crowd. "Damn it, not yet!"

"He'll kill her, just a little girl!"

"I said not yet, that's an order!"

Jessie lay flat against the stone, and her sobs rent Darius's heart. He felt Ezre against him, waiting for him to take the sword, and Gregory's hand on his shoulder, his fingers digging into him with determined strength. Sixty soldiers stood between him and Cyric, not counting Valessa and the lion. Revealing their presence now might doom them all...but why else were they there?

His indecision was enough, his inaction all that was necessary. He clenched his teeth and begged Ashhur not to condemn him for it. Cyric lifted the dagger above his head as he stood over Jeremy. The dark paladin rolled him over to expose his heart. Darius swallowed. The crowd went eerily silent as dark power swelled across the blade.

And then an arrow pierced Cyric's hand, sending the dagger clattering across the altar and to the ground.

"Gavin, you idiot," Gregory said.

Another arrow flew from the window of the home, catching Cyric in the shoulder. The priest roared, all his earlier joy and celebration replaced with mindless fury. Fire spread across his hands, and the next few arrows exploded before reaching him. The two men dove beneath the window as Cyric waved his hand, the arrow piercing it shattering. The building rocked side to side as dark projectiles of fire struck across it, bursting it into flame.

"Warriors of Karak!" cried Kayne, suddenly pulling their attention south. "An army comes along the road!"

"Thank Ashhur," Darius whispered.

The sixty soldiers readied their weapons and rushed to meet the gathered might of those loyal to Sir Robert, two hundred strong. Kayne led the way, and Darius hoped the greater numbers might help them endure his unholy might. The path to the altar was clear. Darius carefully pulled his sword free, and held it high, casting its light across the altar. From high above, the blood moon shone upon him, and he defied it with all his heart.

"With me!" he cried, and together he and Gregory rushed the altar.

Cyric had not yet seen, for he was casting another spell, which exploded the remnants of the home Gavin and Kris were inside. People ran in all directions. Those from Durham not tied were suddenly left unguarded, and many of them fled for safety, but not all. Darius's heart swelled as he saw others rushing the altar, yanking at the ropes to free their families and friends. Many died as the dark paladin swung his axe and Valessa stabbed with her dagger, but then Darius was there, his greatsword clashing against the axe and its dark fire.

"A paladin?" Salaul exclaimed, stunned.

"Damn straight."

Darius shoved the axe aside, stepped forward, and thrust. His foe tried to block, but then Gregory lunged in. His sword could not block, but his body did. As Gregory died, Darius's sword pierced the dark paladin through the belly. Blood spilled across the altar. Darius twisted the blade, then yanked it free. The motion sent Salaul's body tumbling off the side, and he landed beside Gregory's split corpse. Seeing the young man slain only increased his fury, and he turned it on the remaining two atop the altar.

"Darius?" Valessa asked, stunned to see him there. Darius laughed, and he attacked again and again, his sword with greater reach versus her lone dagger. Cyric turned to help, but then Zeke and the others slashed and stabbed with their own weapons.

"You heathens!" Cyric cried to them, falling from the altar to avoid their daggers. They leapt upon him, but he beat them back with fire and shadow. Darius saw only a little of it, for Valessa had jumped off the stone toward him and launched into a vicious series of attacks. His sword shifted side to side, parrying away her thrusts.

"What is this?" he asked her, a grin on his face despite his exhaustion and sorrow. "What good is that armor? What good is that crown? What kingdom do you rule?"

"With your death, I will be redeemed," she said.

"You're wrong, Valessa. You'll be lady of the dead, a princess of graves. All hail her majesty."

He could see the desperation in her eyes and knew she could endure no more. Her thrust came in wild, and he smacked it aside. Stepping in, he swung his sword. It passed straight through her waist, the armor nothing but an illusion, her flesh nothing but shadow. The light of his blade burned, and her form dwindled, changed, became only a beaten woman stumbling naked away from him in fear.

"Give Karak my greetings," he said to her, thrusting for her neck.

She screamed, dropped her dagger, and fled. His thrust missed by an inch. She was nothing but a shapeless darkness as she ran to Cyric, who stood over the corpses of Gregory's three men. All of them were dead, but they'd stopped the sacrifice. Darius lifted his sword, determined to not let it all be in vain. He pointed it at the priest, who looked down at Valessa with disgust.

"A night to remember," Darius said, no humor in his voice. "You were right about that, Cyric."

"I'll rip your heart from your chest," Cyric said. "I'll crush it between my fingers before the altar."

Cyric turned his blade to the side, the light across it burning brighter.

"Try it."

The priest stretched out his hand, and a beam of pure darkness shot from his palm. Darius blocked it with his sword, bracing his legs to endure the blast. He felt his arms jar, felt the incredible strength beat against him, but he held his ground. He thought of the way Jerico had endured far greater, of how he had withstood the onslaught of wolf-men as if it were nothing. Darius would do the same. The magic would not defeat him. He would prove Cyric wrong. The night was theirs, not Karak's.

Cyric ended the attack, instead hurling a curse. Darius felt it latch onto his limbs like invisible chains, but he shrugged it off, breaking the magic with a plea to Ashhur. Lightning followed, but it swirled into the sword and died.

"Where's your strength?" Darius asked, slowly approaching.

Fire this time. Darius leapt to one side, then slammed his sword into the dirt. The light of his blade flared, and the flames could not abide it. Drawing it free, he resumed his approach.

"Where's the awesome power?"

Cyric clapped his hands together, summoning a thick wall of shadow. Darius cut through it like it was paper.

"I thought you were a god?"

Cyric's eyes were full of fear. His strength was insufficient. He'd been challenged, and defeated. To Darius's words, he had no counter. Power swelled across his hands, and Darius prepared for one last barrage, one last attempt to prove his might. Instead, a dark portal emerged behind the priest, swirling with stars. As he leapt through, Valessa grabbed onto him, shrieking for him to not abandon her. Together they vanished within. The portal closed, and with that, they were gone.

Darius fell to his knees and gasped for air. The moment passed, and his exhaustion returned. He could hardly believe what he'd done. Sounds of battle pierced his daze, and he looked to the road leading into the village. The soldiers still fought, and worse, the lion still roared. The paladin forced himself to a stand, clutching his greatsword with both hands. That abomination needed to be returned to the Abyss from whence it came. Blood pounding in his ears, he ran toward the enemy flank.

Most of Karak's soldiers had died, overwhelmed by their sheer numbers. Their bodies lay strewn across the road, still in haphazard lines. Kayne, however, remained. The lion tore through their ranks, their chainmail nothing to his massive teeth and claws. The soldiers struck at his side and thrust for his underbelly, but to no avail. Kayne was too quick, too strong. A few pieces of rock had chipped off his side, and strangely enough, it appeared he bled liquid fire.

"To me, beast!" Darius cried as he came running, trying to sound braver than he felt. "Do not waste your time with pups when you could fight a wolf!"

Kayne heard his voice and turned. A deep snarl emitted from his throat.

"Traitor," he rumbled.

To this, Darius laughed.

"I was loyal to Karak," he said. "Karak turned on me, sent his followers to kill me, and now would have a priest sacrifice hundreds in his name. I dare say Karak's the one who betrayed us."

Kayne tensed, and his claws dug into the hard earth.

"You speak blasphemy and false truths," he said. "I'll tear your lying tongue from your head!"

The lion leapt, reaching his full speed in the blink of an eye. Darius fought his instincts to dodge aside, for Ashhur's voice did not cry retreat in his ear, nor danger. It told him to stand. Trusting it, he thrust his greatsword to meet Kayne's charge, putting every ounce of his strength into the attack. The lion filled Darius's vision, throat full of fire, roar rolling against him like a physical force. But a light shone from his blade, and it grew, and grew. Kayne tried to bat the sword aside as he descended, to clear the way for his kill.

His paws sliced clean off instead. The sword remained unmoved. Mouth open, charge in full, Kayne fell upon Darius. The paladin's blade went up to the hilt inside his jaws, the tip piercing out his back. Fire burned, and Darius felt its heat, but the light enveloped him, protected him. Rock cracked, turned molten and rolled in all directions as the creature howled and broke. In the center of the corpse, Darius stood, sword held in hand as the fire slowly dwindled away. He took a deep breath, then smiled. At his feet, the grass was burned black but for where he stood.

"Thank you," he whispered, then lifted his sword high so all there might see its immaculate shine. Cyric had fled, the lion was dead; Ashhur had not abandoned them just yet.

24

Valessa did not know what to expect as she exited the shadow portal. She could barely think through the pain that filled her. Stumbling out, she fell to knees that became her arms, then her hands, then back again to her knees. Her form kept fighting, twisting, and she could barely remember who she once was. Her eyes opened, and she looked about. They were in rolling hills, the grass a pale yellow. Glancing behind her, she saw a river.

"The Wedge?" she asked. Was that where he'd taken her?

"It seems appropriate," Cyric said. His voice was behind her, and with great effort, she turned to face him. Blood dripped from his hand, and more stained his robe from where the arrow remained embedded in his shoulder. His head dipped low, as if he were humbled for the first time in his life. Most frightening were his eyes: the wild, angry loathing that grew with every word he spoke.

"Is this not where we trap the monsters and other frightening creatures no longer of use to us?"

"Cyric?" Valessa asked, struggling to stand. She felt herself coming together, and pale skin started to form across the shadow that was her. "What are you doing?"

"Ashhur has stolen away my victory, but the blame is mine. Karak does not bestow mercy on those who deserve punishment."

He lifted his hand, and from the center of his bleeding palm she saw stars swirling together amid a black void. And then the pain hit. It was different than when the light of Darius's sword or Jerico's shield touched her. That burned from the outside, dissolving away at her being. This was so, so much worse. She felt the very center of her soul cracking from within, her limbs shaking, her mind breaking into pieces as the very substance holding her together was taken away.

"I should have struck you down the moment I saw you," he said as the pain increased. "The unfinished are all failures in Karak's eyes, unworthy of a place of honor at his side. I gave you a chance, yet now we suffer. *I* suffer! Your burden was to kill Darius, and you did not, you worthless, faithless bitch! What you feel, that is Karak's anger."

His words were becoming a jumble in her mind. Her skin burst, and gray shadows bubbled to the ground. To her knees she went, clawing wildly at the earth. This was how he would repay her? She suffered in agony, denied an eternity with her god, and yet he would blame her for his own failures? Darius had defeated him as well. Where was Karak's fury for him?

"Karak," she whispered. "Please...Karak...save me."

She prayed for strength, for escape from the torment, for the mad priest to suffer...but heard only laughter. Her limbs were gone, as were her legs; she was nothing but a writhing puddle of shadow struggling to retain form. Still she could see Cyric looming over her, nothing but hatred and faith. Yes, she saw it, his faith burning bright, his skin alive with ethereal fire. Karak loved him still, but why?

Then there was no love for her. Closing her eyes, she cursed her god, and fell through the world.

The rock and stone passed over her as she fell. Caverns and empty spaces flew past, but still she fell. She thought to fall forever, to see if at the very bottom she might find the Abyss her god ruled over. But instead she felt water, a great river rolling beneath the surface. This time she did not fight it, despite the horrible pain and discomfort it caused. She didn't care for her form, didn't care for her survival. It carried her for a moment, and then at last, she slipped from its current and into stone.

Something stopped her from falling further. The pain was ebbing, however little. Within the rock, her heart hardened, and with a tentative hand reaching upward, barely more than a tendril of smoke, she yearned for the surface. It was strange, the way it felt as she climbed, melding parts of her body with the stone to lunge higher. But she endured. Crawling, crawling, time meaningless in that darkness, the hours passed. Higher and higher. Many times she thought herself confused, and feared she crawled downward, but she fought through the disorientation.

At last, her hand burst through the grass, and like a woman emerging from a deep river, she crawled upon the surface. She didn't know where she was, saw nothing but trees and thorn bushes in all directions, but it didn't matter. The red star still burned in the sky, and she followed it. Hours passed as she ran, her form steadily regaining strength. Her surroundings grew familiar, and she realized she was on the correct side of the Gihon, thankfully.

On and on, to Darius.

The night was young when she found Daniel's men camped at the outset of Willshire. Darius was among them, she knew, but they would not let her pass, not if they recognized her. Adopting the look and dress of a plain village woman, she wandered through them, smiling meekly at any who looked her way. In the center she found Darius's tent, him sitting within it. His sword was at his side, but so far, it lacked its damnable glow.

"Darius," she said, stepping within. He looked up from his bed, confused, but then she dropped the façade, and stood naked before him, her own body, her own face, with nothing to hide. He reached for his sword, but she did not move.

"Have you not had enough?" he asked, his hand closing about the hilt.

"I have," she said, even as her skin flaked away under the growing light of his sword. "I promise you nothing, for the blood between us remains. But that is not why I am here."

She hated doing so, but she must. Valessa fell to one knee, bowed her head, then looked up into Darius's eyes so he might see the searing hatred in them.

"Help me," she asked. "Help me kill Cyric."

Epilogue

Cyric wandered further into the wild lands trapped between the rivers. There were many creatures there, he knew. He'd read the books, seen the maps. When the gods' war had sundered the land, Ashhur and Karak had given strength and form to the beasts so they might fight as soldiers. But now the creatures had abandoned their gods, or was it their gods who had abandoned them? He didn't know. He didn't care.

The camp of wolf-men was small, but it would grow larger with time. He trusted his strength, the strength of Karak. Darius was only a dying vessel, one of the last paladins of Ashhur that his enemy might throw at him. Desperate, and wild in faith. Such a man would fall in time.

At the edge of their camp the weaker wolf-men slept. Cyric stopped just before them, for he knew his scent would alert them soon. Growls confirmed this. The first to see him snarled, leapt from his sleep, and attacked. Cyric waved his hand, crushing his throat with a heavy stone made of shadow. Two more leapt at him, and with a word he burst the blood from their eyes and nostrils.

"I have not come to fight," he told them as more and more gathered. "Where is your leader?"

"I am pack leader," said a large wolf-man, pushing through the rest. His claws were sharp, his whole body lean with muscle. Cyric smiled at him.

"My name is Cyric, priest of your god, Karak, the god you worshipped before you turned to the moon and in falseness gave her your faith."

"You speak lies," said their leader. "I will enjoy the taste of your blood on my tongue."

"Try, if you wish. The strongest leads the tribe, after all."

The wolf-man feinted a direct rush, then circled to the side before leaping. It was a clever move, but Cyric did not fall for it. Clapping his hands together, he summoned manacles born of dark magic. They broke through the dirt and wrapped about the wolf-man's wrists and ankles, slamming him to the ground. All around him, the rest of the tribe yipped with fear. A small tribe, maybe thirty at most; Cyric knew they would be the first of many. And he also knew that, as a human, he could never inspire their complete loyalty. He looked down at the captured wolf-man, then knelt mere inches from his snapping teeth.

"I will give you great power," Cyric said. "All you must do is accept the love of Karak, and swear your life to me. Can you do that? If you do, I will help you make your tribe a thousand strong. At my side, you will fight as we retake the north in Karak's name. Heathen men will die before you, and your feasting will be great. What do you say?"

The wolf-man looked up at him with startling intelligence in his eyes. The tribe fell silent as they waited for an answer from their pack leader.

"I will serve Karak, if Karak will lead us to blood and battle," he said.

"Excellent." Cyric banished the chains. "Rise, wolf, and tell me your name."

The creature rose to his full height, towering over him. His voice deepened as he spoke, a heavy growl eager for conflict.

"Redclaw," said the wolf.

Luther knelt before his bed, hands clasped in prayer. They were not far from Lord Sebastian's castle, and he expected an envoy from him at any time. Not that it would matter. His host marched beside him, and Sebastian's army had been left tattered and in ribbons. If Sebastian wanted to retain power, he would have to turn to them, regardless of his own feelings.

"All for you," Luther prayed. "All I have done, I do for you. The lawless shall be broken upon the immovable law. In time, the North will be yours, not just in heart but in deed and law. May I remain strong, and break the will of Sebastian. We have left him nothing, as you desired. Let him know his strength is in his loyalty to Karak, not his own might and men."

Movement at the entrance of his large tent alerted him to a man's arrival. Luther turned, saw one of his paladins holding a scroll.

"My priest, forgive me," said the paladin.

"Yes, Grevus?"

The paladin crossed his arms, and he looked uneasy.

"We've received disturbing reports from the towers. It's about Cyric."

Luther sighed, and with a groan, rose from his knees.

"What has my pupil done now? Don't bother reading the message, just tell me."

Grevus's cheek twitched.

"We hear he's overthrown Sir Robert at the Blood Tower, and also assaulted the village of Willshire. Worse...I do not know what to make of this, my priest. Perhaps the messenger lies, or has heard wrong."

"Out with it," Luther said, feeling anger growing in his breast.

"Luther, among many other things, it says Cyric preaches that he is Karak made flesh, now free to walk the land and remake it in his image."

Luther swallowed, his throat suddenly dry. He nodded to the lengthy message the paladin held in his hand.

"Tell me everything."

A note from the author:

I love writing these. Besides the obvious reason (yay another book finished and ready for readers!), these little notes are my chance to sit down, and for maybe a page or two, chat about the work, and try to decide how I really feel about the story. Of course, nearly every author can talk forever about their characters, just like most parents can talk forever about their children. I'll try not to bore you too much, nor will I pull out the wallet photos.

So what have I really learned from Old Ways? Two things. One, no matter if it is the Paladins or the Half-Orcs, Jerico's life often sucks. He's such a fun punching bag, I can't help it. Two, Darius is the man. Parents may have to love their children equally, but I don't have to when it comes to my characters. Some don't live up to expectations. Some cause problems, and keep demanding attention. And then there's Darius. This was supposed to be a series devoted to Jerico and his back-story, but more and more it feels like he'll be stuck in Darius's shadow. The highlight, though, is their interaction, and I'll make sure they meet up once more in what I believe will be the fourth and final book of the paladins.

I wrote earlier about how difficult Clash of Faiths was to write. Looking back, the dark tone was probably much of the reason, an overall grim feeling that, until the last few chapters, I was uncertain whether or not would be denied. But I'm happy to say this one was so, so much easier. Darius might have his struggles, and life isn't a cakewalk for Jerico either, but they're friends now, and united once more against a common enemy. I don't know if this affected the story in any way, but I'm damn proud of it. Every book I release I feel confident it's the best one I've ever done, but with this one, I'm doubly confident.

Which means it might suck all the harder, but hey, if you made it this far, you at least finished the story, so that's still a partial win.

Some of you might have noticed how much longer Old Ways was compared to the previous two. That wasn't intentional. The Paladins series was my attempt to write some shorter, more laid back stories, more fun and less carnage than say, Shadowdance. Well, the story is getting longer, and the emotional stakes have grown far, far beyond what I ever expected. Hopefully you're all happy about that, because it caught me off guard. As Old Ways progressed, I started realizing just how much the scope was widening, and how much more story there was lurking beneath my original ideas. So when I say the next novel should be the last, don't take that as a guarantee. It might not be. I won't know until I write it. Darius and Jerico might end up with other plans...

Some quick shout outs. Thank you, Ramsey, for the awesome maps. I know a few fans should be rather happy about that. Thanks Peter and Terry for the cover, Derek and Ashley for the editing, and Rob for the early critiques to see if I was keeping the story on track. And last, but certainly not least, thank you, dear reader. It's not always fun and games, but I do it for you. I'm a man dancing on the stage, and I'll keep doing it long after the spotlight is off, so long as there's a few of you out there still entertained.

David Dalglish
December 31, 2011

Made in the USA
San Bernardino, CA
20 February 2013